ADDISON COOKE

AND THE
TREASURE
OF THE
INCAS

PHILOMEL BOOKS
an imprint of Penguin Random House LLC
375 Hudson Street, New York, NY 10014

Library of Congress Cataloging-in-Publication Data
Names: Stokes, Jonathan, author.
Title: Addison Cooke and the treasure of the Incas / Jonathan W. Stokes.
Description: New York, NY : Philomel Books, [2016] | Series: Addison Cooke ; 1
Identifiers: LCCN 2015049086 | ISBN 9780399173776 (hardback)
Subjects: | CYAC: Adventure and adventurers—Fiction. | Kidnapping—Fiction.
| Ciphers—Fiction. | Incas—Fiction. | Antiquities—Fiction. | Mystery and
detective stories. | Peru—Fiction. | BISAC: JUVENILE FICTION / Action &
Adventure / Survival Stories. | JUVENILE FICTION / Humorous Stories. |
JUVENILE FICTION / Historical / Ancient Civilizations. Classification: LCC
PZ7.1.S753 Ad 2016 | DDC [Fic]—dc23
LC record available at https://lccn.loc.gov/2015049086
Printed in the United States of America.
ISBN 978-0-399-17377-6
1 3 5 7 9 10 8 6 4 2

Edited by Michael Green.   Design by Semadar Megged.
Text set in 11-point Garth.

AND THE
TREASURE
OF THE
INCAS

JONATHAN W. STOKES

Philomel Books

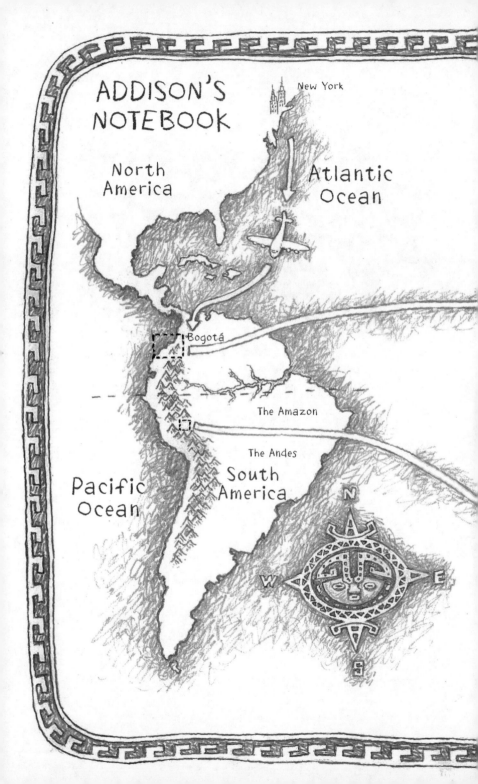

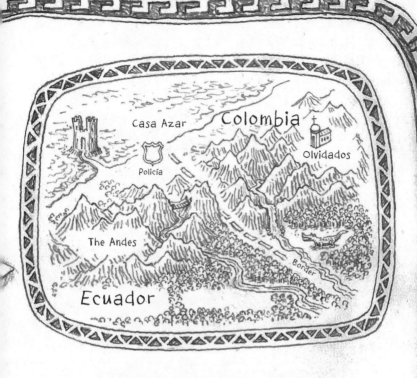

Colombia

Casa Azar

Policía

Olvidados

The Andes

Border

Ecuador

Machu Picchu

I

THE

INCAN

KEY

Chapter One

Fear of Heights

ADDISON COOKE SAT CROSS-LEGGED in the school library, engrossed in an Incan history book. Under the spell of a decent read, Addison could forget meals, forget sleep, and even forget to go to class. He could forget to go to school or, once at school, forget to go home. This was, in fact, the current situation.

The school bell had rung ages ago, and Addison had missed it entirely.

Addison's little sister, Molly, sprinted into the library. She was still wearing soccer cleats and shin guards from intramural practice.

"Addison!" she hissed.

Addison perked up, looked around for the source of the whisper, and spotted his sister.

"Molly, what are you doing down there?"

"Me? What are you doing on top of the bookshelf?"

Addison was, at present, perched on top of a six-foot bookshelf.

"Overcoming my fear of heights. And reading up on Incan history. It's called multitasking."

Addison, like any seventh grader at Public School 141, sported a tidy uniform: a sharp blazer, power tie, and khaki pants. Never wanting to blend in, he topped off his uniform with a smart Ivy cap perched on his head at a rakish angle.

Molly, a sixth grader, had more than a decade of solid experience with Addison's odd behavior. She was more or less used to it. "I ran to your classroom to find you, but Ms. Johnson said you weren't in class all afternoon."

"I got a nurse's pass."

"But you're not sick."

"Naturally. I got the nurse's pass from Eddie Chang," Addison explained. "He was sick last week. I traded him his nurse's pass for an owl pellet."

"What's an owl pellet?"

"You ask too many questions. You should consider a career in tabloid reporting, or criminal investigation."

"Addison, skipping all these classes could catch up to you."

"I've gotten by so far. Besides, I'm only skipping class to further my education."

Addison Cooke possessed infinite confidence in all things Addison Cooke.

Molly Cooke, however, did not share this same feeling. "Well, hurry up," she said, whispering as loudly as the library allowed. "We have two strikes with Aunt Delia already. If we miss the bus again, she'll kill us!"

Even Addison saw the truth in this. He sighed, gathered his library books into his messenger bag, and began climbing down the tall bookshelf.

"No need to panic, Molly."

"I'm not panicking!"

"Sooner or later, you are going to learn that I have everything under control."

Addison stepped on a loose shelf. It overturned, flipping all the books—and Addison—onto the ground.

He landed hard on his back.

"I'm all right."

Molly looked down at him, knuckles on her hips. "And you're supposed to be a good influence on me."

Addison hurriedly reshelved the books before sprinting after Molly.

•••••••

Addison and Molly burst out of the front doors of PS 141, Theodore Roosevelt Middle School, on the Upper West Side of Manhattan. They watched the last school bus disappear, turning right on 72nd Street toward Central Park.

"C'mon, Molly. We'll catch them at Columbus Avenue!"

"We're supposed to outrun a school bus?"

"I could use the exercise—I skipped PE today. Besides, you already have your running shoes on."

"These are soccer cleats!"

But Addison had already taken off running. Molly chased after him, her cleats clacking like maracas on the pavement.

They dashed past the hot-dog vendor with his rolling cart. Past the cook-fire smells of the pretzel vendor. They sprinted past Mr. Karabidian's ice cream cart.

"Missed the bus again, Addison?" called Mr. Karabidian.

"Time waits for no man," replied Addison as he flew by, "and neither does the bus." Addison put on a fresh burst of speed, now struggling to keep pace with Molly.

"The shortcut!" she called, ducking down a service alley. They bolted along loading docks and leapt over shipping flats, Addison desperate not to lose any of his Incan library books.

Turbaned men reclining on blankets played chess in the shade of the alleyway. Women with machetes shaved ice behind the Thai restaurant. Addison and Molly swept past them with the speed of two scalded squirrels.

They emerged from the alley at full tilt, upsetting a flock of warbling pigeons on Central Park West. "There it is!" Addison called, pointing.

Molly watched in dismay as their school bus chugged

uptown, passing the 79th Street Transverse. It trundled into the distance, disappearing in the afternoon traffic.

"Great." Molly squatted down to retie her cleats.

"Never fear, young relative. We will catch a taxi."

"We're not allowed to take taxis."

"I'm glad you mentioned that. Because I cannot afford a taxi."

"We've got to hurry. Aunt Delia will be home any minute!"

Addison surveyed the bustling Manhattan street traffic. "The important thing is to remain levelheaded and to make use of one's environment."

"That's two things. And you sound just like Uncle Nigel."

"Thank you." Addison beamed. "You know, the taxi is not the fastest animal in the concrete jungle. That honor belongs to the bike messenger." Addison knew there were few creatures in any jungle more quick, daring, and potentially lethal than a New York City bike messenger. "I will just flag one down."

For Addison, having an idea was the same thing as acting on it. He jumped in front of the speeding path of a passing bike messenger. The cyclist spotted Addison flapping his arms and swerved hard at the last moment, brakes squealing.

"Watch it, kid!" shouted the bike messenger, skidding to a stop.

"Sir, I apologize, but I require your services."

"You could have gotten me killed!"

"A small price to pay for what is at stake," Addison calmly replied.

"You need a delivery?"

"In a word, yes."

"Got any money?"

"I do."

"I'm listening," said the bike messenger.

"I need you to take me and my sister home."

"I deliver packages, not kids."

"What's the difference?"

The bike messenger considered this question, probably for the first time in his life. "Size, mostly."

"If you take us home, I can pay you when we get there," suggested Addison.

"If you grow wings, I won't need to take you," the bike messenger replied.

"Fair enough." Addison slipped off his school dress shoe and peeled five crumpled one-dollar bills from under his insole. "I keep emergency funds for just such scenarios. How far uptown will five dollars get me?"

"73rd Street," said the bike messenger.

"We're *on* 73rd Street," Addison observed.

"All right, 76th."

"Make it 86th Street, and you've got yourself a deal."

"79th and not one inch farther."

"I'll take it."

Addison climbed on the bicycle seat, which was pretty high off the ground for him. Molly balanced her cleats on the rear wheel axle, her hands on Addison's shoulders. The bike messenger rode seatless, huffing and puffing to get the cycle moving.

Soon they careened through the Manhattan streets at breakneck speed. Pedestrians yelped and leapt out of their speeding path. Molly clung to Addison, who clung to the bike messenger. Addison's tie flapped behind him; Molly squinted her eyes in the headwind. They wove through traffic, slicing within inches of passing cars.

"I could get used to this," said Addison.

"We're there," said the bike messenger, squeaking to a stop.

Molly dismounted, looking grateful to be alive. Addison straightened his windblown hair and thanked the bike messenger.

"Truth is, I was going this direction anyway," said the messenger. "But I figured I might as well get paid for it."

"I respect your entrepreneurial spirit," said Addison.

"Kid, here's my card if you ever need anything."

Addison gratefully accepted the bike messenger's business card and offered his own in exchange. In impeccable felt-tipped penmanship, Addison's card read:

```
┌⁓⁓⁓⁓⁓⁓⁓⁓⁓⁓⁓⁓⁓⁓⁓┐
   Addison Cooke
  ARCHAEOLOGIST
     Rates negotiable
└⁓⁓⁓⁓⁓⁓⁓⁓⁓⁓⁓⁓⁓⁓⁓┘
```

The bike messenger cocked his knuckles to his cap, saluting Addison. He set foot to pedal, ready to cycle north. "Got a tip?"

"Absolutely," Addison replied. "You shouldn't let kids ride without helmets."

......

Addison and Molly raced the final seven blocks to their apartment building on West 86th Street. Addison skidded to a halt, his jaw dropped in horror. Aunt Delia was already climbing the front steps of their brownstone apartment building.

"We're so busted!" Molly exclaimed.

"We can't afford another grounding. Let's try the back door."

"Addison, we live on the fifth floor. There is no back door."

"True. But there *is* a fire escape."

Molly and Addison dashed into the back alley, frightening a skulking cat. The siblings clambered on top of the alley Dumpster to reach the wrought-iron rungs of the fire-escape ladder. Addison began climbing.

"C'mon, hurry up," urged Molly.

Halfway up the ladder, Addison froze. He stared down at the pavement far below, entranced.

"Could you go any slower?"

"Just give me a sec," said Addison.

Molly sighed. "It's your fear of heights, isn't it?"

"I'll be fine."

"Let's call for Raj or Eddie. If their windows are open, they'll come out and help you."

"If you shout for them, Aunt Delia will hear you."

Molly caught up to Addison on the ladder. "Just don't look down. Take deep breaths. You'll be okay."

"I don't need help. I'm fine!"

"Fine."

Addison's legs shook. His heart beat against his ribs like a gorilla rattling the bars of its cage.

"Addison?"

He sighed and shut his eyes, realizing he couldn't possibly climb to the fifth floor. Slowly, Addison climbed back down to the Dumpster, defeated. He carefully lowered himself to the pavement. Feet on solid earth again, Addison took a moment to collect his breath.

"I don't understand it," said Molly. "When are you going to get over this phobia?"

"Forget it. Let's just go in the front door before Aunt Delia calls in the National Guard. We're in deep enough already."

Furious with himself, Addison quietly led Molly out of the alleyway.

······

Aunt Delia shook her head back and forth so that her ponytail wagged. She had the frazzled look of a person with three days' worth of work to do and only three hours to do it. She folded her tortoiseshell glasses and set them loudly on the counter.

Addison and Molly stared meekly at the black and white tiles of the kitchen floor.

"Addison, it's like you never *listen*," said Aunt Delia, wringing her hands.

"I do listen. I just never follow instructions," Addison corrected.

Aunt Delia held up one palm, silencing Addison. "I don't want to hear it."

Addison pursed his lips and did his best to hold his peace.

"You're grounded," said Aunt Delia. "Again," she added. "No television, no sleepovers . . ." Aunt Delia wound up for her knockout punch. "And, Addison—no visits to Bruno's Fossil Emporium for a month."

"Oh, c'mon!"

"No lip, Addison. This is about more than following instructions. When you give me your word, I need to know

I can trust you. You need to start accepting some responsibility. Traveling the city by yourself—what if something had happened to you?"

"I *wish* something would happen to me," Addison blurted out. "School is unimaginably, inconceivably, impossibly boring. You and Uncle Nigel are always leaving the country. Flying to excavations. Seeing the world. If I could leave school, I might actually learn something."

"Is that why you keep getting into trouble? Because your uncle and I have to work?"

"Every time you fly out of the country, you leave Molly and me behind."

"Only during the school year," Aunt Delia countered.

"Well, I'm ready for more. I'm almost thirteen. In some countries, I'd be married by now!"

"Addison missed all his afternoon classes to hide in the library and read about Incan treasure," Molly put in helpfully.

"Molly!" hissed Addison.

"Incan treasure?" cried Aunt Delia.

"Molly wants to get out of here, too. We're tired of being cooped up in school while you and Uncle Nigel trot around the globe."

"Don't drag your sister into this, Addison. Molly—unlike you—has never broken a rule in her life. I refuse to believe she is longing for a life of adventure, when she can't even take the garbage down to the trash chute by herself."

"Can't, or won't?" Addison replied.

Aunt Delia stepped out of her high heels, hung her coat in the closet, and set her briefcase down on the table with a clatter. She took a deep breath and ran a hand across her forehead. "Addison, I will spend more time with you when the museum gets back on its feet. Until then, your uncle and I need to work hard so you and Molly have a roof to eat and food to sleep under."

"I think you got that backward," Molly suggested.

Aunt Delia rubbed the dark bags under her eyes and sighed, exhausted. "Addison, I don't have time to pick you up from after-school detentions. I don't have time for more soul-draining teacher meetings about you getting into trouble with Eddie and Raj."

Aunt Delia took Addison by his wrists and looked him in the eyes. "There is only one of you, and only one of Molly. That makes each of you more rare and valuable than Incan gold. Do you understand why I'm upset?"

Addison nodded.

"I don't make rules just to be mean. I make rules to prevent you from being—I don't know—kidnapped."

Addison nodded again, seeing the sense in this.

"We have to stick together, all right?"

"All right," said Addison. "Stick together. I promise."

......

Addison and Molly shared a bunk bed in their room of Aunt Delia's two-bedroom apartment. Molly's half of the room was strewn with mismatched socks, grass-stained soccer shorts, and mud-caked sports jerseys. Addison's half of the room was as pristine and immaculate as a NASA science lab.

Roosting pigeons cooed on the window ledge, watching the afternoon descend into night. Rising wind and brooding gray clouds betrayed a gathering storm.

"Why do we have to stay with Uncle Nigel this weekend?" Molly asked.

Addison packed clothes and books into his backpack. "Because Aunt Delia's working."

"But why do we have to stay with Uncle Nigel at the museum?"

"Because Uncle Nigel's working."

"Why are they always working?"

"Like Aunt Delia said—to take care of us."

"By ignoring us?"

"More or less," said Addison.

He carefully packed his microscope and calligraphy pens. He swiped a pocket notebook off his desk and tucked it in his jacket. His notebooks contained sketches of birds and mammals he observed in the park, as well as pressed leaves and beetles. Addison's uncle always needled him on the first rule of archaeology: record everything.

Molly collected socks from the floor and tossed them across the room, making three-point shots into her laundry hamper. "I don't want them to get divorced. It will be like losing our parents a second time."

"It's just a trial separation." This was not Addison's favorite topic. "We've never counted on adults before. We take care of ourselves, right?"

Molly zipped up her backpack and sat on her bed. "Why is our family so weird?"

"Because being weird is better than being ordinary."

Molly looked at Addison and frowned. She blew a wisp of hair from her eyes. Somehow, there was always one wisp that managed to escape her ponytail.

Addison wedged a few more Incan books into his backpack, struggling to close the zipper. "Listen, Mo. What's the most important thing in the world?"

"Frank's Pizza on 23rd and Lexington."

"True," Addison admitted. "But the second-most important thing is a good attitude. We can't control what happens to us. But we can control how we feel about it."

Molly considered this. Outside, the clouds burst. She looked out at the first rivulets of rain, tracing tracks down the window, dividing the world into pieces. The tapping drops grew to a drumroll, announcing the storm's arrival with a crashing timpani of thunder.

Chapter Two

The Legend of Atahualpa

AUNT DELIA DROPPED ADDISON and Molly off in front of the New York Museum of Archaeology. It was a sprawling marble building, backlit by lightning strikes in the glowering night sky. Trees bent under the lash of a whipping wind. Addison and Molly dashed through the heavy raindrops of the growing storm, splashing their way through puddles to the basement entrance.

Aunt Delia and Uncle Nigel were museum curators, so Addison and Molly knew the wooded grounds by heart. They cut through a maze of hedges and ducked under an arched portico. Skimming rainwater from his face, Addison found the basement key hidden in a crack of loose mortar. He unlocked the creaking iron door and hauled it open with all his strength. He and Molly slipped inside from the howling rainstorm, the great door booming shut behind them.

The New York Museum of Archaeology was Addison's favorite place in the world. Great echoing halls filled with Egyptian mummies, Mongolian battle armor, a Viking warship, and the eastern wing of an Aztec temple. Deep down in the musty, snaking passageways of the basement archives was a secret underground world the public never saw. A labyrinth of vaults where millions of specimens were filed and stored. This was their uncle's workplace.

Addison and Molly trotted through the dark corridors by feel, listening to the rising thunder rattling the cement walls above. They passed a long hallway crammed with crates of Ice Age bones for the Hall of Paleontology: saber-toothed tiger skulls with teeth curved like Arabian sickle swords, giant sloth femurs heavy as tree limbs, dire wolf claws sharp as switchblades. At last they spotted a light glowing from an office at the end of a dark passage.

"Uncle Nigel, we're here!" Molly called.

······

Professor Nigel Cooke chewed on the stem of his antique calabash pipe, curved like a bull's horn. His eyes gleamed behind polished spectacles as he considered Addison and

Molly. He was the sort of man who knew almost everything about the year 1493, and almost nothing about the year he was currently living in. Today he greeted Addison and Molly in ancient Greek.

"Aspádzomai!"

"Khaîre," said Addison and Molly, heaving aside an elephant tusk so they could sit on the tattered leather couch by the filing cabinet.

"Ti práttete?" Uncle Nigel asked.

"Pretty good," said Molly. "Although Addison made us miss the bus again."

"Molly!"

"I bet your aunt was ecstatic." Uncle Nigel laughed gently. Like Addison's father, Uncle Nigel was from Surrey, England. He was Oxford-educated and spoke with a proper British accent. Addison loved his uncle's speech, each word so crisp it was like biting off a piece of fresh celery.

"'Ecstatic' is not the first word I would use to describe Aunt Delia," said Addison.

"Your aunt has a lot to worry about right now," explained Uncle Nigel. "People don't visit museums as often as they used to. So your aunt and I have to work incessantly, like Slinkies on an escalator. If we don't find a great exhibit that will draw visitors back to the museum, our funding will be slashed and . . ." Uncle Nigel trailed off. Then, looking hard at Addison and Molly, he seemed to decide that honesty was the best policy. "Well, we could lose our jobs."

Addison and Molly weren't sure how to respond. Molly busied herself picking bits of turf from her cleats. Addison drew in his notebook, sketching the Cherokee headdress he saw draped over the filing cabinet.

"The point is," continued Uncle Nigel, "your aunt is on a short fuse. And you'd be wise to be model children for her until we sail through this rough patch."

"I take your point," said Addison.

"Model children," agreed Molly. A waft of Uncle Nigel's tobacco smoke made her crinkle up her eyes and sneeze loudly.

"Benedicite!" said Uncle Nigel, excusing her in Latin.

"Gratias tibi," said Molly, thanking him automatically.

"Well, that's enough serious talk," said Uncle Nigel. "I just returned from a dig in the jungles of Bolivia and found the most improbable relic. An artifact that's not even supposed to exist! I don't suppose you'd like to see it?"

"I don't see why not," said Addison, who could think of nothing better than a strange relic from a distant country.

Uncle Nigel carefully repacked his pipe, using the desk magnifying glass he usually reserved for archeological specimens. As a professor he was absentminded in many tasks, but packing a pipe he treated with surgical precision. "You're familiar with Incan history?"

"That's all Addison's been reading about since you left for Bolivia," answered Molly.

"Then you must know how the Incan Empire fell."

"A bit," said Addison.

"I'd like to hear it," said Molly.

Uncle Nigel struck a match and carefully puffed his antique pipe to life. Aside from his clothes and spectacles, he really owned very little from this century. With thunder rumbling outside like a distant cannonade, Uncle Nigel cleared his throat and began.

"Five hundred years ago, there lived the last king of the Incas . . ."

"King Atahualpa," Addison piped in.

"Precisely," Uncle Nigel nodded. "King Atahualpa battled with his own family for the right to his throne. It was a destructive war. By the time the Spanish conquistador Francisco Pizarro invaded Peru, Atahualpa's army was exhausted. Atahualpa tried to fight Pizarro alone, without the help of his family's armies. But Pizarro easily conquered the divided Incas and threw Atahualpa in a great dungeon . . ."

As Uncle Nigel talked, Addison's eyes darted to the shadowy corners of the office, containing relics from every era of history. Ancient maps, papyrus scrolls, and decaying mummies. Blood-encrusted samurai swords from feudal Japan. Maasai spears decorated in ostrich feathers.

The fossil skeleton of an extinct dodo bird. Even the ten-foot tusk of a narwhal, spiraled like a unicorn's horn.

"King Atahualpa bargained with Pizarro," continued Uncle Nigel. "The king offered to fill his dungeon once over with gold, and twice over with silver, if Pizarro would set him free. Pizarro only wanted treasure, and so immediately agreed. The Incas prepared the enormous ransom: gold vases filled with emeralds, silver chalices overflowing with rubies, and intricately carved golden statues of animals, birds, and the Incan gods. It took sixty thousand Incas to haul the seven hundred and fifty tons of gold across the empire and into Peru."

"How much is seven hundred and fifty tons of gold?" asked Molly.

Uncle Nigel drew on his pipe so the embers glowed. "Picture a hundred and fifty school buses filled with treasure."

PS 141 only had ten school buses. So Addison pictured a nearly endless line of school buses, heavy laden with gold, parked down the entire length of Central Park.

"At the last moment," Uncle Nigel went on, "Atahualpa's bickering family failed him one more time. His brother's army attacked Pizarro before the ransom could be delivered. So the Spanish conquistadors sacked the Incan army and called off the deal. Pizarro burned Atahualpa alive at the stake."

Molly grimaced. Then crinkled up her nose and sneezed again.

"Lots of people were burned at the stake, Mo," said Addison. "It was a popular way to kill people during the Spanish Inquisition."

Uncle Nigel nodded and wound up his tale. "The Incas never delivered their treasure. Instead, they locked it away in a secret chamber and hid three keys across the Incan Empire. Each key contains a clue leading to the next. Locals believe Atahualpa's treasure is cursed . . . Fortune hunters have searched for it over the centuries, and none have returned alive. Legends say the treasure vault will open only for someone who has learned from King Atahualpa's mistakes."

Uncle Nigel gazed pensively at the red glow of his pipe. He blew thin curls of blue smoke from his nostrils that wafted slowly up to the shadowed recesses of the ceiling rafters.

"So what did you find on your dig in Bolivia?" Addison asked quietly.

"Oh, only this," replied Uncle Nigel, unlocking the safe behind his desk and removing a fragile wooden box. He pried open the mildewed lid and tilted it to the light.

Addison's jaw dropped in amazement. Molly's followed suit. Inside the box lay an intricately carved stone, roughly the size of a large chess piece.

"One of the three keys!" cried Addison.

More thunder broke outside the museum. It shook the walls, as if giants upstairs were rearranging their furniture, and repeatedly changing their minds on where to set the couch.

The wind howled so fiercely it could be heard even in the basement. Molly shivered. "Is it real?"

Uncle Nigel allowed himself a smile. "I'm pretty sure it is Atahualpa's first key," he replied, his precise Oxford accent elegantly slicing the words into perfect squares. "Though the key is made of stone, so we can't carbon-date it."

"More's the pity," said Addison.

"Luckily," continued Uncle Nigel, "whoever created the key dated it for us. The Spanish inscription says AD 1533 . . . the same year Atahualpa was murdered."

Addison flipped open his notebook. Using a method Uncle Nigel had taught him, he delicately flattened a blank page over the stone key and rubbed with the side of his pencil to trace an exact copy.

"If the legend is true," Uncle Nigel went on, "the riddle engraved on this first key leads to the second key. The second key leads to the third key. And the third key leads—"

"To the lost treasure of the Incas." Addison's mind reeled, dizzy with the thought. Never in his life had he wanted his uncle's job so badly.

Uncle Nigel carefully retrieved the key from Addison's

grasp, cleaning it with a special brush from his desk. "Treasure hunters have searched in vain for the key for five hundred years," he said. "If the legends are true, the remaining clues to the treasure are still undisturbed, and, well, now you can understand why I have so much work to do. Archaeology is five percent field research and ninety-five percent paperwork. I need to get back to my reports."

"But it's dinnertime," Molly protested. "And we're starving."

"Plus, you deserve a celebration!" cried Addison. "Can we eat dinner in the prehistoric man diorama?"

"Maybe a picnic in the Roman court?" suggested Molly.

"Then we could watch the rainstorm from the greenhouse in the rooftop garden," offered Addison.

"Or go Rollerblading in the Chinese pagoda!"

"You know there's no Rollerblading in the pagoda," said Uncle Nigel, his eyes already fixed on his field notes. "And I'm sorry, guys, but I have too much work to have dinner with you." He tossed his wallet to Addison, who caught it one-handed. "Go grab yourselves some food from the vending machine down the hallway."

"But, Uncle Nigel—"

"I'm sorry. That's final."

Molly and Addison shared a look. Addison shrugged, and they shuffled out.

"You know the drill," called Uncle Nigel. "Don't visit

the museum exhibits after dark. And whatever you do, don't touch anything!"

······

Molly and Addison took their time at the vending machine, debating which snacks might possibly fill them up for dinner. All at once, the lights flickered out, plunging the museum into darkness.

"I guess the storm knocked out the power," said Addison, invisible in the blackened corridor.

"You're a regular Sherlock Holmes," said Molly.

"If I could see you, I'd smack you."

"You wouldn't dare."

"That's true," admitted Addison.

Molly punched a few buttons on the dead vending machine. "Great. Now the vending machine doesn't work. We're going to starve to death in this museum. In a few days, they can add us to the mummy exhibit."

Even in the pitch dark, Addison could sense Molly rolling her eyes.

"This works in our favor, Molly. Let's go find Uncle Nigel—he has no choice but to buy us real food now."

Yet, as Addison crept back through the catacombs, Molly clutched him by the sleeve. "Did you hear that?" she whispered.

"Hear what?" Addison's voice echoed up and down the hollow corridor.

"Shhh. Listen!"

Addison strained his ears over the grumbling thunder. And then he heard. The voices of men arguing in his uncle's office. The men's voices grew to angry shouts. And then Addison heard the violent clatter of furniture being smashed to pieces.

"C'mon," whispered Addison. "Quickly!" He felt his way along the dark corridor, Molly keeping pace. Up ahead, flashlight beams cut the darkness in Uncle Nigel's office. Addison had read enough about Native Americans to know to walk toe to heel when he needed absolute silence. He snuck up to the doorway and crouched low to listen.

"Is anyone else in the museum, Dr. Cooke?" asked a rumbling voice so deep it seemed to shake dust from the rafters. Addison searched his memory, but he had never heard the voice before.

"Yes, Professor Ragar," Uncle Nigel's voice answered, a little shakily. "There are eight armed night watchmen patrolling the museum. I'm sure they will find us soon."

"*Four* night watchmen," corrected the man called Professor Ragar. "And we have already taken care of them."

"My god, you killed them?"

"My men dearly wanted to. Begged me, they did. But for now, your watchmen are only unconscious." The professor's Russian accent was so thick you could cut it with a Cossack's saber.

"Then I guess it's just us left in the museum tonight," said Dr. Cooke.

"Good," Professor Ragar's voice purred, raising the hairs on the back of Addison's neck. "Dr. Cooke, I've tracked you all the way from Bolivia, at considerable expense, and I need everything tonight to run as smoothly as—how do you say?—a Swiss clock."

Addison crept silently into Uncle Nigel's office on his hands and knees, sticking to the shadows. He ducked behind an ancient Greek sarcophagus. Molly followed, heart thumping, moving as quietly as she could. When they peeked over the lid of the marble tomb, Addison and Molly saw a sight that froze the breath in their lungs.

Immense men in dark suits crowded the room. They held Uncle Nigel pinned down, his face pressed against his desk. Two upholstered Victorian chairs were smashed. Uncle Nigel's spectacles lay shattered on the floor. Flashlights were trained on his trembling face.

Professor Ragar stood in shadow. He wore an immaculately tailored gray suit with a matching gray ascot and a silver-tipped walking stick. Addison wasn't sure if the suit fabric was herringbone or glen plaid, but whoever this strange man was, Addison had to admit his taste was impeccable.

"Dr. Cooke," the professor continued, "you beat me to the Aztec treasure at the lost temple of Montezuma. You beat me to the Egyptian treasure ship filled with Nubian gold at the bottom of that—how do you say?—*shark-infested* reef in the Red Sea. But now it is finally my turn." Ragar stepped forward, his cane tapping on the stone floor. He plucked Atahualpa's key from Uncle Nigel's grasp and held it aloft in one gloved hand so that it flickered in the golden yellow gleam of the flashlights.

Molly glanced at Addison behind the stone sarcophagus. She mouthed the words, *What do we do?*

Thoughts tumbled through Addison's head like circus acrobats. He and Molly could try to put up a fight . . . but Addison counted six giant guards, plus Ragar, and he didn't love those odds.

Calling the police seemed a Nobel Prize–worthy idea. But if he and Molly tried sneaking out of the office, Professor Ragar's men might discover them. There was nothing for it; they were stuck. Addison looked back at Molly and simply lifted a finger in the air, signaling for patience. They kept listening.

"I heard you were serving time in a Siberian prison," Uncle Nigel said behind clenched teeth, as Ragar's men shoved him roughly into a chair.

Professor Ragar nodded. "I was arrested in Bukhara. I tried stealing the Jewel of Trust from the Tower of Kalyan."

"Really? What happened?"

"My men betrayed me."

Uncle Nigel paused to considered this. "You used to be a great archaeologist. What happened?"

"There's no money in it." Ragar gestured to the worn elbow patches on Uncle Nigel's threadbare jacket. "I'm sure you've noticed."

"For a thousand years, the Bukharans tossed criminals from the top of the Kalyan Tower, and you thought you could just waltz right in. Prison is better than you deserve."

Professor Ragar silenced Uncle Nigel with a hard slap to the face. "You are playing for time. Is there something you're not telling me, Dr. Cooke?"

Uncle Nigel did not answer.

Ragar slowly circled Uncle Nigel's desk and spotted his still-smoldering pipe. He placed the pipe between his own yellow teeth, drawing a luxuriant puff of smoke and smiling thinly in the gloom, his face still masked in darkness. "If there was anyone else in the museum, you would tell me, yes?"

"I'm alone here tonight," said Uncle Nigel firmly.

Behind the sarcophagus, Molly felt a sneeze coming on from the pipe smoke. She plugged her nose. Addison held his breath.

"Vladimir, you don't understand the Incan treasure or its value to history," Uncle Nigel continued, struggling to keep his voice steady.

"Seven hundred and fifty tons of silver, gold, emeralds,

rubies, sapphires, and pearls. I understand its value perfectly," Ragar hissed. He stepped forward into the crossing beams of the flashlights. His skin was as bone white as a vampire's; his piercing gray eyes flashing with anger. "Ten years I rotted in that hole. Ten Siberian winters." Ragar tapped his dress shoe with his silver-tipped cane. "I lost half my foot to frostbite. But I found my men." Ragar lifted the cane to gesture to the thick-browed men crowding the room. "Russian *vory*, all of them."

Uncle Nigel studied Ragar's mercenaries, prison tattoos peeking from their shirt collars and shirt cuffs. Skulls, iron crosses, and strange Cyrillic script inked on their necks and knuckles. He nodded. "Russian Mafia."

"Ten years we hunted rats in our cells to keep from starving. Ten years we licked ice from our prison bars to keep from dying of thirst. Together, we survived horrors you cannot imagine."

Ragar leaned close to Uncle Nigel, his face finally visible in the flickering light. From her hiding place, Molly stifled a gasp. The left side of Professor Ragar's face was marred by a savage burn scar. His jaw and cheek were a boiled, mottled red. "We have suffered enough. We have *earned* this treasure."

Uncle Nigel held Ragar's gaze and stared him down. "Atahualpa's treasure belongs to the South American people. You have no right to it."

Ragar tucked Atahualpa's key in his chest pocket and turned to his men. "Tie up the doctor."

The gang members yanked Uncle Nigel's arms behind his back and bound his wrists. Uncle Nigel twisted and struggled. "What do you need me for?"

"You, my old friend, are going to help me solve the riddles to the three Incan keys and find the treasure."

"You were an archaeologist once. You don't need my help."

"Incas were always your department, Dr. Cooke. You found the first key, no? And you will certainly help me if you hope to see your family again." Professor Ragar reclined in Uncle Nigel's chair, propped up his feet, and took another deep puff from Uncle Nigel's favorite pipe.

"Why are these men loyal to you, Vladimir?" asked Uncle Nigel. "They must know you're insane."

"When I freed them from prison, they made me their *pakhan*, their boss. They are mine now."

"It's not too late to let me go."

The professor shook his head. "You know how I escaped the Siberian prison?" Ragar leaned close. "Malazar. He rescued me. And I rescued these men."

Uncle Nigel's eyebrows lifted in surprise. His face turned ghostly white. "You work for Malazar?"

Ragar nodded and slowly grinned.

From their hiding place, Molly looked at Addison. He shrugged. They kept on listening.

All the life seemed to have leaked out of Uncle Nigel, like air from a flat tire. He slumped in his chair, his head sinking to his chest. "Vladimir, you've made a deal with the devil."

Professor Ragar drew himself up to his full, towering height. His cold gray eyes narrowed to gleaming crescents. "Take Dr. Cooke to the car," he ordered his men. "If he gives you any trouble, knock him out. But do not kill him, not yet. Dr. Cooke is going to help us find the greatest treasure in the world."

And at that precise moment, to Addison's horror, Molly loosed a sneeze that was only slightly quieter than a sonic boom.

Professor Ragar's six bodyguards spun to face Addison and Molly. A dozen angry eyes locked on their hiding place behind the sarcophagus.

Ragar snapped his fingers at his men.

All six bodyguards lunged for the siblings.

Addison turned to Molly. "Run," he suggested.

And for once, Molly willingly accepted his advice. They flew down the dark hallway as if launched from a catapult.

Chapter Three

On the Run

ADDISON AND MOLLY GREW up in the museum. They celebrated birthdays in the Ming dynasty court. They earned allowance tending the rooftop garden during summer vacation. When Uncle Nigel was out of town, they held impromptu jam sessions on Beethoven's piano in the Hall of Musical Instruments.

When they were young, they played hide-and-seek in the Neanderthal exhibit and King of the Castle in the Aztec temple. When they grew older, they played Capture the Flag in the Roman gladiator arena and Frisbee Golf in the Hall of Crowns and Jewels. It was safe to say they knew every secret passageway and shortcut in the museum. Yet Addison and Molly never imagined this knowledge might one day be needed to save their lives.

Knowing where to go, and how best to get there, made them faster than the men chasing them. They tore through the medieval art wing, flying past tapestries depicting the entire blood-soaked history of the Crusades, zipping through the centuries in a matter of seconds. Addison's dress shoes slipped and skittered on the slippery marble floors. Molly's cleats clomped loudly.

"This would be much easier if Uncle Nigel would let us use Rollerblades in here!" Molly said.

Addison slid to halt in the main atrium. The bodies of the four night watchmen, bound and gagged with duct tape, lay piled on the floor behind the information desk.

Molly dropped to her knees. "Sam, Vinny, Carlos, Tom! Can you hear me? Are you okay?"

One man stirred; the rest were unconscious. Addison spotted nasty bruises swelling on their foreheads. He heard the pounding boot steps of Ragar's guards echoing closer down the marbled halls. "We can't help them right now, Mo. We've got to keep moving."

Ragar's men spilled into the atrium, barking commands in Russian.

Addison yanked Molly to her feet and pointed to three different archways. "Africa, Europe, or Asia?"

"Africa—it has more hiding places!" Molly tore through the central archway, vaulting up steps two at a time, racing to Sub-Saharan Africa.

The Russian *vory* chased them, shouting gruffly into their walkie-talkies. Splitting up, the men circled in on the two young Cookes, cutting off their escape paths.

Dashing through the ancient Zulu gallery, Addison waved Molly behind some rawhide shields and a pile of war drums. He realized they were cornered.

Dark-suited thugs quickly blocked every exit, their alert eyes scanning the gloom. Slowly, they closed in.

Addison summoned all his brainpower, trying to conjure a way out of this delicate situation. "Don't worry, Mo. I've got everything under control." He searched the room in a feral panic. "Environment. Use your environment," he reminded himself.

Addison snatched up a Zulu bow and arrow from a display case and surprised one of the men. "Halt!" Addison notched the arrow and drew the gnarled bow back to his cheek.

The ancient bow creaked, groaned, and snapped in two.

Addison stared in horror at the two pieces of broken bow in his hands. Now just a useless stick tied to a piece of string.

"You just broke a museum artifact!" said Molly, astonished. "Addison, you're gonna get in big trouble."

"We're already in big trouble!" Addison pointed frantically at the advancing bodyguards.

The biggest gangster cracked his knuckles. He pitched

his body forward like a linebacker, took a running start at Addison, and leapt. Addison was no star athlete, but he knew that given the choice, it was prudent to slink out of the way of leaping Russian convicts. Addison dove to one side at the last possible moment.

Airborne, the thug spotted the clear glass display case a little too late. To his immense regret, he found he was unable to change directions in midair. The man crashed through the display, knocking over a platoon of British Redcoats in the Battle of Ulundi. The mannequins scattered like bowling pins while the shattering glass triggered a deafening alarm. Emergency bells blared throughout the Zulu gallery.

Addison and Molly bolted into the Hall of Native Americans, the remaining bodyguards sprinting behind. Addison hefted up a metal trash can and began cracking the window displays protecting Algonquin masks and Apache tomahawks. More alarms wailed throughout the museum.

"Addison, what are you doing?" Molly shouted over the blasting alarms.

"The security alarms, Molly! They must be wired straight to the police station. This will call the police!"

More of Professor Ragar's bodyguards poured into the gallery. With no other escape, Molly and Addison darted upstairs.

••••••

Addison and Molly hid in the medieval armor exhibit, behind a model of a destrier warhorse covered in plated steel. Addison panted for air, his heart thumping against his rib cage like a trapped woodpecker. He struggled to quiet his breathing. At this precise moment, he had the mental clarity of two ferrets fighting in a sack.

"This is a sticky wicket," admitted Addison.

"What's a sticky wicket?"

"An English expression about cricket."

"*Cricket?*"

"A British game, like baseball, but slower and more complicated."

"Addison, why are you telling me about cricket right now? Men are coming, and we should be going."

"I was just making a helpful analogy."

"I would like to remind you," said Molly, "that we are being hunted by Russian convicts."

"Yes, about that," said Addison. "If you have any ideas, I'm open to suggestions."

"Well, I've been thinking," said Molly, "Ragar's men are bigger than we are. But we're faster."

"What do you have in mind?" Addison hoped that perhaps Molly had conceived a brilliant plan.

"Running for it."

"Ah," said Addison. It was not the most ingenious plan he had ever heard, but it held a certain logic. "Well, at least the power is out. The darkness will give us an advantage."

Professor Ragar's bodyguards stormed into the room and immediately turned on all the lights.

"Seriously?" said Molly.

Addison smacked his palm to his forehead. "Backup generators," he sighed. He ducked lower behind the warhorse.

The convicts fanned out across the gallery. The tallest of Ragar's men took charge, spouting orders in a thick Russian accent. "Block all exits. Trap them in here."

"Yes, Zubov," grunted the bodyguards, executing their orders with military precision.

The tall gangster named Zubov wore a long black ponytail. His pockmarked face was marred with the clints and grikes of acne scars. His upper lip was crowned by a supremely unfortunate mustache. It looked like a rodent had curled up under his nose and died.

Zubov's gaunt face wore the steely calm of a cobra uncoiling from a snake charmer's basket. He peered carefully about the room, never seeming to blink. He spun a butterfly knife from his pocket, flicked out the blade, and slowly tapped its metal edge against a suit of armor. "Come out. I won't hurt you. I promise." Zubov held one hand over his heart to signify his deep sincerity.

Safe in his hiding place, Addison held his breath. He listened to the tall man's boot heels echoing across the marble floor, drawing steadily closer.

Zubov scraped his butterfly knife along the suits of armor. The scratching sound jangled the nerves in Addison's teeth.

Molly grimaced and whispered to Addison, "I'm getting out of here."

"Molly, I don't know if you've noticed, but the lights are on. They'll see you."

"Better than waiting here doing nothing." Molly darted across the gallery, ducking behind mannequins outfitted in suits of heavy plate mail.

"Hello, little one," said the tall man, his accented voice grating like crushed gravel.

Molly poured on the speed. She threaded her way between suits of armor, ducking jeweled spears and jagged pikes. She visualized it like a soccer match. If she pushed herself, she thought she had a fighting chance of reaching her goal—the north exit. But Ragar's bodyguards swarmed in, blocking every escape path. Molly quickly found she had nowhere to run. The men in dark suits circled in, grinning.

Zubov reached out a knife-scarred hand to grip her neck . . .

Addison, sneaking unnoticed across the gallery, silently thanked Molly for creating the perfect diversion.

He seized this moment to shut off the lights again, plunging the room back into total darkness.

Molly did not hesitate. She ducked the groping arms of the guards and sprinted directly through the throng, threading the needle.

Guards hissed and shouted in the dark as they crashed into one another, toppling metal suits of armor with deafening clangs.

Addison knew Molly could navigate the museum as well as he could, even in pitch darkness. "Molly, the north hallway!"

Together, the young Cookes darted past the bodyguard blocking the north exit, slipping by him in the gloom. They raced up the north hallway at full tilt.

"Fine work with the diversion, young relative."

"Yes, diversion, right," said Molly, wiping sweat from her forehead. "That was totally my plan."

"Well, don't gloat over it. This is where we make a discreet exit."

Professor Ragar's men tore after them, their predatory eyes adjusting to the dim red light of the exit signs.

"Addison, where to?" asked Molly, fists pumping as she sprinted.

"The place we know best."

......

Addison and Molly, well out of breath, bounded into the

largest room in the museum . . . the vast atrium that housed the Aztec temple.

The giant ziggurat was built of limestone and granite boulders shipped in from Tenochtitlán, Mexico. Even at night, the structure was dramatically lit with floodlights. One hundred steep stone steps led to an altar, where ancient Aztecs once performed thousands of human sacrifices.

The temple was surrounded by a beautiful reflecting pool. Museum visitors often made wishes, tossing in pennies, nickels, dimes, and quarters. Once a year, Addison and Molly rolled up their pant legs and helped the museum staff collect the coins from the water to donate to charity.

Tonight, Addison thought he could use a little charity himself, or at least a bit of luck. He and Molly jumped into the reflecting pool with a splash. Soaked up to their knees, they sloshed across the moat to reach the temple. They climbed the base of the pyramid and watched the remaining bodyguards enter the atrium.

"I like staying with Uncle Nigel for the weekend," said Addison. "Never a dull moment."

"We're cornered."

"I will admit, this is a sticky wicket."

Molly blew the stray strand of hair from her eyes. She knew that once Addison landed on an expression he liked, he stuck with it.

The bodyguards surrounded the moat. Zubov shouted

at his men, "You afraid of getting your little shoes wet? Go after them!"

One by one, the bodyguards waded in, trudging through the knee-deep reflecting pool in their steel-tipped combat boots. They closed in on Addison and Molly like a slowly tightening noose.

Molly considered climbing the steps of the ziggurat, but they would have no retreat. "Any ideas, Mr. Wicket?"

Addison searched for options, his eyes settling on the giant floodlights illuminating the stone walls of the temple. He gripped the metal girder of a floodlight and strained with all his might, trying to wrench the light free of its rocky mooring.

"Addison, what are you doing?"

"Destroying museum property."

Molly shook her head in amazement. "It's like I don't even know you!"

Addison snapped the floodlight free and dragged it to the edge of the moat. He watched the bodyguards splashing closer. "Mo, do you know why Aunt Delia gets mad when you leave the hair dryer near the bathtub?"

"Because it's messy?"

"Well, partly." Addison casually rested his foot on top of the bright floodlight, poised on the edge of the moat. "But also, electricity and water don't mix."

The bodyguards paused, suddenly aware of their danger.

Addison smiled at them and winked.

He kicked his foot and the giant floodlight crashed into the water. Electricity jolted through the reflecting pool with a thunderous zap. Bodyguards collapsed like felled oaks, hitting the water in a sizzling, jiggling mess. They yowled like cats stuck in a clothes dryer. The men raced from the moat, retreating to the safety of the atrium where they crumpled to the ground, shaking and twitching, their hair standing on end.

Zubov stared down at his men in disgust. He raised his cold eyes to glare at Addison across the moat. His face was a pale mask of rage.

Molly joined Addison at the water's edge. "Will those guys be okay?"

Addison nodded. "They will be soon. In the meantime, I suggest we take the fire exit at our earliest convenience."

······

Addison and Molly had never used an emergency exit before. But they felt reasonably sure their situation constituted an emergency. They escaped out the back of the museum and scrambled up the grassy embankment that fed into the wilds of Central Park. The two Cookes knelt in a screen of bushes to catch their breath.

The thunder and rain had fizzled to a drizzle and was now pierced by the din of police sirens closing in from all directions.

"Look—it's Uncle Nigel!" Molly pointed to the service

parking lot behind the museum. Addison watched Professor Ragar shove a handcuffed Uncle Nigel into the back of a stretch limousine with tinted windows. Ragar slammed the door and locked it.

Police arrived seconds later, red and blue sirens flashing on their squad cars. A dozen police cruisers surrounded the museum. Officers aimed spotlights on all the doors.

From the hillside, Addison watched the police commander leap from an armored police van, one hand on his holster. The commander shouted at Professor Ragar, "Hands in the air where I can see them!"

Addison turned to Molly, grinning with relief, "Finally, the police can restore some sanity."

Professor Ragar stepped forward and greeted the police commander affably. "Commander Grady, just the man I want to see."

Commander Grady froze, confused.

"Professor Vladimir Ragar," said Professor Vladimir Ragar. "I sit on the board of the police memorial fund. I believe we met at a recent fund-raiser."

"Professor Ragar, of course," returned the commander, shaking Ragar's hand vigorously. "I'm sorry I didn't recognize you. And thank you, by the way, for your generous contribution. What's the situation here?"

From the hillside, Molly watched, aghast. "Do you think Ragar really donates money to the police?"

"I doubt it. I suspect Ragar is just an extremely smooth

45

talker." Addison shook his head in begrudging admiration. "I can learn a thing or two from this man."

The police commander stood only a few feet from the limousine where Uncle Nigel was hidden, bound and gagged. Professor Ragar acted completely relaxed. He set a friendly hand on Commander Grady's shoulder and led him away from the limousine. "I was just visiting the museum for some specimens and spotted a crime in progress. And I believe I know who the criminals are."

"Who?" asked the commander, who loved a case that solved itself.

"A boy and girl. They broke into the museum, smashed displays, and ruined priceless artifacts. These criminals must be found."

"Of course. Are they nearby?"

"Yes, I recommend you search the grounds, Commander Grady," said Professor Ragar, pointing to the woods that hid Addison and Molly. "These are—how do you say?—urgent circumstances."

"At once."

In the bushes, Molly turned to Addison. "Time to go."

"Agreed."

The two left their hiding place and crept farther up the forested hillside.

"I love it when things get completely bad," said Addison.

"Why would you say that?"

"Because once things are truly awful, they can't possibly get any worse."

At that moment, they heard a shout from Professor Ragar below. "There they are now, Commander! Quickly!"

Ragar pointed his ivory-tipped cane up the hill at Addison and Molly. Police spotlights swept the hillside and lit up the pair like the stars of a Broadway show. Addison and Molly froze in midstep. Addison offered his brightest smile.

A squadron of duty-hardened New York City police officers surged up the hill, batons drawn, closing fast.

"Addison," Molly said, "I think things just got worse."

Chapter Four

A Sticky Wicket

ADDISON AND MOLLY CRESTED the hill, plowed their way through thorn-encrusted briar bushes, and touched down onto a jogging path. Addison searched frantically for a fast escape. "Where are the bike messengers when you need them?"

The shouts of police officers drew closer through the woods.

"C'mon," Molly said. She and Addison tore along the jogging path, heading for the Central Park livery stables.

The two raced past a tourist carriage and ducked into the stables. They crawled under a wooden fence to join a mare in her enclosure. The horse chomped hay and nickered at them cheerfully.

"Shhh!" said Addison.

Policemen surrounded the stable, their voices crackling through walkie-talkies. "They must be inside!"

"Set up a perimeter."

"Cover the exits."

Addison quietly opened the horse's paddock. Seizing the horse's withers, he climbed up onto the mare's back.

"Addison . . . are we going to steal a *horse*?"

"These are—how do you say?—urgent circumstances," explained Addison, imitating Ragar's accent.

"Can you even ride a horse?"

"How hard can it be? I've read about it in books." Addison helped Molly clamber up behind him.

"Go!" said Addison to the horse. "Please," he added.

The mare simply stood there, pleasantly chewing hay.

"Some things you can't learn from books, Addison."

"I will be sure to remember that."

Outside in the corral, dozens of policemen could be heard marching into position, surrounding the stable. A policeman switched on a megaphone, which sparked with static. "Come on out. You're surrounded!"

Addison leaned close to the horse's ear. "Step on it!"

The horse smacked its teeth with its great tongue and did nothing else.

"I think you're supposed to kick it," Molly offered.

"That's your answer for everything!"

Molly decided to take matters into her own hands. Or feet, in this case. She knocked her cleats into the horse's sides.

It did the trick. The mare sprung into gear. With a thunder of hooves, the horse burst from the stable.

Molly and Addison held on for dear life.

Surprised policemen dove from the path of the galloping steed as it vaulted the paddock fence. Addison and Molly clung to the horse like a wet bathing suit. The mare bolted across the baseball diamond and onto the football field, picking up speed. Behind them, a squadron of uniformed officers gave chase.

Overhead, a police helicopter caught them in its searchlight, tracking them across the open field.

Molly bounced along on the horse, hanging on to Addison. "Why am I always in back?"

"Because you're younger!"

"Do you even know how to steer this thing?"

"You ask too many questions!"

The horse plunged directly into the dense foliage surrounding the football field. Soon they were enveloped in the dark forest, tree limbs whipping past their faces. Addison ducked low over the horse's mane, Molly's face catching all the branches that missed Addison.

The helicopter blades grew quieter as Addison and Molly fled deeper into the woods.

Molly's voice shook with each powerful stride of the galloping horse. "Why kidnap Uncle Nigel?"

"Professor Ragar needs his help to track down the treasure. Uncle Nigel is famous among archaeologists. He is the number two Incan expert in the world."

"Who's the number one Incan expert?"

Addison's face slowly turned white. "Aunt Delia!"

Addison reined the horse. "She must be in danger, too. We need to get back home." He tugged on the mare's reins, aiming the horse north for West 86th Street.

······

Addison and Molly cantered north on Amsterdam and hooked a right onto 86th Street. Police helicopters circled in the distance, combing the neighborhood with searchlights.

Addison dismounted, parallel-parking the horse in an empty spot in front of the local deli.

"You can't park there—it's a handicapped spot," said Molly.

"Molly, they're not going to ticket a horse!"

As police sirens swept the surrounding streets, Molly and Addison hurried inside their apartment building.

They bolted up the endless set of stairs and reached the fifth-floor landing out of breath. They rushed down the hall and skidded to a halt. The apartment door was ajar.

Addison lifted a finger to his lips, signaling for quiet. When he crept into the living room, his jaw fell open in shock.

The sofa was overturned, and the coffee table lay broken on its side. A bookshelf was toppled over and ten years of *National Geographic* magazines were scattered across the floor. Aunt Delia's drawings and paintings hung crookedly on the walls. Her well-worn copy of the complete works of Lady Florence Craye lay on the rug, torn into tatters.

Addison and Molly searched the entire apartment. Every room was ransacked.

"Aunt Delia's gone," said Addison. "But her purse and keys are still on the side table."

"She's been kidnapped like Uncle Nigel."

"Well, she put up a better fight than he did," said Addison, considering the wreckage of the apartment. Then, noticing Molly's horrified expression, he added, "I'm sure she's fine. Ragar needs her cooperation to find the treasure."

Addison and Molly righted the overturned sofa so they could sit down.

"This is definitely a sticky wicket."

"Addison, we just fled the police and illegally parked a stolen horse in a handicapped zone! This is more than a sticky wicket!"

"Patience, sister. It is in moments like these that the Addison Cooke brain is at its finest." Addison stood up to pace the floor. "Any moment now, the neurons will click into gear like a well-oiled machine."

Police sirens howled in the distance, drawing closer. Molly stood up, assessing the situation. "Aunt Delia is kidnapped, Uncle Nigel is kidnapped, and we just hijacked a horse." Molly spread her arms wide. "We weren't supposed to be in the museum after hours. We broke expensive artifacts. Professor Ragar tried to kidnap us. And now the entire New York Police Department wants us arrested. We're fugitives!"

"And to think," Addison mused, "just a few hours ago we were worried about being grounded."

Molly flopped back down on the sofa.

Addison clasped his hands behind his back and furrowed his brow. He knew that the solution to a problem often lay at the end of a well-paced floor. He took a few meditative laps around the overturned coffee table. "We need to find that second key," he said at last.

"We need to help Aunt Delia and Uncle Nigel. That's what's important, Addison!"

"Two steps ahead of you, sister. Professor Ragar needs their help solving the riddle and finding the second key. So if we get to the second key fast enough, that's where we'll find them."

Molly weighed the truth of this. "We're just middle schoolers. We can go to the police. We'll explain what happened in the museum. They're not going to throw kids in jail."

"We *are* just middle schoolers. So who would believe us? Molly, listen to all those sirens outside—there's a full-on manhunt. For *us*. Besides, Ragar is practically best friends with the police commander." Addison shook his head. "We can't show our faces. Ragar has seven hundred and fifty tons of treasure at stake. If he can kidnap us, too, he will."

"Why? We're not Incan experts."

"Blackmail."

"Explain it like I'm a sixth grader," said Molly, who was a sixth grader.

"If Professor Ragar kidnaps us, he can get Aunt D and Uncle N to do whatever he wants. They'll be forced to cooperate and help him find the treasure."

Molly nodded. "Those sirens are getting closer."

Addison sighed and shook his head. "In retrospect, maybe I shouldn't have parked the horse directly in front of our building."

"Right," said Molly.

Addison locked the front door. He crossed to the windows and turned off the lights so he could peer out into the night. Flashing sirens paraded up the streets. "The police could be here any minute. We need to slip out of here."

Addison snagged a backpack and fresh clothes from the closet. He fished through his aunt's desk and found his passport. "I'm going after the Incan treasure. That's the only way to find Aunt D and Uncle N."

"Are you serious?"

"As a heart attack."

"Then I'm going with you."

"Mo, you can go stay with our uncle Jasper. I don't need any help—I can do this myself."

"You can't even ride a horse by yourself. How are you going to flee the country, find the treasure, and save Aunt Delia and Uncle Nigel? You're not even old enough to have a driver's license."

"I'll hire cabs."

"We're not allowed to."

"These are urgent circumstances."

"All right, how are you going to hire a cab in South America? You don't speak Spanish."

Addison looked up from his packing. "There's something in what you say, Molly." He creased his brow in thought and gave a deep sigh. Finally, Addison arrived at a decision, his face resolute. "Molly, it's time to assemble the team."

Chapter Five

Code Blue

ADDISON CRAWLED ACROSS HIS bunk bed and cranked open the rear window that faced onto the apartment courtyard. On the window ledge, he kept a rubber ball tied to a long piece of string. When he tossed the ball out of the window, it dropped exactly thirty feet to bounce against the bedroom window three stories below.

Eddie Chang woke to the familiar signal of Addison's rubber ball tapping against his window. He desperately wanted to sleep, rather than get involved in another one of Addison's inadvisable adventures. If seventh grade had taught Eddie anything, it was that following Addison on one of his schemes was a surefire path to a grounding. Eddie hid his head under his pillow.

But the ball kept tapping. And curiosity always got the better of Eddie. He rolled over in bed and switched on the walkie-talkie he kept on his nightstand. "What is it?" he asked sleepily.

"Code Blue!" crackled Addison's voice through the walkie-talkie.

"Please," croaked Eddie, "please no Code Blue." Eddie looked at the alarm clock on his dresser. "Addison, it's after midnight."

"Code Blue is a mission of the highest urgency. You took an oath!"

"I have a piano lesson first thing in the morning. I'm going back to sleep."

"Fine. I guess I don't need your help retrieving seven hundred and fifty tons of Incan gold."

"You are correct." Eddie switched off the walkie-talkie and closed his eyes. After a minute, his eyes flickered back open. Eddie clicked on the walkie-talkie.

"Addison," he said slowly, "did you say seven hundred and fifty tons . . . of *gold*?"

······

At his window ledge, Addison clipped a second walkie-talkie onto a zip line. He gave it a push and watched it whisk along the wire across the apartment courtyard. The walkie-talkie slid directly into the open bedroom window across the way, conking a sleeping seventh grader on the head.

Raj Bhandari woke with a start, rubbing the bump on his temple. He switched on the walkie-talkie and immediately heard Addison's urgent voice. "Code Blue, Raj!"

Raj's eyes opened wide. He'd spent his entire life waiting for a Code Blue. And he was ready.

Raj ripped off his bedsheets, already dressed in his camouflage army pants, combat boots, black T-shirt, and dog tags. He wore a bandana wrapped around his forehead, and another one tied around his bicep.

Raj always kept his bug-out bag waiting by his bedroom door in case of emergency. It was crammed with survival gear: nutrition bars, a Swiss Army knife, a snakebite kit, fishhooks, camouflage makeup, malaria pills, iodine pills, a bear whistle, a passport, waterproof matchsticks, binoculars, ten feet of snare wire, and a pack of Jolly Ranchers.

Raj shouldered his pack and kissed his dog tags. He vaulted out of his window and onto the fire escape. Scaling the wrought-iron railing, he crept around the perimeter of the building. He slipped through the neighbor's fire-escape landing and reached Addison's open window. Raj rolled inside, landing on Addison's bed. Then he bolted across the floor and somersaulted into Addison's living room.

Addison sat comfortably on the sofa, his legs crossed. He checked his wristwatch and cocked an eyebrow. "Thirty-nine seconds. You're getting rusty, Raj."

······

There was a hesitant knock at the door, and Molly let Eddie inside. He still looked bleary-eyed from sleep, his black hair sticking up in back, but he was snappily dressed in his public school uniform. The tallest of the group, Eddie's pant legs showed a few inches of ankle. He scanned the overturned coffee table and books scattered across the room. "I like what you've done with the place."

"We were ransacked," explained Molly.

"Awesome," said Raj, his eyes glittering with excitement.

Addison debriefed the team, bringing them up to speed on the kidnapping, the chase, Professor Ragar, Atahualpa's key, and the Incan treasure. Most people would be astonished by this rapid turn of events, but Eddie and Raj were familiar with Addison's stunning capacity for getting himself into trouble.

"So where do we come in?"

"Raj, you're here because you graduated from survival camp twice, you're a brown belt in karate, you can hold your breath for two minutes underwater, and you're the most highly decorated Boy Scout in PS 141," said Addison.

"Why am I here?" asked Eddie.

"You speak Spanish."

"He does?" Molly asked, incredulous.

"*Sí.*" Eddie shrugged. "Because of my nanny." He had wandered into the kitchen to rummage around in the Cookes' refrigerator. He returned with a tin of olives, some uncooked hot dogs, and a jar of spaghetti sauce.

Addison pulled out his notebook and showed Eddie his copy of Atahualpa's key. "It's a riddle that leads us to the next key. Can you translate it?"

"It's impressive writing," said Eddie, peering at the intricate Spanish cursive inlaid on the key. "It's like cake frosting."

"What does it say?"

Eddie dipped a raw hot dog into the spaghetti sauce, garnished it with a row of olives, and took a bite.

Molly grimaced.

Eddie smiled contentedly. He cleared his throat dramatically and read . . .

"In the seat of the Andes Mountains,
By the *Río Olvidado*,
Lie the bones of the underworld
That guard the key to silver and cheese."

"Cheese?" asked Molly.

Eddie tilted the page to the light and studied the ancient calligraphy more closely. "Gold," he corrected himself. "The key to silver and *gold*."

"Hm," said Addison.

"The whole thing rhymes a lot better in Spanish."

"Thank you, Eddie." Addison paced a fresh lap around the overturned coffee table. "The good news," he announced, "is that I checked out every book in the library on Incan history." Addison frowned, deep in thought. "The bad news is, all the books are in my backpack. And my backpack is in my uncle Nigel's office at the museum."

"Why'd you leave it there?" asked Eddie.

"We were fleeing from kidnappers," Molly answered matter-of-factly.

"Awesome," said Raj.

Addison flipped through his aunt's gigantic copy of *Fiddleton's World Atlas*. "I'm not sure about the second half of the clue, the hidden cave of bones and all that. But the first part seems clear enough."

Molly, Eddie, and Raj crowded around the atlas.

Addison pointed a finger at a map of Colombia. "These are the Andes Mountains. And look—southwest of Bogotá, there is a town called Olvidados."

"'*Río*' means 'river,'" Eddie chimed in, squinting at the map. "And Olvidados is split in half by a tiny river. That could be the Río Olvidado."

"So we have a starting point," said Molly.

Addison addressed the group. "Gentlemen," he said dramatically, "and also Molly," he added, "we are flying to Colombia." He turned and began pulling camping gear from the hall closet.

"Wait, shouldn't we think about this first?" asked Eddie.

"Think about what?" asked Raj, tightening the straps of his bug-out bag.

"I mean, shouldn't we just go to the police?"

"Ragar could be boarding a plane within the hour," said Addison. "Once he leaves American soil, there's nothing the local police can do. We'd just be stuck here praying the Colombian police can be bothered to track Ragar across the Amazon. And frankly, I don't like those odds."

"Well, what are we supposed to tell our parents?"

Addison was not one to be bothered by details. "Eddie, just leave them a note telling them you're with me. It's not lying. Besides, you sleep over here every weekend."

"I know, but Colombia? There's a whole rain forest down there. We could get malaria."

"I've got pills for that," Raj piped in.

"Eddie, I'm an experienced traveler. I'll have you back in time for school on Monday."

"You can't guarantee that."

"I can't *not* guarantee it."

Eddie pondered this.

"Look," said Addison. "If your parents were kidnapped, I'd go and help you."

"That's true," said Eddie. "But you'd do anything that means getting out of school."

Addison felt Eddie had a strong point there.

"I shouldn't even be here," Eddie continued. "You know my mom thinks you're a questionable influence."

"I'm a fantastic influence! Your parents don't let you do anything. I let you do whatever you want." Addison pressed his point. "I'm giving you a once-in-a-lifetime opportunity, Eddie. Your parents are workaholics with seven cats. They practically keep you imprisoned under lock and key. If you grow up sheltered and afraid of taking risks, someday you could end up just like them."

Eddie shuddered. It was all true. "Okay, fine. But South America? Aren't there kidnappers?"

"There are kidnappers here, too." Molly shrugged.

"All right—but it's a different continent. How do we even get there?"

"I'm glad you asked that, Eddie." For this was Addison's trump card, the moment he had been waiting for. "Minutes before my uncle was kidnapped, he gave me one very important item . . ." Addison reached into his back pocket and showed the group. "His wallet."

"So?"

Addison flipped open the billfold and said two magic words: "Credit cards."

Addison could sense Eddie's objections melting away one by one. He forged ahead. "Seventh grade is almost over. We don't know what the future will bring. Even if we find my aunt and uncle, the museum might lay them off. Molly and I might have to go live with our weird uncle Jasper in England. I've known you guys almost all my life. We were raised on 86th Street. We're '86ers,' and this is it. This could be our last adventure together."

Eddie and Raj digested this.

"I'm in," said Raj. "Survival camp is one thing. But now I'll finally get the chance to test my skills in the wild. Besides, when an 86er calls a Code Blue, you help them no matter what." These were words Raj lived by. He placed his hand into the center of the group.

"Addison, how much gold did you say there was?" asked Eddie.

"More than you can spend in a lifetime."

"We'll see about that." Eddie set his hand on top of Raj's. "I'm in, too."

"Me three," said Molly. "I guess we're going to Colombia."

Addison joined his hand in the circle. "To the Incan treasure."

Chapter Six

A Journey Abroad

ADDISON AND HIS TEAM strode through the glittering international airport. Bright morning sunlight flooded the floor-to-ceiling windows of the terminal. "Keep moving quickly," said Addison. "We don't know if the police are looking for us here."

Addison was ten weeks shy of his thirteenth birthday. He wasn't sure if he was legally old enough to fly without an adult. He was about to find out.

The group kept their heads down as they waved their passports and boarding passes before the guard at the security line. They were almost through the X-ray machines before a security guard called to them. "Hey, aren't you guys a little young to be traveling alone?"

"It's okay," said Addison, confidently cocking a thumb at Molly. "She's with us."

The guard nodded and ushered them through.

Molly hurried to keep pace with Addison as they crossed the concourse. "Do you really think we can pull this off and catch up with Ragar?" she whispered.

"We've got to," Addison replied. "We're Uncle N and Aunt D's only chance. But we have two huge advantages over every treasure hunter who's come before us. One: We have the first Incan clue."

"And two?"

"We're Cookes, Molly. This is in our blood. We were born for this."

Crossing the skywalk to their terminal, Addison thought his whole team looked a bit on the nervous side. He secretly wondered if he was biting off more than he could chew, but he quickly banished such thoughts from his mind. If his friends were going to risk all to help him find his aunt and uncle, the least he could do was make sure they enjoyed themselves. It just required leadership.

Addison read the seat assignments on their plane tickets. "These seats are coach. I really prefer first class."

"That costs a fortune," said Molly.

"Not if you ask nicely," Addison responded. He marched up to the imposing doors of the exclusive Ambassador's Club, plucked the frequent-flyer card from his uncle's wallet, and swiped it through the card reader. The great doors swung open, and the team followed him inside.

Classical music hummed pleasantly throughout the lounge. Leather upholstered couches lined the walls. Business people in expensive suits sipped coffee and discussed the price of stocks.

An imperious hostess stood at the check-in counter, frowning down at Addison.

Addison flashed his uncle's frequent-flyer card and his most winning smile. "Beautiful morning, isn't it?"

The hostess checked the frequent-flyer card and examined Addison from head to toe. His hair was neatly parted beneath his Ivy cap, and his school tie was knotted cleanly in a half Windsor.

"Welcome to the Ambassador's Club, Mr. Cooke," said the hostess uncertainly.

Addison quickly read the name tag on her blazer. "Thank you, Nancy. How full is the seven a.m. flight to Bogotá?"

"I'd be happy to check that." Nancy did not look happy to check that. She loudly pounded at the keys of her terminal. "Looks like plenty of room on the flight."

"Perfect. Nancy, I have a special favor to ask."

"Oh, really?"

"This is our first time traveling without an adult. My stepfather would feel more comfortable if we were seated in the first-class cabin, where the flight attendants can keep a better eye on us."

Nancy fixed Addison with a withering gaze. "I'm sorry, it is not our policy to upgrade our coach passengers to first class."

"Of course not. And I'm sure my stepfather would agree with you completely, Nancy." Addison waited to see if she would take his bait. He counted to three in his head.

"And . . . who is your stepfather?"

Addison knew he had her on the line; he just had to reel her in. "We're not supposed to drop his name," he demurred. "Especially on his airline."

Nancy's face drained of color. "Wait, are you saying your stepfather is . . ."

"The chairman of this airline, yes," said Addison, turning to leave. "Don't worry about the seats, Nancy, we'll just be on our way."

"Wait!" said Nancy, typing furiously into her terminal. "Let me just recheck the system. Ah! It looks as though we *do* have some seats available in first class. Would that be acceptable?"

Addison turned to check with Eddie and Raj. They nodded, wide-eyed. He turned to face Nancy.

"That will be acceptable." Addison offered Nancy a reassuring smile. "Nancy, you're a rainmaker. Here's my card if you ever need anything." He slid her one of his uncle's business cards. "Can you point my friends and me to the bar? We are parched and require refreshment."

"With pleasure, Mr. Cooke." Nancy perked up to her most professional posture and gestured toward the bar.

As they walked away, Addison turned to Molly. "And that's how you get a first-class upgrade."

······

Addison sidled up to the bar as if his stepfather owned the entire airline. "Four Arnold Palmers, easy on the ice," he called to the bartender.

Eddie, Raj, and Molly took seats as well. The bartender examined the middle schoolers in surprise.

"An Arnold Palmer is half lemonade, half iced tea," Addison explained to the slack-jawed bartender. "It's named for the legendary golf pro."

"Of course," said the bartender, snapping his jaw shut. "But how will you be paying for this today?"

Addison confidently slid his uncle's credit card across the table.

The bartender eyed the credit card suspiciously. "All right, Mr. Cooke. May I see some ID to verify this card?"

Addison fumbled through his uncle's wallet and handed over his uncle's New York City Public Library card.

The bartender carefully compared the names on the

two cards and decided they matched up just fine. He shrugged. "Four Arnold Palmers, coming right up."

Addison smiled, spinning around in his bar stool to admire the view of the runway. A gaggle of jumbo jets lined up for takeoff. When the Arnold Palmers arrived, Addison clinked glasses with his team. He swiveled the ice cubes around in his drink and took a sip. It was perfect.

······

Addison reclined his seat in the first-class cabin of the jumbo jet. The chair was as large as his bed back home. Molly sat next to him. Eddie and Raj sat across the aisle, trying on their free first-class slippers.

"Breakfast is served," announced a flight attendant, setting steaming plates of eggs and bacon down on their tray tables.

"Free breakfast!" whispered Eddie. "And it comes with miniature salt and pepper shakers!"

"Anything to drink?" offered another flight attendant, making her way through the cabin.

Addison stayed her with a hand. "If you have some orange juice in that trolley, you will win my undying affection."

"At once, Mr. Cooke," crooned the flight attendant.

Addison spread orange marmalade on a muffin,

realizing he had completely missed dinner the night before. He was ravenous. He scooped scrambled eggs onto a slice of toast as he'd once seen his father do. "Mo, why aren't you eating? Breakfast is the most important meal of the day and all that."

Molly held her stomach and frowned. "I can't eat. I'm worried about Aunt Delia and Uncle Nigel."

Addison slowly lowered his fork. He looked down at his eggs. Hot and steaming with just the right amount of bacon. But somehow, Addison found he wasn't as hungry as he'd thought. He turned to gaze out the window. New York faded into the distance as the plane soared over the open ocean, carrying him to a new world.

II

THE

INCAN

TRAIL

Chapter Seven

Welcome to Olvidados

ADDISON PACED IN FRONT of the Bogotá bus terminal, consulting his pocket copy of *Fiddleton's Atlas*. The clouded sky was a gray porridge, the air as warm and wet as a dog's tongue. Addison loosened his tie against the stifling Colombian heat and addressed his team. "Olvidados is just a hop, skip, and a jump away. We'll be there before Molly can say something snippy."

"That's exactly what you said when we left New York," said Molly snippily. "Six hours ago."

"Well," observed Addison, "Rome wasn't built in six hours."

"Maybe. But I bet you can at least *get* to Rome in six hours."

Addison decided to let Molly have this round. International travel was probably enough to make even the Dalai Lama get a bit snappish with his monks. Addison sat down on a bench next to a weather-beaten man sipping a bottle of foul-smelling liquid from a brown paper bag. The leather-skinned man smiled a toothless grin and offered Addison the bottle.

"Thanks," said Addison, waving a hand, "but Arnold Palmers are as strong as I go."

Eddie returned from the ticket counter, beaming with pleasure. "Four bus tickets to Olvidados." He fanned them in his hand and doled them out like a card dealer.

"What took so long?" asked Molly.

"Olvidados means 'forgotten,'" Eddie said.

"So?"

"So," Eddie explained, "I kept asking the cashier for a ticket. She'd say, 'Where to?' And I'd say, 'Forgotten.' And she'd say, 'Where to?' And I'd say, 'Forgotten.' It went on like that."

"Well," said Addison, "how long until our bus gets here?"

"I forget."

Addison clasped his hands behind his back and resumed his pacing.

"Another thing," Eddie continued, interrupting Addison in midpace. "I changed your uncle's cash into Colombian money." He handed Addison his uncle's wallet. "Instead of two hundred dollars, you now have *four hundred thousand* pesos."

Raj tried to let out a low whistle before remembering that he couldn't whistle.

"Well," said Addison, admiring the cash, "Colombia is starting to grow on me. You see, Molly, everything is falling neatly into place."

Thunder exploded, and the clouds emptied their pockets. Torrents of rain hammered the street. The team anxiously eyed the flashing lightning.

"Chin up, everyone!" Addison shouted over the deafening deluge. "I'm sure when we get to Olvidados, it will be a glittering tropical paradise. The perfect vacation after a long week of school."

••••••

Four hours later, Addison stepped off the bus in Olvidados and directly into a puddle of mud. Squabbling chickens and bleating goats exited the bus after him, followed by a very morose-looking Molly, Eddie, and Raj. Addison brushed a few chicken feathers off his blazer and offered his brightest smile. "Well, at least the rain has cleared."

Molly, Eddie, and Raj had the look of people who've been holding their breath for four hours.

"We've been holding our breath for four hours," said Molly.

"It reeked in there," Eddie agreed.

"I found the ride rather pleasant." Addison stretched his aching neck.

"I heard Colombia is dangerous," said Molly warily.

Addison scanned his surroundings. The alleyway seethed with beggars, pickpockets, soothsayers, and knife fighters. Gypsies in brightly colored turbans sold fortunes for copper coins. Fire-eaters belched orange tongues of flame into the air. "It looks like the Bronx." Addison shrugged.

"But what if we get kidnapped?"

"We can't get kidnapped," Addison said confidently.

"Why not?"

"Stick to me like a tick, Mo. What do kidnappers want?"

"Ransom."

"And where do they get it?"

"From parents," said Molly.

"But we don't have parents," said Addison. "And our aunt and uncle are *already* kidnapped, so we're covered."

Molly nodded her head, seeing his logic.

Addison pulled out his compass, gathering his bearings. "The clue said, *'By the Río Olvidado, lie the bones of the underworld that guard the key to silver and gold.'* So our first order of business is finding this Olvidado River."

Addison led the group through the maze of Olvidados, following the local map from *Fiddleton's Atlas*. They wandered past a blind man with a snake coiled around his neck who sang tunes in a tribal tongue and shook his tin cup for change. They edged past local women with gold hoops in their noses who drank corn wine from gourds and gossiped in the ancient Quechuan languages of the Incan Empire.

Like streams feeding a river, the alleys opened to streets that led to the bustling market square. There, dark-skinned women sold tapioca cakes and voodoo dolls. Road peddlers sold strings of glass beads and hawked water snake skins with medicinal qualities. But then Addison saw something truly remarkable: a girl with long black hair and bracelets all the way up her wrists. She was older than Addison, maybe fifteen. In her hand, she held a switchblade, and in her eyes, she held mischief.

Addison found his feet leading him directly to her. "Addison Cooke," he said, extending a hand. "You probably can't understand English. But I had to introduce myself. I'm new to town and could use someone to show me the sights."

The girl ignored Addison's offered hand. With her switchblade, she snapped the bottle cap off a soda and smacked it down on a cardboard box. She produced three conch shells and began shuffling them around on the cardboard.

"My name's Guadalupe," she said in perfect English. "Follow the bottle cap. It's under one of the shells."

Addison watched Guadalupe slide the shells back and forth with dizzying speed.

"If you think you know where the shell is, *amigo*, put your money on the table."

Addison could not resist games of chance. His uncle Jasper loved everything from horse racing to roulette, and Addison had inherited the vice. He placed a few pesos on the cardboard box. "The bottle cap is hidden in your right hand. The one you're holding behind your back."

Uncle Jasper had also taught Addison about confidence games.

Guadalupe frowned. "I see you've played this game before."

"We're from New York," Molly explained, taking her place next to Addison, who gathered up his money.

Guadalupe nodded. "We don't get many tourists. The only famous things to see in Olvidados are the cathedral, the llama farm, and the giant pile of rubber tires."

"Your English is really good," said Molly.

"It should be," said Guadalupe. "I'm from Cleveland."

Molly processed this. She glanced around at the derelict shop fronts and seething, trash-strewn alleys. "How did you end up *here*?"

"It's complicated."

Addison nodded appreciatively at Guadalupe, liking her more and more. Here was a person with a few decent stories to tell.

"We're interested in looking for the bones of the underworld," Eddie said. "Can you help us?"

"Bones of the underworld?" asked Guadalupe. "What kind of tourists are you?"

"It's complicated," returned Molly.

"Bones of the underworld aren't my specialty, *chica*, but I can show you the sights," said Guadalupe. "For a price."

"Why should we hire you?" asked Eddie. "You just tried to cheat us."

"You said you're looking for the underworld. I know every basement, alley, and gutter in this town."

Addison admired street smarts and pluck. He beamed at Guadalupe. "I am an astute judge of character, and I think you will make an excellent guide."

"I'm an astute judge of money. Show me yours, so I know I'm not wasting my time."

Addison pulled out his uncle's wallet and opened it wide.

Guadalupe eyed the contents and made a quick mental calculation. "My price is four hundred thousand pesos."

Addison considered himself a shrewd negotiator. Four hundred thousand pesos seemed just a bit steep. "Can I get a student discount?"

"Sure," said Guadalupe. "Even better, how about a five-finger discount?"

"What's a five-finger discount?"

"This is!" And with her five fingers, Guadalupe snatched the wallet from his hand.

Before Addison could blink in surprise, Guadalupe was already hightailing it across the crowded market.

"John Wilkes Booth!" cried Addison.

"Who?" asked Eddie.

"That's what Addison says instead of swearwords," Molly explained. "So he doesn't get in trouble."

Addison darted after Guadalupe. Within seconds, she vanished among the throng of con artists, vagabonds, and thieves.

······

Fuming, Addison led his crew along narrow alleys, waded through a flock of passing sheep, and crossed a junkyard where a forlorn mule chomped at crabgrass.

"It's getting dark," said Molly, blowing the stray wisp of hair from her eyes. "We have no money and nowhere to stay."

"Molly," Addison said, impatiently raising one hand in the air, "you're very quick to take a glass-half-empty view of things. I prefer to say we have nothing tying us down." He consulted his map. "We'll find the location to the next key. It's near the river. We've come this far. It must be close."

"We don't even have money now. How are we supposed to get out of here?" Eddie was a champion worrier, and once his thoughts began spiraling, they often flew into a tailspin. "We could be stuck in Colombia for years. And we're supposed to be back in school on Monday! I need to get good grades so I can get into a decent college."

"Take a good look around, Eddie." Raj gestured to the festering warren of alleyways, teeming with cutpurses and desperados. He breathed deeply. "You're in life's classroom."

Following his compass, Addison led the band through the shantytown in the gathering darkness. Sinewy women with cracked mahogany skin ground cassava in mortar bowls and boiled malanga leaves. The evening air smelled sweet with the fragrance of gardenias.

"Here we are," Addison announced at last, looking up from his map. He reached the end of a trash-cluttered lane, turned the corner, and spread his arms dramatically. "The Forgotten River!"

To his amazement, the river was just a trickle of muddy ooze.

"No wonder they forgot about it," Molly said.

Addison struggled to hide his disappointment. "To be fair, the clue was written five hundred years ago. I'm sure back in the day it was a fantastic river. The Frank's Pizza of rivers."

Bells tolled from the cathedral. The team trudged up to the front steps of the church and flopped down in a tired heap.

"We found the Forgotten River," said Eddie. "Now what?"

"I'm not sure," Addison admitted, rubbing his tired legs. "The Cooke brain runs more smoothly after a moment's rest."

"I'm hungry," said Eddie. "I miss Restaurant Anatolia. Best Turkish restaurant in the city."

"Eddie, when we find that treasure, you can afford all the Turkish food you want. You can buy Restaurant Anatolia and sleep on a bed of kebabs."

"I could settle for that."

"We shouldn't be thinking about ourselves," said Molly. "Aunt Delia and Uncle Nigel have been kidnapped for nearly twenty-four hours."

"Molly, I haven't even begun to think about *not* thinking about thinking about our aunt and uncle." Addison took off his wingtips and felt the cool cobblestones through his dress socks.

Eddie plopped down beside him. "I don't mean to sound defeatist, Addison, but this is completely impossible. If this Incan treasure's been around for centuries, how come no one's found it yet?"

"Because no one had my uncle's key. Any treasure hunters who came before us were just fumbling around in the dark. They didn't know where to begin."

"We *have* the key, and we don't know where to begin." Molly shrugged.

Eddie bobbed his head in agreement. "What if Ragar beats us to the punch? He has a head start. Plus he has your aunt and uncle—and they're Incan experts."

The sunset cast long shadows across the cobbled courtyard of the cathedral. Darkness was falling fast. Addison could tell his team felt just as frazzled as he did. He shook his head. "My aunt and uncle won't help Ragar. They'll provide clever clues that sound right, but are deliberately wrong."

Molly sighed. "They can't fool him forever."

"Probably not. But they *can* slow him down. And that gives us a chance."

Raj could never sit still for long. He explored the looming walls of the ancient cathedral, peppered with Gothic spires, snarling gargoyles, and vaulted archways. "Eddie, can you read that plaque by the door?"

Eddie glanced up. "Probably. It's in English."

"Oh," said Raj, embarrassed. "For tourists, I guess." Raj crossed to the sign and read it aloud. "This church is the Cathedral of Lost Souls. It was built in the time of Francisco Pizarro."

"What's that about Frank's Pizza?" Eddie asked.

"Built just after Pizarro's conquistadors defeated the Incas," Raj continued, reading the chiseled calligraphy on the plaque.

Addison turned to examine the cathedral with sudden interest. "So this old heap is five hundred years old." His eye zeroed in on a carved stone crest that crowned the portico over the massive double doors. And the Addison Cooke brain finally flicked into gear. "Benedict Arnold!" he exclaimed, leaping to his feet. "I've seen that crest before. Raj, you're a genius!"

"I am?"

"Well, one of us is. Because we now have a clue."

Addison flipped through the sketches in his pocket notebook until he found the right page. He pointed a finger triumphantly at the coat of arms—a shield supported by two fire-breathing dragons. It matched the crest on the cathedral. "There. The crest of Diego de Almagro II!"

"Diego who?" asked Eddie.

"I think maybe Addison has heat stroke," Molly said.

"I copied this down from one of my Incan books. Do you guys realize who Diego de Almagro II is?"

"Diego de Almagro I's son?"

"Diego," Addison announced, pausing for dramatic effect, "is the man who killed Francisco Pizarro!"

"That is so rock-and-roll," said Raj.

Molly, mystified, mulled this over. "Wait, so how is this a clue?"

"Look," said Addison, his four-cylinder words struggling to keep pace with his six-cylinder brain, "Diego's father was Spanish, but his mother was a local tribeswoman— Diego sided with the Incas. He helped them kill their greatest enemy—Pizarro."

The light snapped on in Molly's eyes. "So if Diego built this cathedral . . ."

"It was a safe place for the Incans to hide their second key." Addison grinned.

"That makes sense," said Eddie, bobbing his head. "Guadalupe said there were only three things worth seeing in Olvidados: the cathedral, the llama farm, and a giant pile of rubber tires. If I had to find a five-hundred-year-old Incan key in this town, I'd start with the five-hundred-year-old cathedral."

Addison hastily slipped his shoes back on. "We've got to get inside this church."

Molly hesitated. "If we want to rescue Aunt Delia and Uncle Nigel, why not just hide here until Professor Ragar arrives? Why go after the key?"

"We don't want to risk the treasure falling into the wrong hands," Addison declared. "We want it to fall into the right hands."

"Our hands," Eddie specified, rubbing his hands together.

"Well, the Cathedral of Lost Souls is closed for the night," said Molly, pointing to the sign over the door.

"Nothing is closed to the open mind," said Addison.

Chapter Eight

The Cathedral of Lost Souls

ADDISON CONFIDENTLY LED THE team up the front steps of the cathedral. He adjusted the peak on his Ivy cap and buttoned his school blazer. "Straighten your ties, and look respectable."

"I'm not a hundred percent sure about this one," said Molly.

"Molly, when have I ever steered you wrong?"

"Do you really want me to answer that?"

"I've got this under control," said Addison. He reached up and clanged the heavy brass door knocker. After a moment, the oak doors creaked open.

A priest with a short white nose and a long black cassock poked out his head.

Addison offered a cheerful hello in Latin. *"Salve, quid agis. Bonum est vespere!"*

The priest appraised the group suspiciously with his dark beady eyes. He rattled off a curt reply in Spanish.

"He has no idea what you're saying, Addison," Eddie explained.

"I thought priests spoke Latin."

Eddie spoke to the priest in Spanish and blanched at the priest's tart reply. "He says they speak Latin in the service," Eddie translated. "But they don't go around making chitchat in a language that's been dead for two thousand years."

The priest barked a few questions at Eddie.

Eddie turned to Addison. "Who are we? And what do we want?"

"Tell him we're the Vienna Boys Choir," said Addison with an elaborate bow. "We know his cathedral is closed for the night, but we've traveled a long way. We'd love to view his beautiful church and maybe sing a free concert in exchange."

The frowning priest listened to Eddie and rolled this new information around in his mind for a moment. At last, he spoke in broken English. "The Vienna Boys Choir. Here. In Olvidados."

"Quite." Addison smiled ingratiatingly. "We just flew in and have no place to spend the night."

The priest peered into the darkness and snapped a few words in his halted English. "There are four of you. Shouldn't there be a hundred?"

"We're actually the Vienna Boys Barbershop Quartet," Addison offered.

The priest pointed at Molly. "That one is not a boy."

"True, but she sings like one."

"I kick like one, too," Molly growled at Addison.

The priest crossed his arms and looked sternly from Eddie to Raj and back to Addison. He was having exactly none of it. "You," the priest said flatly, "are from Vienna. In Austria."

"Vienna, South Carolina," Addison clarified.

"The New York chapter," Eddie added.

"In America," Molly said, to round things out.

"I sing tenor," Raj put in helpfully.

"Enough," said the priest, pushing his spectacles up his short, piglike nose. He jabbed a finger in the air and unleashed a blistering tirade of fiery Spanish that left Eddie dabbing a mist of spittle from his forehead. Addison only recognized the words *"prisión"* and *"policía."* The priest slammed the heavy oak doors so that they cracked like thunder.

Addison stared at the shut door, inches from his face.

"I don't think I should translate some of that," said Eddie.

"We really could have thought that one through better," said Molly.

Addison was stunned. It was the first time he could remember not being able to charm his way into a place. "I guess my infectious good nature only works on people who are fluent in English." He clasped his hands together, warming them against the cool night air. "Well," he said brightly, "if at first you don't succeed, try the back door."

••••••

The team climbed over a crumbling piñon fence into the cemetery behind the cathedral.

Under the cloak of night, they ducked behind gravestones that slumbered in silence and sneaked to the rear of the vast building.

"I don't know if the Olvidados police department will appreciate this," said Eddie, staring uncertainly at the ominous shadow of the dark cathedral.

"What they don't know can't hurt them," said Addison. He scraped old leaves aside to reveal a wooden cellar door leading down to the cathedral's basement. He tested the heavy doors with his dress shoe. "Raj, can you get these doors open?"

"Can I ever!" Raj's eyes bulged with excitement. He

threw open his backpack and began unpacking matches, fuses, bang snaps, sparklers, electrical tape, batteries, goggles, and at last, his prized possession—a lock-picking set.

"Never mind," said Molly, trying the door handles. "It's unlocked."

"Ah," Raj said, a little deflated.

Molly quietly hoisted open the rotting cellar doors. Addison drew a flashlight from his blazer pocket. The team followed the flashlight's beam, descending into the darkness.

······

Together they crept through the musty cathedral basement. Addison listened to the sound of men's voices upstairs and gestured the group for silence. He moved stealthily, the echoing stone walls amplifying his every footstep.

"Addison, what are we looking for?" whispered Eddie.

Addison closed his eyes and quoted the Incan key from memory. " 'In the seat of the Andes Mountains, by the Forgotten River, lie the bones of the underworld that guard the key to silver and gold.' "

Addison scanned the room with his flashlight and shouldered his backpack. "The clue says 'the bones of the underworld.' Lots of cathedrals have crypts—basement rooms filled with bones. We need to figure out if there's a basement to this basement."

"This is all just a hunch," said Eddie skeptically.

"There's a chance," said Addison.

They tiptoed past rusted candelabras, clothing racks of faded priest robes, and antique incense burners of burnished copper. Parchment maps with burnt edges adorned the walls. Hundreds of dog-eared books lined dusty shelves.

Molly sneezed repeatedly. "It smells just like Uncle Nigel's office."

Raj opened a rotting oak door and discovered a spiral staircase, leading both up and down. "Which way?"

"Down," Addison whispered, "to the underworld." The steep stone steps coiled their way underground, into a deep cellar.

The team emerged in a dank hallway beneath the exposed foundation of the cathedral. Addison cast his flashlight about the sagging beams and cobwebbed stone pillars.

"Do you see anything that looks like a clue?" Molly whispered, peering into the gloom.

"I don't know what we're looking for, but I know we'll know it when we see it."

They reached the end of the cellar and stopped.

"It's a dead end," said Raj.

"I don't see any crypt in here," said Eddie. He peered about the dingy room, draped in cobwebs and shadow. "Maybe we should just leave?" he added hopefully.

Addison took a closer look at the stone cellar. On the far wall stood an oak cabinet, piled with dusty jars of pickled herbs and ancient bottles of wine. Addison rapped the sturdy oak with his knuckles. "This wood isn't too old. It was built much later than the cathedral." He turned to face the group. "It's the one thing that doesn't belong. We have to move this cabinet."

Eddie groaned. "It's gigantic."

"We can see the other three walls of the cellar," said Addison. "We have to make sure there's nothing hidden here. On the count of three. One . . . two . . . three."

They heaved against the cabinet with all their strength. One of the jars of pickled herbs wobbled a bit, but nothing else moved.

"Let's get rid of these bottles."

They stripped the shelves bare, moving the jars to the floor, careful to keep quiet. Eddie, miraculously, didn't drop a single bottle.

"That should do it," said Addison. "Take two."

Again the team pushed with all their might. Slowly, they managed to scrape the wooden cabinet away from the foundation wall.

Addison swept his flashlight beam over the stone masonry but saw nothing to write home about. He sighed.

"Wait!" cried Raj. He wiped dust from the stone with his palms, revealing a large symbol faintly etched into the rock wall of the foundation. A life-size shield supported by two fire-breathing dragons.

"Diego de Almagro II's coat of arms," Addison gasped.

"It's still a wall and not a crypt," said Eddie.

Addison could not argue with Eddie's astute observation. Still, he peered hard at the ancient symbols carved on the stone shield, "Something about the crest seems different . . ."

"There," said Molly, pointing to the design at the center of the shield. "That part looks just like Atahualpa's key."

Raj let out a low whistle. This time, he managed to get a few notes.

"Good eye, Mo," said Addison. He aimed the flashlight on the center of the crest. And there, inside a ram's skull with twisted black horns, was a piece of stone carved in the shape of the Incan key.

"What does it mean?" asked Raj, his voice trembling with excitement. "Is it some kind of clue?"

Addison reached out a cautious hand and brushed cobwebs from the stone wall with his fingertips. If there was a puzzle to the design, he could not figure it out. Finally, unable to think of anything better, he pressed the stone key firmly with his thumb.

Dust shook from the wall. And with a low rumble, the entire shield swiveled inward, revealing a dark cavern.

"A secret door!" Eddie whispered.

"I've waited my whole life for a secret door," said Raj, his eyes glowing.

Addison carefully studied the cobwebbed doorway under the glow of his flashlight. "What do you make of it, Raj?"

"I don't think this door has been opened in a long time. If we're on the right track, Ragar hasn't been here yet."

"Then we're in the lead," said Addison.

Molly peered into the dark tunnel. She could resist no longer. "Ladies first." She grinned, and stepped inside.

······

Molly led the team down a long stone shaft carved through the limestone bedrock.

Addison played his flashlight over the walls. They were covered in painted murals, faded by time, depicting Incas and Spaniards locked in battle. "Look at these, Molly! At least five hundred years old! Aunt Delia would lose her mind if she saw these."

"Aunt Delia would lose her mind if she knew we were down here," Molly countered. "We're not allowed south of 42nd Street."

The tunnel was so cramped even Molly had to stoop. She waved the group forward.

"You're lucky to be raised by archaeologists with exciting jobs," Raj said. "My mom is just an anesthesiologist."

"What's that mean?" asked Molly.

"It means she literally puts people to sleep."

The tunnel finally opened into a chamber where they could stand. As everyone gratefully stretched their backs, Addison panned the flashlight beam across the room.

One wall was dominated by a huge iron cross. Swords, pikes, and javelins were leaned against a rack. On the far side of the room were jail cells with corroded iron bars.

"A torture chamber!" Molly gasped.

"Awesome," said Raj.

"They kept people in these cages?" Eddie asked.

"Most cathedrals had a tribunal like this," said Addison. "The Spanish Inquisition killed people for not being Catholic. Often by burning them at the stake, like King Atahualpa. People would say they were Catholic to avoid being killed. So the Inquisition would torture them to find out who was telling the truth."

"Aunt Delia used to tell us about the Inquisition whenever Addison said her punishments were too harsh," Molly explained.

"Diego de Almagro was part Native Indian," said Eddie. "Why would he want to torture people?"

Addison shrugged and shook his head. "Maybe he tortured the torturers."

"I don't feel hungry anymore," Eddie announced.

Raj crossed the narrow chamber, peering closely at the rough-hewn stone walls. "Looks like another dead end."

"I still think we're looking for a crypt. Everybody search for a trapdoor." Addison shone his flashlight on the torture equipment, hunting for a concealed switch or a hidden panel. He eyed iron cudgels, spikes, sticks, and chains. Handcuffs and manacles anchored to the rock walls. A medieval rack for stretching people.

Raj, unable to resist, picked up a heavy sword and gave it a few swings. Molly found a rusty dagger and practiced a few stabs at the air.

Eddie searched the far wall of the chamber for any telltale cracks in the mortar. A bat flew out from a corner, and Eddie shrieked. The group jumped.

"Jeez, you scared me," said Molly.

"*You* were scared," said Eddie, clutching a hand to his chest.

Addison's eyes lit up with excitement. "Where did that bat fly out from?"

"I don't know," said Eddie. "I didn't ask."

"Eddie, bats live in caves. If there is a secret tunnel, that bat will know all about it." Addison stood stock-still. He licked his thumb and held it in the air. "Does anyone feel a draft? A current of air?"

Molly closed her eyes, concentrating. "Maybe. It's hard to tell."

"Raj, you wouldn't happen to have a box of matches on you?"

"Safety matches, long-reach matches, or strike-anywhere matches?" asked Raj, producing three boxes from his backpack.

"This will do the trick," said Addison, selecting a regular safety match and striking it on the edge of the box. He stared at the tiny blue flame and sure enough, the flicker betrayed a slight breeze in the underground chamber.

The group held its breath.

Addison followed the dancing flame to the far wall of the torture chamber, next to the iron cross. He held the burning match up to tiny fissures in the cracked stone masonry. The blue flame wiggled and leapt where fresh air hissed through. "This isn't just a cross," said Addison. "It's a door handle."

Addison tossed his flashlight to Molly and doused the match. He stepped up to the iron cross, gripped it with both hands, and tugged with all his strength. Nothing much happened. "Eddie, little help?"

Eddie added his grip to the cross, braced himself, and pulled.

There was a low grumble of scraping rock. A circular section of the wall swung open, revealing a hidden tunnel.

"Dibs," said Raj. He climbed into the hole first, followed by Molly.

"What's in there?" Addison called down the dark shaft.

After a few seconds, Raj's breathless voice echoed back. "Skulls! Thousands of them!"

"I'm not going in there," Eddie declared.

"You never know, you might like it," said Addison.

Eddie fixed him with a steely glare.

"Won't know unless you try." Addison followed Raj and Molly inside.

Eddie, left alone in the dark torture chamber, weighed his options. He quickly scurried after Addison, leaving the door open behind him.

······

The team crawled a few feet through the passageway. The air was cold so deep underground. The tunnel opened into a large cavern, part of the natural caves worn into the limestone by the Olvidado River.

Molly handed Addison the flashlight. He held the beam high to fill the room. Addison brushed a comma of hair from his forehead and gasped. He marveled at the underground chamber.

Raj wasn't kidding. The vault was crammed with skeletons—tens of thousands of them. Entire vats piled high with skulls. Towering pillars ringed with rib bones. Chambers decorated with spiraling patterns of leg bones. Intricate ceiling mosaics of finger and toe bones.

"What is this place?" Molly whispered.

"An ossuary," said Addison. "An underground room

decorated with bones. And you need to bone up on your vocabulary," he added.

"What kind of person uses skeletons to decorate?"

"This is just how they buried people." Addison removed his Ivy cap as a sign of respect for the dead. He took the lead, picking his way along the cavern. "Careful, everyone, this place is sacred."

They followed a winding footpath marked with leg bones. The femurs were still attached to the tibias. Complete skeletons leered from stone alcoves, their ghastly teeth frozen in permanent grins that appeared to laugh in the flickering light.

"All these skeletons are short," said Raj.

"They're ancient Incas. You can tell from the jewelry." Addison pointed to a turquoise bracelet wrapped around a skeleton's ulna.

The team inched slowly along the path, keeping carefully within the glow of Addison's flashlight.

Eddie, craning his neck to stare up at a rib bone chandelier, somehow contrived to catch his shoelace on a stray collarbone. He tripped headlong, landing in the arms of a cobweb-covered skeleton. Eddie screamed, tangling himself up with the dead body. "Help!"

"Careful, Eddie!" Addison hissed. "This is an archaeological site. Do you have any idea what these skeletons are worth to historians?"

But Eddie had already lost his balance again. He

tumbled into the vat of skulls, the mummy on top of him. "Get it off me!"

The skull bin tilted, pulling an ancient trip wire, releasing a boulder. The falling stone yanked a rope through a pulley, sending a massive scythe blade whipping through the air.

"Look out!" Raj took a running start and leapt for Eddie, tackling him to the ground. The scythe sliced inches over their heads, the jagged blade imbedding itself in the soft limestone wall with a quivering thud.

"Eddie, what were you thinking?" asked Addison. "This is a sacred burial ground."

"I thought that mummy was going to kill me."

"He's been dead for five hundred years," said Addison. "He's at a huge disadvantage."

"I didn't know this place was booby-trapped," said Raj, delighted.

"Don't move, you guys. Stay right where you are." Addison aimed his flashlight up at the dark recesses of the cave ceiling. The narrow beam illuminated a fretwork of guy-ropes, barely visible in the shadows. "Each pile of bones is rigged to a trap. The Incas did not want anyone disturbing their remains."

Raj was still lying on top of Eddie, whose face was squished into a dusty rib cage. They were fifteen feet off the path. "Well, what do we do?"

"You need to get back to the path, touching as few bones as possible."

Raj helped Eddie back to his feet. "Let's just run for it."

"Are you sure that's the best plan?"

Patience was not Raj's strong suit. "Three . . . two . . ."

"Raj, let's think this through, first!"

". . . one!"

Raj sprinted and Eddie followed, their feet dancing across the piles of bones. A massive blade sprung from the ground, splitting every bone in its path. Raj and Eddie dove to either side of the blade's deadly course. They rolled and scrambled back onto the stone trail. It was a close shave.

"I can't believe we're not dead yet," marveled Eddie.

"The night's still young," said Raj. He dusted off Eddie's back for him.

Sticking close together, the group crept slowly forward.

At the end of the burial chamber, they reached a narrow staircase. Addison took a careful look. The steps were paved with skulls. At the top landing was a small doorway carved into the cave wall. "Let's climb up and see what's inside."

"Let's not and say we did," said Molly.

"There's that can-do Cooke spirit."

"I'll go first," said Raj.

"Wait!" Addison stayed Raj with his hand. "We have

to assume this is a trap. The Incas didn't want us touching any bones, so why would they let us just fox-trot up a staircase of skulls?" Addison and Raj dropped to their knees and examined the steps under the glow of the flashlight.

"There," said Raj, his eyes gleaming. "Some of these steps are the tops of skulls. And some are just polished limestone rocks."

Addison smiled and turned to the group. "Everybody got that? Step only on the rocks, and we'll live to tell the tale."

The team gingerly climbed the skull staircase, carefully choosing their steps. At the top landing stood a doorway marked with a skull and crossbones—an actual skull with actual crossbones. Addison reached for the door handle.

"Let's take a second," said Raj. "We don't know what's waiting for us behind that door."

"Nothing good, I'm guessing," said Eddie.

"Well, we've come this far," said Addison. "Everybody ready?"

Addison heaved open the final door. Everyone ducked.

A moment passed.

Addison was shocked by how little happened. The door simply stood there. An empty dark space gaping at them.

Eddie stood up from where he was crouching. "Well, I don't know what I was so afraid of." He strode confidently through the doorway and screamed as a hundred bats flew out of the cavern, screeching like wailing banshees. He covered his head from their flapping wings and clawing feet. The first hundred bats were immediately followed by several thousand more.

Addison ducked and waited for the storm to pass. It was hard to tell what was more terrifying: the bats' high-pitched screeching or Eddie's high-pitched screaming.

At last, the cloud of bats tapered off. Eddie slowly regained his breath. And then a few hundred more bats flew shrieking out of the cave for good measure.

Eddie sat down on the cold rock. "I liked the dead people better." A big, slow bat loped out of the cave, squawked at him, and flapped down the tunnel. "I think that's the last of them," Eddie sighed.

Addison's team ducked as another thousand bats rocketed past Eddie's head.

••••••

The group entered a final chamber with a high, arched ceiling. Raj found an ancient torch that he managed to light after snapping a few matches. He held the flickering torch aloft.

The hall was flanked by thirteen suits of armor, covered in the dust of centuries. Each medieval gauntlet clutched a rusted ax or broadsword. Their jagged shadows lurched and danced in the torchlight.

Eddie stared transfixed at the plumed Spanish helmets.

He rose on his tiptoes to peer through the slats of a visor . . . then yelped as he spotted a skull inside, leering back at him.

"There are skeletons in this room, too!"

Addison blew dust from a knight's shield and examined the coat of arms. "Francisco Pizarro's Famous Thirteen," he said reverently. "The Spanish knights who stuck by him at Isla de Gallo. These were the conquistadors who overthrew Atahualpa and conquered all of Peru."

"Why are they in an Incan burial ground?" asked Molly. "I thought Diego hated Pizarro."

"It's a mystery," Addison admitted. "There are wheels within wheels." He led his team down the center aisle, where the tattered remains of a red carpet crumpled to dust beneath their feet.

At the end of the chamber stood a raised platform. And on the platform was a single pedestal, guarded by the silent shadows of the knights.

Addison slowly lifted his gaze . . .

On the pedestal, glittering in torchlight, lay Atahualpa's second key.

Eddie gasped. "It's pure silver. Just that key alone will make us rich!"

Addison, keeping his distance, carefully studied the key, the pedestal, and the raised platform. "Raj, what do you think?"

"I think we didn't come all this way to waltz into a booby trap."

"Agreed," said Addison. He swung his flashlight beam up to the ceiling but could not spot any hidden wires or guy-ropes. "Raj, can you borrow a sword from one of those knights?"

"With pleasure." Raj had already been eyeing the heavy bronze broadswords with admiration. He wrestled one from the rusted gauntlet of the shortest knight and passed it hilt-first to Addison.

Addison hefted the sword, his arms shaking from the weight. He gingerly poked the stone platform. Eddie ducked and covered his head, expecting bats.

Nothing happened.

Addison prodded the marble pedestal with a few cautious taps.

Again, nothing happened.

"If a booby trap doesn't kill me, the tension will," said Eddie.

Addison shushed him; he needed to concentrate. Arm muscles trembling, Addison raised the sword to the top of the pedestal and gently, ever so gently, nudged the key.

A massive explosion rocked the room with a blinding flash.

Addison's team hit the deck, clutching their ringing ears.

"I think I just had a heart attack," Eddie gasped.

"What *was* that?" asked Molly, waving acrid smoke from her nose and sneezing.

Addison picked up his Ivy cap from the floor and stared at it in astonishment. He poked his finger through a seared hole in the peak. "A bullet hole," he whispered.

He aimed his flashlight at a small loophole concealed in the far wall. "That blast was a musket shot." Addison panned his flashlight around the room, revealing a dozen gun bores burrowed into the wall. "Spring guns," said Addison, his voice shaky with fear and wonder. "Move the key and a musket fires."

Raj took Addison's cap and turned it over in his hands, staring at the bullet hole in amazement. "Addison, if you were as tall as a grown-up, you'd be dead."

"We've found an advantage." Addison tucked his cap back on his head. "These traps aren't designed for us. The Incas counted on conquistadors, not middle schoolers."

Addison handed the sword to Molly. "Mo, you're the shortest. Would you do the honors?"

Molly blew the hair from her eyes. She grunted as she hoisted the long sword.

Everyone else ducked and covered their ears.

Molly swung the sword like a baseball bat. She knocked the key clear off the pedestal. The muskets fired in a deafening blast that echoed around the stone room. By the time Molly's ears stopped ringing, Addison held the key safely in his hand.

It was heavy in his grip. Addison hardly dared to believe it was real. He wiped away the dust with the heel of his palm.

"Solid silver," Eddie said, his eyes glowing.

"Do you think anyone upstairs heard that blast?" asked Molly.

"It doesn't matter," said Addison. "We have the key now. We're through the worst of it."

Chapter Nine

Things Get Worse

ADDISON FLIPPED OPEN A fresh page in his notebook and took a rubbing of the key with the side of his pencil.

"Voices!" whispered Molly.

The group strained their ears. Sure enough, shouting voices echoed through the cavern.

"It could just be the priests," said Eddie hopefully.

"We have to assume it's Professor Ragar," said Molly.

"Either way, we have worn out our welcome." Addison slipped the Incan key into his pocket. "If we stay in this chamber, we're trapped. C'mon!" He strode across the cavern and waved the team back into the ossuary.

"Not the skeletons again!" Eddie whimpered.

"Eddie, hurry!" said Molly, yanking him along by the collar.

Addison and his team ducked through the chamber door and picked their way down the booby-trapped steps, carefully skipping the skulls. They reached the chamber floor only to discover they were too late.

The bespectacled priest stepped into the ossuary, flanked by six of Professor Ragar's bodyguards. There was no escape.

"There they are!" thundered the priest in his accented English, his voice rebounding off the stone walls. "The Vienna Boys Choir!"

Ragar's men swung their industrial flashlights on Addison's team. Addison recognized Zubov, the tall man with the black ponytail and the unblinking, lifeless eyes of a predator.

Addison squinted at the priest through the blinding beams. "How did you find your way down here?"

"You left every door open behind you," said the priest.

Addison shot an accusatory look at Eddie. "Eddie, you were the last through every door."

"What?" Eddie shrugged. "I didn't want us to get locked in."

"Who are you really?" demanded the priest. "How did you find these secret chambers?"

"That," said Addison dramatically, "is a secret."

Zubov shouted to his men. They lurched forward, moving in on Addison's team.

"Addison, what do we do?" asked Molly.

"I am open to suggestions."

"We need a miracle," said Molly.

"I don't believe in those." A plan simmered in Addison's mind and slowly came to a boil. "They don't know the bones are booby-trapped, but we do. We split up and lure them onto the bone piles."

The four members of Addison's team scattered. Ragar's men chased them onto the stacks of bones, struggling to find their footing.

One guard, webbed with Mafia tattoos, made the considerable mistake of chasing Molly. In her cleats, her fast feet found purchase on the skittering bones. The burly guard tried to race up a mound of mandibles, but the harder he ran, the farther he slid.

Molly crested the pile, her eyes darting back and forth for a hidden trip wire. The man climbed closer, reaching out a calloused hand to grab Molly's ankle. She spotted a trip wire, yanked it hard, and dove aside as a steel scythe rocketed toward the surprised guard. Terrified, he leapt from the path of the shrieking blade and tumbled down the bone mountain, striking his head on the rocky ground. The man lay crumpled in a heap of clattering foot bones.

Raj, clinging to the cave wall, visualized a plan. He would get a running start, leap off the nearest bone pile, grab the closest guy-rope, shimmy up, swing to the opposite pillar, and jump down on the tallest guard. The plan was flawless.

He took a running start, slipped on a femur, and crashed down the mountain of bones. The avalanche of shattering bones triggered several booby traps. Boulders tumbled from the ceiling, pelting a guard on the head. The man sank to his knees, stunned senseless.

"Great work, Raj," said Addison, impressed.

"Don't mention it," said Raj from underneath a pile of patellas.

Addison's team, faster and lighter than Ragar's men, formed up at the far end of the chamber. Zubov shouted at his guards to stop chasing the kids and to block the only exit. With a sinking feeling, Addison realized his predicament. His group was hemmed in, with no hope of escape.

Zubov fixed Addison with the cold stare of a hunting shark and circled in.

"We're boned!" said Eddie. "There's no other way out of here!"

"Of course there is," said Addison, trying to sound more confident than he felt. "We're 86ers." Simply saying the words inspired him, and to his immense relief, Addison discovered that he had an idea. He rapped his knuckles against the rock wall at his back. "This is a limestone cave—formed by water."

"That's great, Addison." Molly pointed an impatient

finger at the guards rapidly picking their way through the bone piles, edging ever closer. "Can we focus on the issue at hand?"

"Water flows through the limestone for millions of years—it forms a cave." Addison could see his team was still not following. "The water needs both an entrance and an exit. There must be another way out!"

Raj was readying himself in a fighting stance, preparing for the onslaught of guards.

"If we all run in different directions, they can't catch all of us!" shouted Molly.

"That's not fair—they'll catch whoever's slowest," cried Eddie. "Me!"

"Everybody be quiet and listen." Addison lifted a hand in the air and cocked his ears. And then he heard what he wanted—a faint trickle of water. "This way!"

Addison shimmied along the cave wall until the sound of water grew louder. He knelt down and scooped away bones as fast as he could. A thin channel of water gurgled beneath the heaps of bones, escaping through a hole in the rocks. Addison helped Raj squeeze into the narrow chute.

Eddie backed up a step. "Are we really going in there?"

"You can stay here, Eddie. It's your choice!"

Ragar's men tightened their cordon, closing in on Addison's team. They moved carefully to avoid trip wires, until they were almost within arm's reach.

"Hurry!" Addison called, pushing Eddie in after Raj. Molly crawled in next, headfirst.

Zubov reached the edge of the bone pile, leapt clear of any remaining trip wires, and dashed for Addison.

Addison ducked into the narrow cave and discovered his team had formed a traffic jam. "Keep moving!" he shouted. He turned in time to see Zubov lunge a knife into the opening of the cave.

Zubov was too large to crawl into the passage, so he simply reached a tattooed arm inside and slashed with his knife. Addison crab-walked backward on his hands, the knife barely missing his throat.

Addison turned in the narrow tunnel and crawled forward as fast as he could, the rock pressing in on him from all sides.

Raj's voice carried through the darkness. "I hear the river up ahead!"

The limestone chute grew wet and slippery. One by one, Raj, Eddie, Molly, and Addison lost their grip and began sliding down the slick tunnel. They screamed as they slipped out of control, the water flushing them down the channel, twisting and turning. Their voices grew hoarse until the wet tunnel finally spit them out, sending them splashing into the muddy Olvidado River.

Addison's team gasped for breath, treading water in the marshy stream. Addison gazed up at the starry night sky, thrilled to be aboveground again. "Let's get out of here."

The group sloshed to the shore. They scrambled up the slimy mud embankment, picked their way through brambles and briars, and burst onto the cobbled square in front of the cathedral.

"We got the key!" Eddie exclaimed, jumping up and down.

"We escaped!" Raj offered Eddie a high five that Eddie connected with on his third try.

"We really did it!" Molly cheered.

"That was pretty close," said Addison, beaming.

He turned and ran smack into Professor Ragar.

●●●●●●

The first thing Addison did was yelp in alarm.

The second thing Addison did was try to run.

The third thing Addison did was yelp in alarm.

Professor Ragar's extra bodyguards surrounded the group, blocking off any escape. Addison swiveled his head, searched for a direction to run, and came up empty. Switching tactics, he attempted diplomacy.

"Well, here we are," said Addison, struggling to regain his composure. "A fine evening, don't you think?"

"You made it all the way to Colombia, just to save me the trouble of finding the second key," Ragar said in his deep, accented voice. He wore a stylish gray derby hat pulled low over his scarred face. Addison could not help but admire the sterling silver tie bar pinned to a flawless silk tie. "The Cooke family never ceases to—how do you say?—*astonish* me." Ragar extended his open palm to Addison and raised his eyebrows expectantly.

Addison, not missing a beat, gave Professor Ragar a high five. "Thanks. Your praise means a lot. And I love your tie bar."

Ragar wound up his open palm and slapped Addison across the face.

Addison's cheek stung, and his head rang for a few seconds. He bit his lip and kept his voice steady. "I can usually get along with most people, but I am having trouble finding your good side."

The professor motioned to his bodyguards, who grabbed Addison by the arms. Addison squirmed, but the men were four times his size.

Ragar fished in Addison's blazer pocket and removed the Incan key. He admired its glittering silver skin in the moonlight. "Thank you."

Addison could think of nothing polite to say, so he settled for a dignified silence. He studied the burn scar etched into Ragar's face. The professor's gray derby hat partially concealed where the patchy hair had been seared from the scalp, leaving only red and mottled flesh.

The rest of Ragar's bodyguards burst from the front door of the cathedral, covered in bone dust and gasping for breath.

Ragar smiled at Addison. "I would like to introduce

you to someone." He gestured to Zubov, who sauntered forward.

Addison already felt fairly well acquainted with the tall, pockmarked man. His slick black ponytail looked like a tenacious ferret clinging to the back of his head. Zubov glared at Addison. Try as he might, Addison could detect no hint of goodwill in that gaze.

"His name is Boris Rachivnek," Ragar continued, "but in the Siberian prison, his nickname was Zubov. 'Zubov' means—how do you say?—'*teeth*.'"

Addison assumed this was meant to sound sinister. He raised his eyebrows appreciatively and nodded to Zubov. "Nice to meet you, Teeth."

Professor Ragar frowned at Addison and continued. "Zubov graduated from the highest level of the Russian special forces. He won medals in every form of combat. He is a world-class tracker, and deadly with a knife."

Addison nodded his head, duly impressed, though he wasn't sure he liked where any of this was going.

"Zubov wasn't seeing enough action in the military, so he turned mercenary, fighting in armed conflicts around the globe until he was imprisoned for arms trafficking. He has no hobbies, the poor creature. Violence is the only thing he finds interesting."

"Well, Teeth," said Addison. "It is a pleasure to make your acquaintance."

Zubov only stared at Addison, a single vein bulging angrily in his temple.

"I am going to leave you alone with Zubov," said Ragar. "But first, I am curious. Why did you come for the key? You could not possibly hope to find the Incan treasure."

"We just want to get our aunt and uncle back," said Molly.

"You came to Colombia to free your relatives and now you yourselves are captured. In Russia, we call that 'irony.'"

"We call that 'irony' in English, too," said Addison.

Ragar frowned. "You are saying the word 'irony' is the same in English as it is in Russian?"

"Where are my aunt and uncle?" Molly demanded, getting things back on track.

Ragar gestured to his black stretch limousine, parked in the shadows. Addison strained his eyes, but couldn't see in through the tinted windows.

"Your aunt and uncle have not been very helpful so far, but I possess the gift of persuasion." Professor Ragar nodded to his guards, who stood at attention. "They are all deadly men like Zubov, who have survived the Siberian prisons." Ragar leaned close to Addison, his scarred face ghostly white in the dark of the night. "I will keep your aunt and uncle alive as long as they help me solve the clues. But the second I don't need them anymore, they will join your parents on the other side."

Addison stiffened, straining against the men who gripped his arms. "What do you know about my parents?"

Ragar's laugh was a raspy, joyless wheeze like a car engine that won't quite start. "Zubov, do what you like with these kids. I never want to see them again." He gestured to his men, who released Addison.

The professor stepped into his stretch limousine. For a brief moment, Addison caught a glimpse of his aunt and uncle, blindfolded and gagged, before Ragar slammed the limousine door shut. The bodyguards climbed into a caravan of black Jeeps that trailed the limo. The motorcade rumbled across the muddy square. The Jeeps turned the corner and disappeared into the labyrinth of Olvidados.

Chapter Ten

Zubov

ADDISON TURNED TO FACE ZUBOV. "Addison Cooke,"
he said, offering his business card. "Pleasure to meet you.
I admire a man of talent." Addison felt if he could get a
conversation going, cooler minds might prevail.

Zubov stared down at Addison with the speculative
look of an underfed tiger.

Molly looked up at the giant man. "How come they
call you Teeth?"

Zubov grinned, revealing teeth filed down to points.

"Ah," said Molly.

Raj stared up at Zubov in amazement. He could not
help but feel impressed. "How did your teeth get that
way?"

Zubov turned his predatory gaze on Raj. When he spoke, his accent was even heavier than Ragar's. "I was locked in Zinsk gulag, in Siberia, sharing bread and water with deadliest criminals in Russia. I needed weapon to stay alive. I stole iron file from work mine, but had no metal to sharpen into a shank. Not even spoon or fork. So I file my own teeth. Now I always have weapon."

Zubov smiled again and clicked his teeth.

Addison respected a man of resource. He was pleased to have Zubov opening up about himself. The thing was to get on Zubov's good side. Perhaps Addison could begin to soften him up. "We're just seventh graders. You're not really going to hurt us, right? You could just let us walk away and never see us again. Less work for you, less hassle for us—everybody wins. Deal?"

Zubov leveled his slow gaze on Addison. The icy glare did little to inspire Addison with confidence.

"There were children in Zinsk." Zubov eyed Molly. "Even women and girls. None were shown mercy."

"Why work for Ragar?" asked Addison, looking for the angle. "What's in it for you?"

"Ragar freed all of us from Zinsk. We owe him our lives."

"Will he share the Incan treasure with you?"

"Every day I am free is a treasure I owe Ragar."

"So, I'll take that as a 'no,'" said Addison.

Zubov reached out one gigantic paw and grabbed Addison by his necktie. He lifted Addison off the ground.

Addison's feet dangled helplessly, pedaling the air. He realized, to his immense regret, that he had completely failed to get on Zubov's good side.

With his free hand, Zubov flicked out his butterfly knife, the steel flashing brightly in the moonlight. "You're going to have ten less fingers by the time I'm finished."

"Ten *fewer* fingers," Addison corrected.

Zubov began squeezing Addison's windpipe. "Forget fingers. I start with your tongue."

Addison twisted and kicked, but could not shake free of Zubov's iron grip.

Zubov pressed his knife to Addison's cheek.

For once, Addison shut his mouth tight.

Eddie and Raj were paralyzed with shock. It was Molly who acted.

Her first instinct was always to run. But to her amazement, she found herself sprinting toward Zubov, rather than away. She took a running start, wound up, and kicked Zubov hard in the kneecap. Her soccer cleat struck home with a satisfying crunch.

Zubov barked with rage. He hurled Addison to the ground and whirled to face Molly, whipping and spinning his butterfly knife.

Raj snapped out of his daze and snapped into action.

He had spent countless hours of his life daydreaming about being in a knife fight. He wasn't about to let this golden opportunity pass him by. He stepped forward. "I've got this."

"Raj, no," Addison croaked, clutching his bruised throat.

"It's okay, everyone. I read a survival book with a chapter on knife fights." Raj shed his jacket and wrapped it around his arm as a shield. He squared off with Zubov, who welcomed the challenge with a wolflike grin.

Addison watched in horror. "Raj, are you sure? I don't want to sound negative, but you're five foot two and weigh ninety pounds."

"So?"

"So the smart money's on Zubov."

"The human body is capable of incredible feats when its survival is threatened," said Raj.

Raj and Zubov slowly circled each other, Raj watching Zubov's every movement. Zubov swiped, and Raj dodged. Zubov slashed, and Raj rolled. Zubov jabbed like a fencer, and Raj somehow scrambled past him.

"Enough of this," said Molly, with annoyance. And with all her strength, she stomped on Zubov's foot with her soccer cleats. There was an audible snap. Zubov howled in pain and surprise. In the same split second, Molly swatted Zubov's hand. His butterfly knife clattered to the ground.

Addison quickly scooped up the knife and pocketed it. He watched Zubov sink to the ground, clutching his broken toe. "Zubov, sorry we got off on the wrong foot."

Raj stared at Molly in wonder, and then at Addison. "You Cookes are amazing."

Zubov gritted his sharpened teeth and swallowed down his pain. He tested his weight on his foot and rose back to his full height.

Eddie hopped nervously back and forth. "What do we do now?"

Addison narrowed his eyes, weighing the options. "Run!" he suggested.

And with that, they turned and bolted.

······

At that exact moment, several blocks away, Guadalupe was running for her life. *Policía*, waving their batons, chased her through the night market. All Guadalupe had done was relieve a street vendor of a single churro. Well, maybe a handful of single churros. The point, in Guadalupe's opinion, was that the street vendor possessed altogether too many churros. Whereas Guadalupe possessed far too few. In her hunger, she had done him the favor of rebalancing this equation. It seemed like a keen idea at the time.

The *policía* surrounded Guadalupe. She frantically

crammed an entire churro into her mouth before they could take it from her.

The lieutenant stepped forward. He glared down his long nose at her. "Stealing again," he said in his Bogotá dialect. "This is your third strike, Guadalupe. I'm going to lock you up for a long time." To emphasize this point, he took a long time saying the word "long."

Guadalupe kissed the toasted sugar from her fingertips and swallowed down the last of the delicious churro. "It was worth it."

"I've been saving a spot in my jail for you."

The *policía* closed in on all sides. Guadalupe saw no way out. Sighing, she lifted up her wrists for the handcuffs. Her wrists were already covered in bracelets; two more couldn't hurt.

Guadalupe believed in fate. Whatever will be, will be. Life, it seemed to Guadalupe, was often nothing more than a series of random coincidences, and it was not for her to stand in the way of chance. As it happened, in fact, she did not have to stand at all.

At that precise instant, Addison, Molly, Eddie, and Raj barreled around the corner, pursued by a limping Zubov. They collided with Guadalupe and the *policía* like five bowling balls striking seven bowling pins. Everyone was knocked off their feet entirely.

Addison sprawled on the muddy ground. He looked up

from the general tangle of limbs to find himself face-to-face with Guadalupe.

"You!" he growled.

"You!" she gasped.

"Addison, c'mon!" shouted Molly, grabbing his arm and yanking him to his feet.

Guadalupe, Addison, Molly, Eddie, and Raj sprinted through the market pursued by Zubov and the *policía*.

••••••

Guadalupe hotfooted across the bazaar, her feet barely touching the ground.

Addison tore after her, like a cheetah chasing the world's last gazelle.

"Why are we following her?" called Molly, pumping her fists for speed. "We can't trust her!"

"She knows this town better than we do, and she's not interested in getting pinched by the police."

Molly took Addison's point. They loped after Guadalupe, the *policía* fast at their heels.

The market was as noisy and colorful as a circus. Salted fish and skinned venison hung from shop rafters. Barefoot children rolled spices onto smoked mutton, agouties, and pacas. Barking venders shilled bananas, oranges, and mangos. Wrinkled Quechuan women hunched over cooking fires, smoke-curing beef and drinking white rum.

"Left," Molly called, watching Guadalupe skitter down a side alley.

"Stop following me!" Guadalupe called over her shoulder. "You'll lead the *policía* right to me!"

"You owe us," shouted Addison. "We just saved you from being arrested!"

"Not yet, you haven't!" Guadalupe dodged as the *policía* nearly tackled her from a side lane. She whipped open the back door of a house, surprising a family over dinner. "Just passing through," she called, sprinting through their dining room.

Addison and his team chased Guadalupe through the living room and out the front door, followed by a dozen *policía* and one rather furious Zubov.

Guadalupe hurtled between the tin-walled shacks of the shantytown. "You keeping up?"

Addison's group gasped for breath. They darted past dark-eyed men hunched over dice games. Past bandits rolling corn-husk cigarettes with shreds of rope tobacco. Past tattooed desperados cheering over ten-peso cockfights.

"See if you can follow *this*," cried Guadalupe just as Addison could feel the *policía*'s breath on the back of his neck. Guadalupe sprinted along an overpass, leapt the guardrail, and jumped off the bridge.

With no time to consider a better idea, Addison and his team dove off the bridge after her.

••••••

For a few seconds, Addison plummeted through the air. This gave him plenty of time to reflect on the wisdom of his actions. They might fall ten feet, or a hundred feet. They might land in a raging river, or a rocky ravine. Addison had simply not taken the time to check before leaping off a bridge. It was like Aunt Delia always told him: he had to learn easy lessons the hard way. Whatever happened, Addison decided, it was probably going to hurt.

A split second later, the group landed in what can only be described as a giant pile of tires.

It did not hurt at all.

Addison bounced a few times and came to a stop.

Guadalupe brushed herself off and looked at Addison with begrudging respect. "Not bad for a tourist."

The *policía*, high on the overpass, weren't so inclined to take the jump. They circled to find another way down. Zubov, gritting his pointed teeth, faded silently into a darkened alleyway.

"It's Guadalupe, right?" ventured Addison.

"Yes."

"I like your style."

Guadalupe looked Addison up and down, appraising him. "I guess you did help me escape." She climbed down from the heap of tires and turned toward a warren of wooden huts. "Try to keep up."

She led the group through a maze of alleys. They climbed a storm drain and crossed a row of rooftops overlooking the town. Spanish tiles creaked under their feet, followed by stretches of flat white stucco where they moved as quickly and quietly as cat burglars. At last, they reached a rooftop with a sprawling view of the Andes Mountains.

"This is where I sleep," Guadalupe announced.

Addison scanned the village below. He watched the *policía* running to and fro, blowing whistles and searching the surrounding streets.

"Is it safe?" asked Molly.

"The *policía* are like cattle," Guadalupe sniffed, "they never look up."

"Either way," said Addison, "I think this is a good time for us to take our leave of Olvidados."

......

Addison and his team sat behind the parapet, catching their breath. Guadalupe set to work on a churro she had hidden in her pocket.

"Well, where do we go now?" asked Molly.

Addison opened his pocket notebook and examined the sketch he made of Atahualpa's second key. "Eddie, have a whack at translating this."

Eddie tilted the notebook to read by moonlight:

"Across the mighty Amazon,
Through the jungles of the headhunters,
Follow the footsteps of the Incas;
In a castle at the end of the world
The key is hidden closest to the gods."

"It sounds better in Spanish," commented Guadalupe, reading over Eddie's shoulder.

"That's what I've been telling them!" Eddie agreed. "Wait a second, this doesn't concern you!" He hid the notebook from her.

Guadalupe smiled at Eddie, sizing him up. She took him for an easy mark. "How did you learn Spanish so well?"

"Guatemalan nanny," Eddie said guardedly.

"Your reading is excellent."

"Thanks," said Eddie, warming to Guadalupe. "I also speak Chinese, from my parents."

"Cool. Any other languages?" Guadalupe sidled closer.

Eddie lifted one shoulder and dropped it. "Some Turkish."

"You had a Turkish nanny, too?"

"Nope. But my apartment's right over Restaurant Anatolia. So."

Guadalupe looked at him quizzically.

"My parents both work," Eddie explained. "So sometimes after school, I hang out in the restaurant kitchen to do my homework. I learn Turkish from the cooks. It's *harika*. That's Turkish for 'great.'"

Guadalupe nodded. "So what's this about ancient Incan keys?"

To Eddie's amazement, the notebook was suddenly in her hand. She held the sketch of the Incan key up to the moonlight, eyeing the writing.

"We're on a treasure hunt," said Molly.

"Bacán," said Guadalupe, smiling at Eddie. "That's Colombian for 'cool.'"

"Guadalupe doesn't need to know what we're up to," whispered Addison.

"It's none of her business," said Raj, snatching the notebook from Guadalupe and handing it back to Eddie.

Guadalupe shrugged and returned her attention to her churro. She made a convincing show of ignoring their conversation.

Eddie studied the Incan clue. *"'Across the mighty Amazon, through the jungles of the headhunters, follow the footsteps of the Incas; in a castle at the end of the world . . .'"*

"Across the Amazon," Molly piped in, "that gives us a starting point."

Addison shook his head. "From Olvidados, we could cross the Amazon going south or going west."

"Well, if we knew where the 'jungles of the headhunters'

were, that would narrow it down," Raj put in. He was rather hoping to encounter some headhunters.

Eddie examined the key again. "*'Follow the footsteps of the Incas; in a castle at the end of the world . . .'*"

Addison snapped his fingers. "I think I have an idea where we're going. Give or take fifty miles."

"Where?" asked Molly.

"Glad you asked, young relative, or this would have been a short conversation. Now, stick to me like shoe gum. This bit about crossing the Amazon seems clear enough . . ."

"Crystal," Molly agreed.

"We just don't know whether to go south or west. Well, we're supposed to follow the Incas 'to the end of the world,' if you're still with me."

"Sure."

"And the Incas believed the Pacific Ocean was the end of the world."

"Okay," said Molly.

"So, I think we cut across the Amazon rain forest to Ecuador, all the way to the Pacific Ocean. And then we look for this castle."

The team silently considered this.

Finally, Guadalupe burst out a gale of churro-spitting laughter. "Cross the Amazon, just like that?" She stood up so she could gesture to the distant jungle. "What about the fire ants, the crocodiles, and the jaguars? What about the poachers, the Máloco tribesman, and the cartel smugglers? What about the hundreds of species of snakes?" She worked herself up to a shout, "There are *frogs* that can kill you in the Amazon. *¡Está berraco!* It's a big problem. You can't just cross the Amazon like you're crossing the street. You won't last an hour!"

"She's right," said Raj. "On average, every year, thirty-six hikers go into the Amazon and never come out."

"Raj, why do you even know these things?" asked Molly.

Addison studied Guadalupe. She was older than he was and a few inches taller. Her head was wrapped in a bandana like a swashbuckling pirate, and she kept one hand cocked confidently on her hip. Addison could see from her worn gypsy clothes, tattered at the ankles, that she'd seen more than a few adventures in her life.

"What do you suggest, Guadalupe?"

"This is my country, and I'm an expert in the Amazon." Guadalupe set both her hands on her hips, her bracelets tinkling. "I will be your guide."

"I thought you said you're from Cleveland," said Eddie.

"Teddy Roosevelt was from Manhattan," Guadalupe returned, "but he's still the world's most famous Amazon explorer."

Addison considered Guadalupe's line of reasoning. "We're not paying you this time."

Eddie was beside himself. "Addison, you're not honestly considering this, are you? The last time you hired her to be our guide she stole your wallet!"

Guadalupe shrugged. "I will be your guide for free. You saved me from the *policía* tonight, so I owe you. Besides, I've been thinking about a change of scenery from Olvidados."

"Naturally," said Eddie. "The *policía* probably have a price on your head."

"Won't anybody miss you?" asked Molly. "What about your parents?"

"Haven't got any." Guadalupe shrugged again.

"Molly and I are running low on family members, too," said Addison.

"Sometimes I wish I didn't have three sisters," Raj put in, hoping to add to the conversation.

"Addison," Eddie said desperately, "you're not seriously hiring her."

"I don't see what choice we have," said Addison. "I don't have any money, and she's the only guide who will work for free."

"She's a professional thief. We can't trust her!" Eddie pleaded.

"You can't survive the Amazon without me," said Guadalupe.

"It's a deal," said Addison. "Welcome aboard."

Chapter Eleven

The Amazon

THE NEXT MORNING, THE team gathered by a road-side shack at the edge of the jungle. Guadalupe emerged carrying armloads of water bottles and food.

"Here," she said, passing out the food, "so we don't starve to death in the jungle."

"Thanks, Guadalupe, that's really thoughtful of you," said Addison.

"Don't mention it," she said, tossing him his uncle's wallet.

Addison checked the wallet. It was now half empty.

The team loaded packages of food into their backpacks.

"What'd you buy?" asked Eddie, licking his lips.

"Corn, chicken, and *cuy*," said Guadalupe.

"Sounds delicious," said Eddie. "What's *cuy*?"

"Guinea pig."

"Wait, what?"

"Guinea pig is a local delicacy—very popular in the mountains. You're welcome."

Eddie swallowed hard and experienced one of those rare moments when he found he had no appetite.

Addison gripped the straps of his backpack. "Well, let's get going. This rain forest isn't going to cross itself." He eyed the morning sun in the east and pointed the group due west. A field of yellow maize grew behind the row of shacks, and behind them, the Amazon rose up like a green tsunami.

Addison marched a few steps into the cornfield before realizing the group was not following. He turned back to see them gazing uncertainly at the jungle. "What's wrong?"

"How far is it to the ocean?" Molly asked.

Addison studied his copy of *Fiddleton's Atlas* and measured the map key with his thumb. "At least twenty-five miles, give or take a few dozen. A bit of exercise is just the thing to lift the spirits."

Raj stretched his legs, limbering up. The rest of the group stared at Addison gloomily.

Eddie groaned. "We could be killed in there. If we take a wrong turn, we could hike for years and never find our way out."

Addison took a deep breath, summoning his powers of persuasion. He needed to come up with something truly compelling, rewarding, and inspiring to sway the group.

"Police!" shouted Raj, pointing to a patrol car speeding down the dirt road.

The group grabbed their backpacks and scrambled into the underbrush, diving for cover. They flattened their bodies to the ground. The patrol car zipped past. Addison's team stayed hidden until they were sure the *policía* were gone.

"Well," said Molly. "We can't go back to Olvidados."

They walked to the edge of the forest and paused to take in the view. Kapok trees, hundreds of feet tall, stretched in a green canopy as far as the eye could see. Tangled vines, thick as suspension cables on the Brooklyn Bridge, clung to the brindled bark trusses and dank, mossy rafters of ancient mahogany. The jungle was eerily silent, as if a million unseen eyes were watching and waiting.

Guadalupe pulled her hair back into a ponytail.

Eddie nervously chewed his lower lip.

Raj tightened the red bandana around his forehead.

The team looked to Addison.

"Every ladder has a first rung," Addison said optimistically. And with that, he plunged into the jungle.

••••••

The forest floor was silent and intensely green. Clouds of humidity hung heavy in the air. Addison's team was immediately drenched in sweat. Entering the rain forest was like climbing into a giant wet sock.

Guadalupe slashed at the underbrush with a stick, beating a path through the tangles of ferns. Monkeys gossiped in the canopy far overhead. Carpeted in moss, the jungle seemed to soak up all sound.

Addison followed Guadalupe's path, marveling at the wealth of exotic plants. The farther he walked, the more he noticed. What first seemed like an empty forest was teeming with wildlife. Colorful birds flicked and flitted across the vaulted boughs of rubber trees. Millions of beetles scuttled along damp trails of rotting bark, bustling through traffic more crowded than the 42nd Street subway stop.

Passion flowers poked their crimson heads through the foliage, blossoms spread out like ten-legged starfish. Heliconias, lobster red and tipped with gold, sprouted from tree trunks. Rafflesias, spotted like whale sharks, flaunted petals larger than Eddie. Addison felt he was no longer on Earth, but exploring some distant planet.

"Out of curiosity, how many animals here can eat us?" Eddie asked.

"Oh, most of them!" said Raj, thrilled that Eddie had introduced the topic. "There are jaguars, cougars, and vampire bats that carry rabies."

"No more bats!"

"All three of those animals come out at night, so we're okay for now," Raj said.

"That's a relief."

"Now, your big problem is really the snakes," Raj continued excitedly. "You've got coral snakes that can kill a man in ten seconds. You've got bushmasters, the largest venomous snakes in the western hemisphere. And don't even get me started about the anacondas."

Nobody prompted Raj about the anacondas, but he continued anyway.

"You've got green anacondas, yellow anacondas, and spotted anacondas. Anacondas are constrictors. They wrap around you with lightning speed and choke the air out of your lungs until you suffocate." Raj's eyes seemed to swell like balloons as he warmed to his topic. "The first rule of survival is not to panic. Unless you're being attacked by an anaconda. In which case, panic."

"Raj, this is the most sentences I've ever heard you say in a row," said Addison.

But Raj was only just slipping into gear. "Some anacondas can grow up to five hundred pounds and twenty feet long! There was one case of a village woman in Cartagena who was swallowed whole by an eighteen-foot—"

"Raj, enough already!" Molly fixed him with a glare that would make an anaconda decide to carry on with business elsewhere.

"Jeez, sorry."

"Molly is not on good terms with snakes," Addison explained.

"Well," said Raj diplomatically, "I'm sure we won't see any."

......

Toward midmorning, Guadalupe struck upon a wide trail heading due west through the jungle. She sighed in relief. Her arms were exhausted from beating a path through the thick vegetation.

Addison examined the path with excitement, scraping away dirt and grubs to reveal an ancient stone trail marker. "Do you realize what this means?"

"That your hands are filthy and there's no soap for fifty miles?" guessed Molly.

"Besides that," said Addison, rising to his feet. "Look at this trail marker—we're following in the footsteps of the Incas!"

"What do you mean?"

"The clue said, *'Follow the footsteps of the Incas.'* This is an ancient Incan roadway." Addison swept a hand from east to west. "We must be on the right track, heading closer to the heart of the Incan Empire."

Addison forged on, following the path. "Just imagine," he said breathlessly, "five hundred years ago, this was a major highway connecting Incas from Colombia to Ecuador."

Eddie ducked under tangled vines that clawed at his face. "Not much now, is it?"

"It makes you think," said Addison. "Five hundred years from now, what will our own highways look like?"

The team marched more quickly on the open path. It wasn't long before Addison reckoned they had put a few miles behind them. Being from Manhattan didn't give them many advantages in the jungle, but at least they were all experienced walkers.

Eddie peered nervously into the depths of the passing foliage. "What about the headhunters?"

"What headhunters?" asked Molly.

"The clue said, *'Across the mighty Amazon, through the jungles of the headhunters,'*" Eddie quoted. "They're probably extinct by now, right?"

"Oh, no—the Máloco are still here. Every few years, we hear stories of people going missing," Guadalupe said, eyeing the impenetrable screen of the jungle. "But the Amazon is a huge place. They may never cross our path."

The group dropped into a thoughtful silence, checking over their shoulders for signs of danger. Their winding route led through a sunny glen, across a mountain stream, and into a thick grove of hundred-foot Platonia trees wrapped in curry-yellow bark.

Molly fell into step beside Addison as they plodded westward through the deepening rain forest. She lowered her voice so only Addison could hear. "At the cathedral, when Professor Ragar climbed in his limousine, I saw Aunt Delia and Uncle Nigel in the backseat. Their wrists were tied."

"I'm sure they're okay," said Addison as convincingly as he could. "They've been in tough situations before."

"If something happens to them, what will we do? I don't want to live with Uncle Jasper. He can't even drive a car."

"They're going to be fine, Molly. In fact, this might even be good for them."

Molly looked at Addison skeptically.

"Look, they're spending time together, right, Mo? They're having an adventure together, whether they want to or not."

"You think it will bring them back together?"

Addison shrugged. "Ragar may be doing us a favor."

Molly crinkled her brow, weighing the situation. "How do you think Uncle Nigel even knows a person like Professor Ragar?"

"I've been pondering these same puzzles, Mo. In the museum, Uncle Nigel said Ragar works for someone named

Malazar. And this seemed to terrify Uncle Nigel. Which begs at least two questions. Namely, who is Malazar . . ."

"And what does he have against Uncle Nigel?"

"These are deep waters," Addison nodded. "Altogether, Ragar is a man who raises far more questions than he answers."

The team trekked onward through the darkening woods.

······

The Incan trail led all the way to a wide branch of the Amazon River and promptly dead-ended. The group stood by the river's edge, scratching their heads.

"Presumably," said Addison, "a few hundred years ago there was a bridge."

"Doesn't help us much now, does it?" said Guadalupe.

"Quite," agreed Addison, glancing down at his compass. "One way or another, we do need to get across."

"The current's pretty fast," said Molly doubtfully.

"Nothing like a refreshing swim to spur the circulation," said Addison. He studied the silted brown water. "Raj, what are we likely to find in this river?"

"The arapaima is the largest freshwater fish in the world," said Raj. "Ten feet long and four hundred and fifty pounds."

"Maybe we can catch one," said Eddie. "I'm starving."

"What I mean," said Addison, "is how many things in this river want to eat *us*?"

"Well," said Raj, delighted the conversation had finally circled back to his favorite topic, "you've got schools of razor-toothed piranhas that can reduce a cow to a skeleton inside five minutes. You've got electric eels that can shock you. And then of course you've got the snakes."

"Again with the snakes," said Molly.

"And alligators, lots of alligators," Raj added.

"Maybe we can go around the river?" suggested Eddie.

"The Amazon River's a few thousand miles long," said Addison. "We should probably take the shorter route."

"You're saying we swim," said Eddie cautiously. "But what happens if we're attacked by piranhas?"

"Death," said Raj, staring into the murky brown waters. "Oblivion's icy kiss."

"No thank you. I pass."

"Well, I don't know what to tell you, *amigos*," said Guadalupe. "We're on this side of the river. And Ecuador's on the other. And we're going to Ecuador." She headed down to the river.

"I wouldn't do that," said Raj. "Worldwide, alligators and crocodiles kill over a thousand people every year."

"I have a personal preference," Eddie announced, "for not being eaten by crocodiles."

"Then I've got good news for you, Eddie," said Addison.

"The Amazon is freshwater, so you don't need to worry about crocodiles."

"Excellent."

"What you *should* worry about are the caimans."

"Caimans?"

"South American alligators," Raj piped in. "They grow up to twenty feet long and can weigh over a thousand pounds. They're called black caimans to be precise."

"I don't care what you call them," cried Eddie. "I care about them not eating me!"

"Eddie, all you care about is what you want to eat and what wants to eat you," said Molly.

"What can I say, I'm a pragmatist!"

"We have no choice," said Guadalupe, losing all patience. "Talking about it's not going to help. We have to cross."

"Black caimans are man-eaters," Raj protested. "We really shouldn't go in the water."

"Está berraco," said Guadalupe, rolling her *r*'s with exasperation. "I would rather be eaten by twelve alligators than stand here another minute listening to you babies whine. Besides, I'm your guide. And I'm absolutely positive there are no alligators, crocodiles, or caimans in this river." She fixed her ponytail, hiked up her pants, and sloshed into the water.

"This is my favorite blazer," sighed Addison. He loosened his tie and stepped in after her.

••••••

All things considered, there were any number of places Addison would rather have been. His dress shoes sunk into the muddy bank, suctioning his feet with every step. The water pooling around his ankles and drenching his dress pants was surprisingly cold. He clung to clumps of reeds for balance until the murky water rose to his chest and the current took him.

Addison doggy-paddled into the wide river, unable to see what swam beneath his feet. "The current is pretty strong," he said, trying to sound relaxed about it.

Guadalupe paddled ahead. "Then you'll just have to swim strong. Keep going!"

The team reached a weed-covered sandbank, where the current slowed.

"You know, maybe this isn't so bad," said Eddie, getting used to the temperature.

"Don't get cocky," said Molly. "We've still got a long way to go!"

Guadalupe swam to the far side of the sandbank and froze. "Hey, *amigos*, remember when I said I was absolutely sure there were no alligators in the river?"

"Vividly," said Addison.

"It's possible I wasn't being completely straight with you."

The team turned to look where Guadalupe was staring.

A pair of sixteen-foot black caimans slid off the far mud bank into the river. The man-eaters floated toward the group, gliding like silent submarines, only their eyes and nostrils visible above the muddy brown tide.

"John . . . Wilkes . . . Booth," Addison breathed, watching the caimans drift closer.

"What do we do?" Eddie called, his voice rising an octave.

"Just stay quiet and slowly back away," said Guadalupe.

"That's for bears," said Raj.

"Okay, wave your arms and make a lot of noise to scare them," Guadalupe offered.

"That's for mountain lions."

"Well, what are we supposed to do for alligators?" Guadalupe demanded.

"Not go in the water," Raj said flatly.

$$\cdots\cdots$$

The caimans closed in on the team. There was no turning back. Addison's group turned and swam downstream as fast as they could, into the deepest part of the river.

The swift current caught them and swept them into the churning white waters of the rapids. Waves frothed and boiled, sliding the group between jagged boulders. Paddling furiously, they spun ever faster down the whirlpool currents of the raging river.

"We're out of control!" shouted Molly.

"Yes," yelled Addison, "but we're getting a lead on those caimans!"

Addison heard the rush of a waterfall looming ahead. Rising cliffs funneled the wide, roiling river down to a narrow point, forcing the water ever faster. The violent torrent built to a deafening roar.

"Everybody take a deep breath!" called Raj.

"We're all going to die!" shouted Eddie.

Addison gritted his teeth and watched as his friends were swept, screaming, over the edge of the falls. He shut his eyes tightly and felt the current take him.

His screams were cut short half a second later.

To Addison's astonishment, the waterfall had been all of three feet high. "You see, guys? That wasn't so bad," he sputtered. "You just need a positive mental attitude."

And with that, they all plummeted over a twelve-foot waterfall.

The pounding water held Addison under until his lungs burned. Thousands of gallons crashed continually over the falls. Addison kicked and flailed, not sure which way was up.

At last, he surfaced downstream, coughing and gasping for air. He wiped water from his eyes and searched the river. To his relief, his friends' heads bobbed above the waterline. Everyone appeared to be more or less alive. "You see?" he said. "Again, really not so bad."

"It's worse than bad!" yelled Molly, pointing her finger. "There are more caiman coming after us!"

"Molly, can't you just let me have this?"

The current drew the team more swiftly, but it pulled the caimans more quickly as well. Their powerful tails drew S-curves through the water, their long mouths bristling with teeth.

"Raj, what are our options?" gasped Addison, pulling hard through the water. "Don't you have firecrackers in that backpack?"

"Couldn't get them through customs!" shouted Raj.

Addison pumped his arms, swimming faster. He glanced over his shoulder to check on the caimans and watched in surprise as the beasts suddenly broke off their pursuit. "Finally, we get a lucky break!"

It was at this point Addison realized he could hardly hear his own voice over the growing roar of an even more massive waterfall.

"Addison!" Molly hollered.

"I know, I know! But look on the bright side—no more caimans!"

"The first rule of survival is not to panic!" Raj shrieked at the top of his lungs.

The whole world trembled with the rising din of pounding water. Addison spun around and saw his team was heading for oblivion. "Hold hands! Grab hold of anything you can!"

The team reached out to cling together. Yet Guadalupe, a little farther downstream than the others, couldn't free herself from the raging current. She hurdled toward the hammering waterfall. Addison saw she was done for.

"Addison, take my hand!" Molly called. "Hurry!"

Addison hesitated. Guadalupe was paddling for her life, but couldn't fight the current sucking her toward the brink of the falls. Before he could think, Addison turned and swam after her. Within a few strokes, he reached her and grabbed her by the hand.

But it was too late.

The greedy current drew Addison and Guadalupe ever closer to the roaring edge. Addison kicked hard and lunged. At the last moment, their clasped hands managed to snag onto a jagged boulder that pierced the waterline like a shark's fin. The angled rock held them pinned, mere feet from the dizzying precipice of the eighty-foot waterfall.

"If I let go," Guadalupe shouted over the roaring waterfall, "you'll go over!"

"If you let go, we'll *both* go over." He quoted Guadalupe. *"Está berraco."*

Guadalupe nodded. *"Está berraco."* She held on.

Addison held on.

Raj reached the opposite bank. He found a long tree branch, cast it at arm's length like a fishing pole, and managed to snag Eddie.

Eddie grabbed Molly's hand, forming a human chain in the water.

Molly held out her free hand. "Addison, grab hold!"

"I'm not letting go of Guadalupe!"

Molly stretched, but she could not reach Addison. "Raj, get me closer!"

Raj waded deeper into the water. Eddie spread his arms as wide as they would go. Molly reached just a little bit farther. Her fingers latched onto Addison's.

Addison clutched tight.

Raj hauled Eddie toward the shore. Eddie dragged Molly. Molly reeled in Addison, who towed Guadalupe with him. Hands clasped together, they fought the eager pull of the current and tugged one another to the river's edge. One by one, the group crawled up on to the muddy bank and collapsed, gulping for breath.

Eddie turned on Guadalupe. "You nearly got us killed! What kind of guide suggests crossing an alligator-infested river!"

"It doesn't matter," said Addison, still getting his wind back. "She got us to cross it. And we did. We made it."

Guadalupe stood up, wringing the water from her clothes, a look of triumph on her face. "You're welcome."

Chapter Twelve

The Máloco

GUADALUPE LED THE GROUP deeper into the jungle. With the detour downriver, they'd lost the trail entirely. Addison navigated by compass and hope.

The rain-forest canopy grew so dense it blocked out all light. The forest floor was a twilight world wriggling with innumerable insects and reptiles. The group picked their way around kapok trees tall as skyscrapers, with trunks wider than city buses. They feathered their way past venomous plants, bloodsucking horseflies, and strangely painted birds that Addison longed to sketch in his notebook if he only had the time.

"I think we'll catch the trail if we keep bearing north," he said at last.

"We don't even know if there is a trail on this side of the river," said Guadalupe.

"Well, you're the guide. Which way do you think we should go?"

Guadalupe turned in a slow circle and then shook her head. "It's possible I haven't been completely straight with you guys."

"Again?" said Eddie.

"Look, it's not so much that I'm an expert Amazon guide. It's more that I just really, really needed to get out of Olvidados." Guadalupe shrugged. "They could have put me in jail for months."

"But we could be in *here* for months," said Molly.

"Harika," Eddie groaned. "Even our guide is lost."

"The first rule of survival is not to panic," Raj said, repeating his favorite mantra. "The jungle can provide all our needs! Look," he added, kneeling down beside a puddle of water in the mossy undergrowth, "the jungle is providing a cooling drink of water." He bent low and began lapping from the muddy puddle.

"Raj, what are you doing?" said Addison, aghast. "We have water bottles in our backpacks!"

Raj paused, muddy water dripping from his chin. "That is true," he admitted. "Well, the jungle is providing a napkin." He wiped his mouth with a palm frond.

"The jungle is also providing a spider," Molly said, pointing at Raj's chin.

Raj yelped and leapt backward, stumbling over an enormous tree root. He rolled to his feet, smacking and scratching at his face. "Did I kill it?"

"I think you just scared it to death. Anyway, it's gone now."

"First rule of survival," Raj said with a satisfied smile.

Molly blew the strand of hair from her eyes and shook her head.

The group forged on, following Addison's compass. They crossed forests of red mangroves and dark mahogany and clambered over tree roots as massive as the twisted, gnarled fingers of giants. They wandered through hazy green dells of palms and ferns so monstrously large, they looked as if they were transplanted from primeval worlds.

Parting her way between towering fronds, Guadalupe caught a sight that made her jump back in fright. The group gathered at her side.

A ten-foot statue of a demon barred the way. It was carved from stone, with the head of a jaguar and the wings of a bat. Addison's group gaped in terror and fascination.

"Who made this?" Addison wondered aloud, fearing the answer.

"Máloco Indians." Guadalupe turned and spat. "Cannibals."

"You're kidding," said Eddie. "Is there anything in the Amazon that doesn't want to eat us?"

Blood dripped from the mouth of the statue. Addison reached out a finger and dabbed at it. "It's fresh."

"Gross," Molly declared. "And you touched it."

"Is it human blood?" asked Raj, a bit too hopefully.

"It's probably from an animal sacrifice. Maybe a bird or a frog." Addison studied the strange symbols carved into the sides of the statue.

"What does it mean?" asked Eddie.

"It means 'keep out,'" said Guadalupe. "The Máloco fight anyone who crosses their land. They say not even cartel smugglers will use this part of the jungle."

Addison's team was silent for a moment, peering nervously into the unfathomable depths of the rain forest.

"Well, this is great news," said Addison brightly.

"Addison, how is this great news?" asked Eddie. "Even smugglers won't go here."

"The Incan clue said *'through the jungles of the head-hunters.'* This means we're on the right track."

"But there aren't really such things as cannibals, right?"

"The Wari' people eat their own relatives after they die, as a sign of respect. The Jivaroan tribes shrink the heads of their enemies to keep as trophies." Addison smiled, marveling at the statue. "The Amazon is lousy with cannibals."

This was not at all what Eddie was hoping to hear. "But even in this day and age?"

"There are protected Amazon tribes who've never had

contact with our civilization." Addison traced some of the strange symbols into his waterlogged notebook and stood back to admire the demon statue, with its bared teeth and bulging eyes. "Aunt Delia would love this."

"What do we do, Addison?"

"We've come this far. We can't very well go back." Addison turned to look at the frightened faces of his team. He pocketed his notebook and shouldered his pack. "Look, we're going to get out of here. It's as simple as getting back on the Incan trail."

"How?" asked Eddie.

Addison set a course and began walking deeper into the jungle. He moved with enough confidence that the group followed. "The Incan trails were used by Chaskis," he spoke over his shoulder, "ancient runners who delivered messages across the empire."

"Is he giving another history lesson?" Guadalupe interrupted.

"This is how my whole family talks," Molly sighed.

"One Chaski would run to a relay station, where he'd hand the message off to the next Chaski—"

"Like a pony express," Raj cut in, "but with people instead of horses."

"Exactly. The upshot is, the Incas usually built their roads along the tops of ridges. That way, the relay stations could see when a Chaski was incoming."

Molly looked at Addison doubtfully. "You're saying if

we keep heading uphill, we'll cross the Incan trail again?"

"Absolutely." In truth, Addison had no idea. But he knew that choosing a direction and sticking with it was better than choosing no direction at all.

······

The land sloped uphill. Parrots and toucans chattered in the canted afternoon light that sifted through the primordial trees.

Guadalupe fell into step beside Addison. "What happened to your aunt and uncle, anyway?"

"They were kidnapped in New York."

Guadalupe considered this. "Usually, New Yorkers have to come to Colombia to get kidnapped."

"We do things differently in my family." Addison parted his way through the overhanging vines, careful he was not accidentally grasping at tree snakes.

"You must be close to your aunt and uncle, to come all this way."

Addison weighed the question. "Well, they're separated, so we only see my uncle on weekends. And they work a lot. But they're the closest thing to parents I've got."

Guadalupe nodded.

Addison knew Guadalupe lived on her own. He felt she might understand his situation. "Molly and I are on our own a lot. They're hardly around. It's kind of selfish, right? People who raise kids and never see them. Like they're only thinking of themselves."

Guadalupe hiked for a moment in silence. She studied Addison thoughtfully. "They didn't choose to have you, right? I mean, they're not your real parents."

"Exactly."

"And yet they took you in when you needed them. Even though they have to work harder. They don't sound like they're only thinking for themselves," said Guadalupe. "But you do." She walked on ahead.

Addison watched the afternoon sunlight filter through the wind-rippled leaves. He plodded along in thoughtful silence, the gently sloping forest floor muffling the sound of his footfalls.

······

The sun drew lower, and the group made camp for the night. Raj collected stones to build a fire circle. Eddie and Molly gathered firewood. Addison and Guadalupe walked to a nearby creek to refill the water bottles.

Addison sat down on the mossy bank and stripped off his shoes and socks. He stared in dismay at his jacket and trousers, caked in mud. "This is the dirtiest I've ever been."

"You can wash your jacket in the creek," said Guadalupe.

"Will that work?"

She shrugged. "It can't get any dirtier."

Addison felt she had a point so he waded into the cooling water. The evening air hummed pleasantly with a chorus of crickets and cicadas.

Guadalupe followed him into the shallows, scrubbing dried mud from the knees of her pants. She waded past her hips and elbows until the water reached up to her chin.

"How did you end up here from Cleveland?" Addison asked.

"I told you before, it's complicated."

"Try me."

"When my parents divorced, my mother left Cleveland and took us to live with her parents here in South America. She only waited a year before getting married again. I didn't like my new stepfather. I couldn't stand being in the house. So I left."

"But you said you're an orphan?"

"After I left, they were in a car accident," said Guadalupe.

Addison slipped deeper into the water. He watched the gently running creek slowly dissolve the caked mud from his jacket. He tried to think of the right thing to say. "That's terrible. I'm really sorry."

"What do you know about it?" snapped Guadalupe. "You're just some rich boy from New York."

"I'm not rich."

"Compared to me, you are."

Addison treaded water and did not look at Guadalupe. Her words bothered him. She probably saw his blazer and tie and assumed he led a charmed life. Somehow, Addison wanted her to know he shared the same problems she did. "My parents died when I was eight," he said finally.

Guadalupe swam in silence, the water lapping against the edges of the tidal pool. Crickets and night frogs heralded the dusk with chirps and purring trills. "What happened?"

"We were in Cambodia," Addison began. "In the Dângrêk Mountains. A site called the Temple of God."

Guadalupe squinted her eyes and looked at him closely.

"Molly and I grew up all over the world," said Addison. "My parents were like gypsies. We lived on hippie communes, slept on steamboats, and once crossed Egypt with a Bedouin caravan. My parents would do whatever they needed to reach an archaeological site. I come from a very weird family."

"That explains a lot."

"All the Cookes are archaeologists. My father, mother, aunt, and both my uncles. It's sort of our family business. It takes us around the globe."

"Why were you in Cambodia?" asked Guadalupe.

"My parents wanted to find an artifact called the Crown of Sita. I didn't know at the time, but later my uncle explained it. Khmer smugglers were looting artifacts and selling them to buy weapons. My parents wanted to rescue the crown from the temple and secure it in a museum before the smugglers could steal it."

"This was your childhood?" She stifled a laugh.

"Look, do you want to hear my story or not?"

"I do," said Guadalupe. "Sorry. So what happened?"

"Everything went wrong. The sky went dark, and we were trapped by monsoon rain. We couldn't escape. Khmer smugglers surrounded the temple and attacked."

"Your parents put an eight-year-old in this situation? Addison, you may have worse parents than I do!"

"They couldn't have known we'd be ambushed."

"I guess," said Guadalupe, shaking her head.

"My uncle Nigel ran with Molly and me. We hid in the jungle. All we could do was watch from the trees."

Addison treaded water silently for a while before he continued. "Molly was too young to remember, but I can close my eyes and see it like it was yesterday."

He took a breath. "I remember the mountains, thunder and lightning crashing all around. I remember my mother using vines to climb the temple wall on the edge of the cliff. She was trying to escape before the smugglers could catch her. The cliff was thousands of feet high. Just as she made it to the top of the wall . . ."

Addison's voice trailed off.

Guadalupe watched him quietly. "What about your father?"

"I never saw him again."

The crescent moon rose high above the palms, reflecting its pallid light in the purling ripples of the tidal pool.

"I've never told anyone about that. Not even Raj or Eddie."

"You probably want me to say something kind or thoughtful," said Guadalupe. "Or to tell you it will all be okay. But I don't believe that. *Algunos cortes son demasiado profundas para sanar.* Some cuts are too deep to heal."

Addison listened to the lapping of the water and the breeze wafting palm fronds in the darkly suspirant forest.

Finally, Guadalupe spoke again. "At the waterfall, you swam to help me. Why did you do that?"

"I'm not sure. It just happened."

"Well, you could have died. A person should look out for themselves."

"Guadalupe, I don't know how we're going to make it through this if we don't help each other," said Addison.

Moonlight played on the water, casting dancing reflections on Guadalupe's face. At last, she swam close to him. She fished in her pocket for a moment. "Here," she said, handing Addison his uncle's wallet. "I picked it from you when you pulled me from the river today."

"Thanks," said Addison.

······

Night fell, and the hushed forest came to life with hoots and howls in the darkness. Guadalupe had forgotten to bring forks, so the group ate dinner with their hands. They hunched over the fire, gulping down beans, rice, corn, chorizo, plantains, and *cuy*.

"Whoa," said Eddie, covering his mouth and grimacing. "Do *not* eat the *cuy*."

"Way ahead of you," said Molly.

"I don't know. I kinda like it," said Raj, helping himself to more.

The tired group gazed into the campfire, watching it crackle and snap.

"We never found that Incan trail you promised," said Molly.

"We'll reach it tomorrow," Addison replied, in what he hoped was a confident tone. "I'm sure of it."

"Do you think it's true what Uncle Nigel said about the Incan treasure being cursed?" asked Molly.

"Well, no treasure hunter who's gone after it has made it back alive." Addison tried a little *cuy* just to be openminded. He decided it tasted like chicken.

"Nobody told me about a curse," said Guadalupe, finishing her dinner and leaning back against a log.

"Yeah, me neither," said Eddie. "You somehow left that part out, Addison."

Addison poked the fire with a stick. "Three hundred years ago, a Spanish adventurer named Valverde married an Incan princess. He led an expedition into the mountains to the secret spot where she claimed the treasure was hidden. They never returned."

Raj busied himself in the dark, setting protective booby traps around the camp. He had already dug several deep pits, bristling with sharpened bamboo stakes, and was now struggling to engineer a complex snare trap of saplings and vines.

"A hundred years later," Addison continued, "a pair of treasure hunters named Captain Blake and Lieutenant Chaplin claimed they found Valverde's map. They led a party into the mountains and disappeared in a rockslide."

Raj, now thoroughly intrigued, joined the campfire and listened eagerly with the rest of the team.

"In the 1930s," said Addison, "a Scotsman named Erskine Loch mounted a treasure hunt in the forests of the Andes. Torrential rains drove his men to fever and hallucinations. His porters deserted. Loch was found stabbed to death through the heart."

"Death . . . the long sleep of the hereafter," said Raj, wide-eyed. "So there *is* a curse!"

The fire crackled in the lonely night.

"Look," said Addison, sensing the fearful mood of his team, "none of those explorers found what we found: the first two Incan keys. This gives us a huge competitive edge. Besides, I don't believe in ghost stories."

It was at that moment that Molly split the night with a bloodcurdling scream.

······

A spotted anaconda, coiled around a low-hanging tree limb, dropped onto Molly. The ten-foot constrictor wrapped its muscled body around her legs, then waist, and worked its way up her chest.

Molly hollered again.

"Don't shout!" yelped Raj, leaping to his feat. "The snake will squeeze the air out of your chest."

"What should I do?" gasped Molly, struggling against the wriggling snake.

"Just fill your lungs and hold your breath!"

Guadalupe felt a flood of adrenaline surge through her body. Thinking quickly, she grabbed a flaming brand from the fire and lunged at the great serpent. It hissed viciously, tightened its grip on Molly, and wrapped a coil around her throat.

Addison followed Guadalupe's suit. He snatched a glowing stick from the fire, danced from foot to foot like a fencer, and slashed at the reptile's face.

Raj hefted a burning log, half his own size, and speared it toward the snake.

"Ow!" snarled Molly, grasping a free hand toward her singed leg.

"Sorry!" Raj called, hopping backward for balance. He held the burning log to the anaconda's tail, branding its mottled skin so that its flesh sizzled and filled the night air with a faint smell of barbecue.

The snake tightened its grip on Molly's throat. Her face began to turn blue.

Raj grabbed more burning sticks, handing them to Guadalupe and Addison. They singed the snake again and again. At last, the enraged serpent decided that enough was enough. The Amazon was a big place, and there were easier meals to be had. The anaconda released Molly with a savage hiss and retreated from the flaming brands. The massive snake barber-poled up a mahogany tree and vanished into the slithering shadows.

"Got to watch out for those," said Guadalupe.

"It's a jungle out there," Addison agreed.

"Thanks," breathed Molly, panting for breath. She clutched her burnt leg.

"I have a first-aid kit!" Raj cried, still jittery from the attack. He riffled through his backpack and came up with iodine and bandages. He examined the red and swollen burn. "Does it hurt?"

"I'll give you one guess." Molly gritted her teeth and didn't make a sound as Raj cleaned the wound and bandaged it up.

"Molly," said Raj, shaking his head in admiration, "you're not like any of my sisters."

"Thanks," Molly said again. She climbed to her feet and tested her leg.

"Chin up, Mo," said Addison. "Nobody said discovering seven hundred and fifty tons of treasure would be a walk in the park."

"Nobody said it'd be a walk in the jungle, either," Molly grumbled.

"I need to get back to a city," Guadalupe said, staring distrustfully at the overhanging branches. "Even getting pinched by the policía is better than this."

Addison could find no flaw in her reasoning. "The good news is, we now know the snakes are afraid of fire." He sat down and made himself look as relaxed as possible. "We just stay close to the campfire tonight, and we'll be fine."

Molly sat down and inched as close as she could get to the flames without catching fire. "Thanks, Guadalupe," she said.

······

It took the team a long time to fall asleep that night. They stared up at the few stars visible through the jungle's curtain.

"Raj," asked Eddie at last, "what will you do with your share of the Incan treasure?"

"Rent my own apartment so I don't have to share space with my three sisters."

"You really have three sisters?" asked Guadalupe.

"It's my cross to bear."

"What else would you do with the treasure?" asked Eddie. "It could be worth millions."

Raj scratched his chin thoughtfully. "I'd change my last name to 'Dark Star.' And then I'd go to survival camp in Montana. What about you?"

"With that much gold, I'd buy a glass submarine. I'd build a Jacuzzi you can drive down the street. I'd buy Restaurant Anatolia. I'd buy our school, tear it down, and turn it into a skate park. I'd build a mansion out of cupcakes and eat my way through it. I'd buy a skyscraper and fill each floor with water and goldfish. I'd hire the Dallas Cowboys to be my personal bodyguard. I'd build a fire engine that shoots Nutella from fire hoses."

"You've given this some thought," said Guadalupe.

"A bit," Eddie admitted. "I don't have brothers or sisters, so I have time on my hands."

"Addison, what will you do with the treasure?" asked Raj.

"Probably give my share to a museum," said Addison. "What I really care about is finding it before Professor Ragar."

"And what about you, Molly?" asked Raj.

"I don't care about the treasure," she said simply. "I just want to rescue Aunt Delia and Uncle Nigel."

......

Addison woke the next morning pleased to find he was quite alive and not being digested inside the belly of a snake.

Raj checked his booby traps. Guadalupe stoked the campfire back to life, heating up rice, beans, and corn for their breakfast. Eddie watched the food steam, his mouth watering.

Addison rose and stretched his sore muscles. He opened his notebook and read the second Incan clue for the forty-seventh time . . .

"Across the mighty Amazon,
Through the jungles of the headhunters,
Follow the footsteps of the Incas;
In a castle on the edge of the world
The key is hidden closest to the gods."

Molly raised herself up on one elbow and squinted her eyes. "Addison, did you hear something?"

"Nothing in particular."

"In the bushes over there. I heard a mumbling."

"That's just your stomach," said Addison. "Rise and shine, Mo. Shove a little breakfast into the Cooke stomach and enjoy this beautiful morning."

Molly sat up and rubbed her eyes. "It's funny. It's just that I'm pretty sure I heard something."

"I'm sure it's nothing," said Addison.

The next second, the air was filled with deafening war cries.

......

Fifty Máloco headhunters sprouted from the jungle, spears held high over their heads. Their faces were painted red, and their ears and noses pierced with bone. They barreled full speed toward Addison like stones from a slingshot.

"John Wilkes Booth!" yelped Addison.

"See, I told you!" shouted Molly, jumping to her feet.

"A brisk run will aid the constitution," suggested Addison, taking flight.

Addison, Molly, Raj, and Guadalupe plunged headlong into the underbrush. Eddie brought up the rear, huffing and puffing.

"Run like the wind, Eddie!" cried Addison.

"I'm trying!" gasped Eddie.

"You run like a mild breeze!" shouted Molly. She was pleased to find that her burnt leg didn't seem to slow down her feet.

The Máloco tribesmen were not kidding around. They hurtled right over the booby traps Raj had set, catching up quickly. Their screams rattled in Addison's ears, chilling him to the bone.

Addison's team leapt over tree roots and ducked under branches, and sometimes were forced to do both at the same time. The vegetation grew so thick, Addison couldn't see three feet ahead of him. So Addison was as surprised as anyone when he and his group raced right over the edge of a ravine.

They skidded down the steep dirt slope on their backs, grasping at roots and stones to slow their descent. The Máloco lost ground, choosing a more sensible detour down to the gully.

Addison's group scrambled to their feet, clumps of leaves matting their hair, and kept right on moving. Their route led them directly up the next steep hill. Soon they were out of breath, gulping for air like beached trout. Addison was already sore from yesterday's hike and this life-or-death sprint was not particularly helping matters. He wondered how long he could keep running without any breakfast.

"Look out this time!" cried Guadalupe, skidding to a halt. The jungle opened up to reveal a hundred-foot drop to a deep rocky gorge, a fast-moving river gushing far below.

"Benedict Arnold!" cursed Addison.

Raj found a dangling jungle vine and took a running start. He screamed his battle cry at the top of his lungs: "BHAAAAAAAANDARI!!!!"

The team watched in amazement as Raj swung all thirty feet across the rocky chasm. He crashed into the bushes on the far side in an explosion of leaves and squawking birds.

"Let's just take this footbridge," Molly suggested, pointing a few feet to the left. The team wasted no time in agreeing. The hemp rope bridge danced and shivered as they raced across, the raging river rushing a dizzying hundred feet below.

"Destroy the bridge!" Addison called.

Reaching the far side, he and Guadalupe dropped to their knees and tugged out the stakes anchoring the rope bridge to the cliff. Just as the Máloco reached the bridge, it snapped apart, wilting to the far wall of the gorge.

The furious tribesmen shouted at Addison from across the canyon. They sent poison-tipped spears and darts raining down on the group.

"We should probably keep moving," said Guadalupe, ducking an incoming arrow.

"Wait," said Addison. "There wouldn't just be a footbridge here for no reason." He squatted low to the ground, scanned the terrain, and cried out in triumph. "There!"

he cried, pointing to a stone marker. "The Incan trail! I knew it!"

"Sure you did," said Molly. She took off down the trail, the group following at her heels.

"Some people are so hard to impress," Addison muttered. A Máloco spear clattered to the ground by his feet. Addison scurried after Molly.

A few miles later, the team relaxed to a slow march, exhaustion written on their dirt-lined faces. The Incan trail petered out to a pathway, dwindled down to a rut, and finally fizzled out altogether.

Raj beat a path for them through the jungle, pounding the vegetation with a stick. The forest grew lighter up ahead. Suddenly, Raj stopped and uttered a cry. The group caught up to him and peered through the bushes.

"What is it now?" gasped Eddie, wheezing for air.

"The end of the world," said Addison.

The team gazed beyond the edges of the jungle. Sheer cliffs dropped away a thousand feet below them. The Pacific Ocean spread its arms ten thousand miles wide to embrace the curve of the world. Majestic waves rolled across the panorama to pound the rocky shore.

"Look!" cried Molly, pointing to an outcropping along the coastline below. A stone bridge joined the land with a small island. And on the small island stood an impossibly large stone structure perched impossibly high on an impossibly thin jetty of land. Waves crashed against its stone foundations, casting rainbows glinting in the midday sun. Like an image from a fairy tale, its rounded turrets and pointed spires proudly presided over the gray-blue sea.

It was a castle.

Chapter Thirteen

The Castle on the Edge of Forever

THE GROUP PICKED THEIR way down the rocky bluffs to a winding road along the barren beach. Scavenging seagulls hovered on the blustering wind.

Guadalupe pointed to a street sign. "The next town is Casa Azar! This is great news—in the jungle we must have crossed the border into Ecuador!"

"You seem pretty excited about Ecuador," said Molly.

"Well"—Guadalupe grinned—"I'm not wanted by the *policía* in Ecuador."

"Give it time," said Eddie.

Guadalupe shrugged and nodded. "I give it about twenty-four hours."

Addison thumbed through his copy of *Fiddleton's Atlas* and found the castle listed under "Places of Interest." He cleared his throat dramatically. "Ladies and gentlemen, I give you the Castle on the Edge of Forever."

"Are we sure it's the castle we're looking for?" asked Molly.

Addison's eyes popped as he read the description in *Fiddleton's Atlas*. "It must be," he said, tapping the page. "This castle was built by Diego de Almagro II."

"The conquistador who built the Cathedral of Lost Souls!"

"The very same. And Diego built this castle in the same year, 1541."

"Wow," said Eddie, impressed. "What have *I* done this year?"

Addison examined the castle through his field binoculars. Sandstone towers ringed with bastions. Curtain walls pocked with arrow loops. Battlements, saw-toothed with stone merlons, flanking the tower gates. If this was any indication of what Ecuador was going to be like, Addison was ready to give up New York for good.

He zoomed in the binoculars, training his focus on the causeway connecting the highway to the castle. "There's a lot of activity down there." Limousines and luxury cars rumbled over the stone bridge onto the fortified island.

Eddie borrowed Addison's field binoculars and peered at the castle. "I don't see anything."

"I put the lens caps back on." Addison turned to face the group. "The third key is in that castle. We have to find a way to sneak in there and grab the key before Professor Ragar."

......

Addison's team crouched in the underbrush watching the castle gatehouse at the foot of the bridge. Security guards inspected a line of black limousines before waving them onto the island. Each limo was filled with dangerous-looking men in tuxedoes, accompanied by dangerous-looking women in colorful dresses.

"Está berraco," whispered Guadalupe, ducking low into the bushes. "Do you realize who these people are?"

"It just looks like a wedding," said Addison. "A very *expensive* wedding, but just a wedding."

"These are bad people," Guadalupe said, shaking her head. "Even by my standards."

A stretch limo pulled up to the gatehouse. Guards circled the limo with bomb-sniffing dogs.

Guadalupe pointed out the new arrivals through the open windows of their black limo.

"That's Héctor Guzmán, head of the Guzmán cartel."

"Is a cartel like a gang?" whispered Molly.

"A huge gang. They say Guzmán kills his rivals by locking them in a freezer."

"That'd have to be a pretty big freezer," said Raj skeptically.

"Maybe he uses a walk-in freezer, like at a restaurant," Molly reasoned. "How do you recognize all these people, Guadalupe?"

"TV." Guadalupe studied the gang members arriving in the next limousine. She solemnly crossed herself. "I just figured out whose wedding this is . . . Don Miguel's daughter."

The name Don Miguel meant exactly nothing to Addison. "I'm very happy for Don Miguel . . . and his daughter. But we still need to get into this castle."

"Fat chance. That's Don Miguel's castle."

"He's allowed to own a historical site?"

"In Ecuador, you can buy anything. Don't you realize who Don Miguel is?"

Addison's group blinked at Guadalupe.

"No?" said Eddie.

"Not even a little bit," Addison admitted.

Guadalupe stared at them in amazement."Don Hernando Miguel?"

"Still not ringing any bells."

"We're from America," said Eddie. "All our famous criminals are TV stars or professional athletes."

"Don Miguel is the boss of all the bosses," Guadalupe whispered in something approaching superstitious awe.

"He's marrying his daughter off to his biggest rival, Héctor Guzmán. I saw it in the news. Their two gangs have feuded for years, but this wedding could bring them together. Then they can stop shooting each other and get back to shooting other people. It's beautiful really."

"I love a good wedding," Addison agreed.

"The point is," said Guadalupe, "you're looking at the two most violent gangs in South America. Everyone at this wedding is armed and dangerous."

Addison looked across the bridge. A massive tent filled the courtyard. Guests arrived in tuxedos and evening gowns. A twelve-piece band played a sizzling samba.

"I hear what you're saying, Guadalupe," said Addison. "I really do. But just think of the hors d'oeuvres . . ."

"What kind of hors d'oeuvres?" asked Eddie.

"Oh no," said Molly. "I know that look on Addison's face. He's forming a plan."

"Hush, young Cooke. The wheels are turning."

"Addison, you expect us to just mambo into a castle filled with rival gangsters, find the third key, and cha-cha right out?"

Addison studied the guards spread out across the grounds. He considered the odds. He gave it six to four against. "I give it six to four in favor," he said confidently.

"These are dangerous criminals," said Guadalupe. "You'll find more killers at that wedding than at a state penitentiary. You couldn't throw a brick in that wedding without braining a criminal."

"I'm not suggesting we throw bricks at criminals in weddings," said Addison. "Besides, you don't have to come along. You helped us across the jungle—if 'help' is the word I'm looking for—and that was our deal."

Guadalupe stiffened. "I'm not chicken. Besides, I bet they have a lot of excellent merchandise in that house." She squinted at Addison. "How do you plan on getting inside?"

"Through the front door." Addison turned to inspect his comrades, brushing the dirt from their school uniforms. "Eddie, be a gentleman and straighten your shirt cuffs." Addison tightened his half-Windsor knot, sculpting the perfect tie dimple. "In my nearly thirteen years on this earth, there are two things I've learned beyond a shadow of a doubt. The first is that you can get in anywhere if you dress sharply enough."

"And the second?" asked Eddie.

"There is no sweeter food than free food." Addison buttoned his blazer. "Besides," he added, "I love a good wedding."

••••••

Addison confidently led his team up the driveway to the gatehouse. Raj tried frantically to spit-shine the mud stains from his shirtfront. Eddie picked brambles and thorns from his socks, hopping from one foot to the other, trying to keep up. Together, they approached the head security guard.

"I don't know about this one," muttered Molly.

"Mo, try and keep an open mind."

"Addison, you're so open-minded your brain's fallen out."

"Molly, I am going to make that guard beg to let us into the wedding." Addison strolled up and offered a cheerful grin. "Fine weather."

The guard barked a sentence in Spanish.

"He wants to know if we are guests of the wedding," Eddie translated.

"Of course we are," said Addison immediately.

The gate guard eyed them suspiciously and spoke to Eddie.

"He needs to see our invitations," Eddie said nervously.

Addison made a show of patting down his blazer pockets. "Eddie, do you have the invitations?"

"Nope." Eddie shook his head.

"Are you kidding me? What did you do with them?"

"I never had them!" Eddie insisted.

"I cannot let you into the wedding without invitations," said the guard in thickly accented English.

"That's excellent," said Addison with sincerity. "I was hoping you'd say that."

"Why?" asked the guard, squinting at Addison.

"We don't want to go to this boring wedding. We're just stuck here because of my uncle. Can you tell us the best way to get to Casa Azar? We want to sneak out and do something fun."

The guard sized up Addison uncertainly. "Why are a bunch of American kids coming to this wedding, anyway? You don't even speak Spanish."

"My uncle Héctor flew us in from America for the wedding. It's all a big waste of time, but at least we got out of boarding school for a week." Addison smiled ingratiatingly. "Can you order us a cab to Casa Azar, so we can ditch out of here?"

The guard frowned.

Inwardly, Addison held his breath.

Finally, the guard took the bait. "What did you say your uncle's name was?"

Addison stifled a yawn, as if bored. He casually played his ace. "Héctor Guzmán."

The guard's face turned instantly white, like he'd been slapped with a cream pie. His lower lip trembled in fear. Sweat sprouted from his forehead like morning dew.

"Anyway," Addison continued, "we can always just hitchhike to Casa Azar." He turned to leave, waving his friends to follow.

"Wait!" called the guard. "You must go to the wedding!"

"No thank you," said Addison firmly. "We're going to go have some fun."

"Please, you must!"

"Absolutely not. Out of the question."

"If Don Guzmán discovers I let you sneak out of the wedding," the guard pleaded, "I won't just lose my job . . . I will lose my life!"

Addison sighed and crossed his arms. He pretended to weigh the issue over in his mind.

"I am begging you," said the guard. "What if something happened to you in Casa Azar? My life is in your hands. Please, you must go to this wedding! I don't want to end up in a restaurant freezer!"

Addison spread his arms and let them collapse at his sides. "Well, it was worth a shot. But you owe us one."

"Thank you," said the guard, clasping Addison's hand and shaking it gratefully.

Addison smiled warmly and returned the shake. He nodded to his team, and together they strode past the guardhouse and over the stone bridge to the castle.

Guadalupe cast a sidelong glance at Addison, a look of wonder in her eyes. *"Bacán."*

Addison smiled.

"Please!" the guard called after them. "Put in a good word for me with Don Guzmán!"

······

Addison, Molly, Guadalupe, Eddie, and Raj strode toward

the castle's entrance. A security guard waved them past a velvet rope.

"Not too shabby," said Eddie.

"We're not through the woods yet," Addison whispered.

Security guards waved them through a metal detector. Addison and Molly made it past without issue, but Raj lit up the metal detector like a Christmas tree. Perplexed guards began frisking Raj's pockets, removing fishhooks, sewing needles, iron pills, snare wire, bear spray . . .

One sharp-eyed bodyguard put a hand on Addison's shoulder. *"¡Deténgase! ¿Quién es usted?"*

Addison unleashed his warmest smile on the guard. "Addison Cooke. *¿Cómo está?"* He held out his hand for a shake. The guard only stared at the hand, and then went back to staring at Addison.

"I have never seen you before," said the guard, peering closely at Addison's group. "You are not with Don Guzmán's party and I have never seen you with Don Miguel."

"We're the band," said Addison.

The guard cocked an ear to listen to the Latin big-band music blaring from inside the wedding tent. "The band is already inside," growled the guard. "Plus, you don't have no instruments."

Addison tilted his chin so he could look down his nose at the guard. "We're the a cappella group," he said imperiously. Addison was still a bit stung that the choir ploy hadn't worked at the Cathedral of Lost Souls, and he was determined to give the scheme a second shot. He patted the guard on the cheek. "I assume dinner is included with our fee." Without waiting for a response, Addison snapped his fingers at his friends who trailed him inside.

The guard eyed them suspiciously. He spoke rapid Spanish into his walkie-talkie. A team of guards circled in, handguns bulging under their blazers. They followed Addison's group into the party.

······

Addison strolled into the most magnificent party he'd ever seen. A massive tent, as big as a circus big top, covered the entire courtyard of the castle. The tent arched over a stage where the band hammered out a rhythmic rumba. Guests in black-tie formalwear glided around the dance floor. Waiters passed glittering platters of pricey beluga caviar, fried calamari, and oysters on the half shell. Addison had to hand it to Don Miguel—he must be pretty good at his job to foot the bill for a wedding this posh.

The nine-foot wedding cake stood on a gilded pedestal. Addison spotted the bride shaking her fists and shouting at the wedding photographer. The poor photographer was having trouble fitting both the cake and the bride into his photo.

Don Hernando Miguel greeted guests with a double

kiss, greasing their cheeks with his oiled mustache. Puffed up in a tight tuxedo, his black hair slicked tight against his scalp, Don Miguel looked every bit like an overfed penguin.

Addison carved a path through the crowd, smiling, waving, shaking hands, and aiming finger guns at guests as if they were old friends. "I love a good wedding," he said again, to no one in particular. Eddie's eyes swam as they reached a buffet table piled high with French cheeses, Italian meats, and Swiss chocolate strawberries.

"*Harika,*" Eddie gushed. "They even have Turkish kebabs!"

Addison helped himself to a shrimp cocktail. "Finally, a civilized environment where one can relax."

Molly pointed a finger across the crowd. "There's Professor Ragar!"

Addison nearly choked on a shrimp. His eyes followed the line of Molly's finger.

Sure enough, Professor Ragar swaggered into the party, surrounded by his men. Ragar leaned heavily on his silver-tipped walking stick and adjusted his cocked derby hat. In the midday light, his mottled burn scar had the crimson hue of barbecued ribs.

"This is bad news." Addison grimaced. "Ragar must have cracked the last clue. He knows the key is in this castle."

"It's also good news," whispered Molly. "It means Aunt Delia and Uncle Nigel are close."

Addison spotted Ragar's black limousine, all bullet-proof glass and armor plating, idling in the driveway. The chauffeur circled the massive car around to the parking lot. Addison squinted hard at the dark-tinted windows but couldn't catch a glimpse to see if his aunt and uncle were trapped inside.

"Well, Don Miguel won't be happy when he discovers Professor Ragar crashing his party." Addison watched in dismay as the professor kissed Don Miguel on both cheeks, murmured a few words in Spanish, and then embraced him like a long-lost brother. "Guy Fawkes! Ragar is smooth as silk!"

Guadalupe sized up Professor Ragar's group, noting their tattoos. "Russian Mafia, right?"

Addison looked at her, impressed. "You really know your gangsters."

Guadalupe only shook her head. "Those guys don't mess around."

Addison noted, with growing alarm, the wedding security guards whispering to Don Miguel and pointing toward Addison's group. Professor Ragar's piercing gray eyes lit up and scanned the crowd. By the time he glanced over at the buffet table, Addison's team had vanished. With a flick of Ragar's hand, bodyguards fanned out and began searching the party.

Addison's team squatted uncomfortably underneath the buffet table, Raj peering out from the folds of the tablecloth. "I don't think he saw us."

"Good," said Addison. "Keep a lookout."

It was dusty under the table and Molly found herself gearing up for a sneeze.

"What's our move?" asked Guadalupe.

Addison reached out a finger and thumb and pinched Molly's nose, stifling her sneeze at the last second. "We find the Incan key before Ragar."

"Thank you," said Molly, recovering. "What about Aunt Delia and Uncle Nigel? They could be right outside."

"Follow me like a ninja. Which sounds easier: finding the key, or rescuing Aunt D and Uncle N from two dozen armed men?"

"Well, when you put it that way . . ."

"Look," whispered Addison, "Ragar said he'll keep them alive until he finds the treasure. So if we find the treasure first, Ragar has no reason to hurt them."

Molly weighed the sense of this.

"Meanwhile, it buys us time to think up a plan for rescuing them."

"All right," said Molly. "So how do we find the key?"

"There's nothing to it, Mo. It's like falling off a log. We just nip about the old castle, nibble a few shrimp cocktails, steal an ancient Incan key, snag a few more shrimp cocktails, and tap-dance out of here."

"You couldn't steal an ape from a chicken," said Molly.

"It's true I don't have experience with nicking things," Addison allowed. "There isn't a book on it. I've checked."

"A book on stealing?" Guadalupe had been silent for a while. But now her face brightened with interest. "You don't need the book when you've got the author."

Guadalupe crawled from the buffet table and snuck into an open door of the castle. The team hurried after her.

......

Addison's crew padded silently through French doors and into an ornate dining room. A thirty-foot-long oak table was laid with bronze candelabras and hand-painted porcelain.

"There must be good money in crime," said Addison. "Don Miguel is doing okay for himself."

"It's a growth industry," said Guadalupe. "Smuggling, extortion, kidnapping . . . How else can anyone pay for a wedding these days?" She cased the joint like a professional. "Wow," she said in awe, "I've never seen silverware that was actually *silver*."

"C'mon, Guadalupe," said Addison, "we're on the clock."

Guadalupe stared longingly at the flatware before following the group into the library.

Now it was Addison's turn to stare in wonder. The library's wall-to-wall bookshelves were crammed with books. They were stacked two stories high, with a rolling ladder to reach them. The wood-paneled room was dominated by a giant oil painting of a young Spanish nobleman.

"There he is," said Addison. "Diego de Almagro II. Otherwise known as El Mozo."

"'The lad?'" Eddie translated.

"That's right. Diego had the same name as his father, like me. So they called him El Mozo."

The group gathered under the painting. El Mozo's hand rested on the pommel of his sword, a red plume blossoming from the steel helm he cradled in the crook of his arm. His skin was dark and his expression darker. He looked ready to draw his sword and skewer the portrait artist.

"He killed Pizarro?" asked Molly.

Addison nodded. "El Mozo's father and Pizarro were like brothers until they started fighting over the Incan treasure. Pizarro imprisoned El Mozo's father and cut off his head."

Raj let out a low whistle. He smiled; he was getting better at it.

"El Mozo raised an army of rebels to avenge his father. They assassinated Pizarro. It makes sense to hide a key here. El Mozo wanted to ensure Pizarro's knights never found Atahualpa's treasure."

"Seems like this castle would be the first place Pizarro's knights would look for clues," said Molly.

"True. But a lot of them were killed or vanished during the civil war."

Molly nodded solemnly. "Maybe it was El Mozo who hunted down Pizarro's thirteen famous knights and hid them in that cavern under the Cathedral of Lost Souls."

"I can believe it." Addison gazed up at El Mozo's fierce eyes glaring down from the portrait. "Let's keep moving."

"Wait," said Molly. She pointed to a grisly ram's skull with black horns painted on El Mozo's shield. "That symbol was carved on the shield door in the basement of the Cathedral."

"Good eye, Mo." Addison examined it closely. "It's the symbol for Supay. The Incan god of the dead."

"Why would El Mozo paint the god of the dead on his shield?"

Addison was pretty sure he knew the answer. "Revenge."

●●●●●●

The team waited for an armed patrol guard to march past before sneaking out of the library and into the massive center hall of the castle. One grand staircase led to the higher floors. The other descended to the basement.

"So where do we find the key?" asked Eddie.

Addison recited the clue from memory. *"'In a castle at the end of the world, the key is hidden closest to the gods.'"*

"*'Closest to the gods.'* Which way's that?"

Addison pointed a finger at the first staircase. "Up."

The team prowled up several flights of stone steps, past the second, third, and fourth floors, until they reached the attic. There, they found a landing with three wooden doors.

"One of these must lead to the top of the tower. The highest point in the castle . . . That's where I bet we'll find the key," said Addison.

Guadalupe tried all three doors and pointed to the first one. "It's not that door."

"How do you know?"

"Because it's unlocked. Any door that's unlocked doesn't have anything good behind it." To demonstrate, Guadalupe opened the door, revealing a bathroom. It was a tiny room, with hardly enough space to swing a cat.

"Okay, that leaves two doors," said Molly. "But even if you're right, Addison, how do we even know the key will still be here after so many years?"

"My guess is Don Miguel doesn't know there's an ancient Incan key hidden in his castle. I mean, if the third key is half as well hidden as the first two were, we have a pretty good shot."

Guadalupe knelt down and peered at the two door

locks. "I can jimmy open the second door, but not the third. It's a dead bolt."

"Okay, we'll start with the second door and see where it gets us," said Addison. "Can you open it?"

"Who's got a knife?" Guadalupe smiled.

"We can use my lock-picking set!" Raj exclaimed, beaming as he dug through his backpack.

"I'm better with a knife."

Addison drew Zubov's butterfly knife from his trouser pocket. He flicked it open. "Will this do?"

Guadalupe raised her eyebrows, impressed. "It'll do. Somebody count to ten." She set to work picking the lock, her tongue curled in the corner of her mouth for concentration.

Eddie began counting, *"Uno, dos, tres . . ."*

"Are you sure you don't want my lock-picking set?" asked Raj.

"Done," said Guadalupe. And the wooden door creaked open.

The team stared down a musty hallway hung with old framed portraits of Spanish noblemen. The ceiling was rotted and mildewed. The red carpet was frayed and rat-chewed. Addison smiled; it looked promising. He stepped inside.

"Guadalupe, aren't you coming?" he asked.

"No thanks. I'll just keep a lookout here."

"She's going downstairs to nick the silverware," said Molly.

"Guadalupe," said Addison, "we've got a mission to do!"

"It's not my mission. And I need some kind of reward for risking my life here. Besides, I'll be right back."

"Ragar's men will be searching the castle, Guadalupe. Stay out of trouble."

"Me? Trouble?" Guadalupe looked deeply offended. She pulled her long hair back into a ponytail, rolled up her sleeves, and slipped on a pair of gloves she kept buttoned in her back pocket. She darted back downstairs, making a beeline for the dining room.

······

The rest of the group made their way down the narrow passage. The smell of rot assaulted their nostrils, and rats could be heard scuttling to and fro under the floorboards. Stepping into the hallway was as pleasant as rear-ending a hearse.

The corridor was lined with doorways revealing compact bedrooms furnished with simple cots. "Maybe these are for wedding guests," Addison whispered.

"It could also be where the guards sleep," said Eddie warily.

The crooked attic hallway meandered crazily back and

forth like a man who'd been beaned by a brick. As they rounded a bend, a bedroom door burst open, bathing the passage in light. Addison's group froze.

A handsome young man in dark glasses with slicked-back hair and a flashy suit strode down the hallway, flanked by security guards.

Addison had to admire the moxie of a man who would wear sunglasses in such a dark hall.

The man flicked off his shades and glared down at Addison. *"¿Qué estás haciendo aquí?"*

"We were just looking for the bathroom," said Addison.

"You're not allowed to be here!" the man answered in English. "This floor is off-limits."

"Yes, if you could just point us toward the facilities . . ."

"This hallway is locked—how did you even get in?" The man waved to his security guards, who grabbed Addison and Molly, pinning their arms behind their backs. "Who are you?"

Addison puffed up his chest with indignation. "I," he announced, "am Don Héctor Guzmán's son!" The words did not have quite the effect Addison was hoping for.

"You are lying," said the handsome man with the slicked-back hair.

"How would you know?" asked Molly.

"Because *I*," said the man, "am Don Héctor Guzmán's son."

Addison winced. Sometimes you roll the dice and come up snake eyes.

"Don Miguel will want to hear about this," Guzmán's son declared.

"*Señor,*" said a tall security guard with a shaved head. "We can not bother Don Miguel in the middle of the festivities."

"That is true," said Guzmán's son. "We will lock them up."

Security guards dragged Addison and Molly back down the winding passage and onto the landing. Eddie and Raj were herded before them.

"Whatever you do," said Addison, gesturing anxiously to the third door on the landing, "please don't lock us in that tower."

"Why not?" Guzmán's son leered. He slid on his shades and smoothed his hair in one practiced gesture.

"I can't stand closed spaces! I have claustrophobia."

Don Guzmán's son looked at Addison, perplexed.

"Eddie," said Addison, snapping his fingers, "what's the Spanish word for claustrophobia?"

"*Claustrofobia,*" said Eddie.

Addison turned back to Guzmán's son. "I have *claustrofobia.*"

The man shook his head. He'd known Addison for thirty seconds and had already lost all patience for him.

The bald security guard grabbed a set of keys from his belt and unlocked the third and final door. He gripped Addison by the neck, far more painfully than was absolutely necessary.

"No! Please!" said Addison. "I can't!"

"You will!" shouted Guzman's son.

One by one, the guard shoved Addison, Molly, Raj, and Eddie through the open doorway.

"You will stay locked in here until Don Miguel is ready to deal with you," said Guzmán's son, smoothing his slicked-back hair. "Then, whoever you are, you will be punished."

The door slammed shut. The key turned in the lock, the dead bolt slid home.

"Great," said Eddie. "This is just *harika*."

"This *is* harika," said Addison, rubbing his aching neck. He turned in a full circle, taking in his surroundings. "That helpful gentleman put us exactly where we want to be . . . the high tower."

······

They mounted the dusty wooden stairs that spiraled upward toward the tower eyrie. It looked as if no one had climbed the tower in centuries.

The stairs hugged the curved castle wall, each oak plank slotted into the stone masonry. Several rotten boards were missing entirely, and there was no railing to prevent someone from plummeting down the center of the shaft. Addison tried not to picture this, but it was easier said than done. Every few steps one of the warped and worm-eaten planks would creak underfoot, ready to snap.

"I hope Don Miguel has good liability insurance," said Eddie.

Addison trudged up the stairs, growing dizzier with each footfall. The higher they climbed, the more his stomach filled with dread. He kept his eyes trained on each step before him, trying to ignore the gaping abyss a few inches to his right.

Halfway up the tower, Eddie stumbled on a loose plank. The team watched it fall, tumbling end over end, disappearing into the darkness below. Addison counted six Mississippis before he heard the echo of its landing.

Addison panted for air, fighting his panic. He pressed both hands against the outer wall, steadying himself for balance. "It's times like these I wish I'd listened to what my aunt Delia told me about becoming an archaeologist."

"Why, what did she say?" asked Raj.

"She said, 'Don't become an archaeologist.'"

Despite his gnawing fear, Addison forced his feet to keep lifting, carrying him higher. At last they made it to the highest landing. Addison collapsed on the wooden floor and put his head between his knees to keep from fainting. The floor was covered with an inch of dust. There was nothing to see except abandoned rat nests, and rat nests that Addison wished were abandoned.

The oak plank ceiling was so low it was easier to sit than stand.

"A trapdoor!" Raj cried, excitedly.

He clawed at the rectangular seam in the ceiling, and an old rotten trapdoor swung open, revealing nothing but a thick roof of stones and mortar immediately above.

"I guess it's a dead end," said Molly.

"Does this mean we have to go all the way back down now?" asked Eddie.

"You know, it's a bit odd," said Addison, still trying to steady his breathing. "From the outside, this tower was domed. But on the inside, this ceiling is flat."

"I think you're right," said Raj. He moved to an arrow loop cut in the stone wall of the tower, thrust his head outside, and peered upward. "We're nowhere near the top," he reported. "There has to be another thirty feet of tower above us!"

"A false ceiling," Addison concluded. "Look for another trapdoor."

The team examined the flat oak beams of the ceiling, searching for any loose plank, trigger, or hidden switch. "Nothing," Raj concluded. "The ceiling's completely solid."

Addison studied the way the rafters joined with the masonry. He placed his palms flat on the wooden ceiling and rotated, counterclockwise. Pushing with all his might, the entire ceiling shifted an inch.

"Help me! Rotate the ceiling like you're winding a clock."

The team pushed, and with a grinding of wood, the ceiling swiveled a few feet on its axis. The rectangular opening of the wooden trapdoor moved to reveal an empty space in the stone ceiling. Addison's group pushed until the two holes lined up flush.

A single ladder led upward into a hidden eyrie.

"I wish I knew El Mozo's interior decorator. He must have been worth every penny," Addison said.

"Let's keep moving," said Molly.

Addison rested a hand against the rickety old ladder, but found he could not take a step.

"You can do it, Addison," Molly said quietly. "Every ladder has a first rung, right?"

Addison's hands trembled. "It's not the first rung I have a problem with. It's the third, fourth, and fifth rungs." His arms shook.

"What's wrong with him?" Eddie asked.

Addison took a deep breath. "I'm afraid of heights," he admitted. He shut his eyes and turned his head away.

Raj and Eddie scaled the ancient ladder. Eddie called back down, "Well, are you coming or not?"

"I'll be down here," said Addison. "Keeping a lookout."

Molly stayed by his side for another moment. "I wish I knew why you had this fear of heights, Addison. Maybe then I could help you get better."

Addison only shook his head.

Molly climbed the ladder to the eyrie.

······

The eyrie was lit by a single shaft of light from an arrow loop in the masonry. The floor held little of interest. Ditto for the sandstone walls. It was the domed ceiling that was spectacular.

It glittered with tens of thousands of painted tiles, every color of the spectrum. The mosaic depicted a radiant blue sky with brilliant white clouds. Angels with trumpets soared in the heavens. And floating in the clouds rested dozens of Incan gods. Some gods were male and some female. Some were part jaguar, llama, or snake. Molly, Eddie, and Raj stared upward with their jaws agape.

"What do you see?" Addison called up from the bottom of the ladder.

"A painting of the sky," Molly replied.

"Remember—look *closest to the gods.*"

"There are too many gods," said Molly, searching the

painted sky. "There's nothing *but* gods."

"Do any of them point to a key?"

Molly, Raj, and Eddie searched. But none of the gods appeared to have anything to do with keys.

"I see a deer god and a monkey god," called Eddie, "but I don't see any key god. Addison, is there an Incan god of keys?"

"I can't remember." Addison shut his eyes and concentrated. He called up the ladder. "What other gods do you see? Call them out for me."

"I see a thunder god," said Molly, pointing to a god riding on a rain cloud. "And a sea god, an earth god, and a moon god. Which god would have the key?"

Addison, at the foot of the ladder, took a deep breath to relax his mind. "King Atahualpa," he said at last. "He would have the key."

"But he wasn't a god."

"He was to the Incas."

"All right. So what does he look like?" called Molly.

Addison opened his eyes. He was pretty sure he knew the answer. "The Incan emperor was considered the child of the sun. Inti, the sun god, the most powerful Incan god."

"You want us to look closest to the sun?"

"Yes."

Addison's team studied the sun in the center of the

mosaic, spreading its rays to all points of the compass.

"There," said Molly at last. She pointed to a single discolored tile. "That tile, in the middle of the sun. It's a slightly different yellow."

The team looked closely to where Molly was pointing. And sure enough, the tile in the center of the sun was not a tile at all . . .

It was in the shape of a key. And it was made of solid gold.

······

Molly piggybacked on Eddie's shoulders and carefully chiseled mortar from around the Incan key using one of Raj's fishhooks. The ancient masonry crumbled away, releasing the key from the mosaic. Eddie lost his footing; he and Molly tumbled to the floor. They held their breath, waiting for a booby trap that never came.

Molly, Eddie, and Raj carefully passed the key back and forth, feeling the weight of the solid gold. Then they raced down the ladder to show the key to Addison.

A clue was engraved on the flat golden surface of the key.

Eddie squinted at the tightly scrawled calligraphy. "I think some of these words have ancient spellings."

"Do the best you can," said Addison.

Eddie took a deep breath and read aloud:

"The top of the world holds the treasure of
the Incas.
Above the sacred valley in a palace in the sky,
Supay's mouth is open wide to swallow up the
brave.
Beware the curse of Atahualpa or you will
surely die."

"Eddie, this clue actually rhymes in English," Molly said.

"Yeah, I guess so. I like that bit about the palace and
the treasure. I'm not sure I like the part about the curse
and the dying."

"That's just to scare away the amateurs," said Addison.

"It's working," said Eddie.

"The clue mentions that Incan god Supay," said Molly.
"I think El Mozo's obsessed with death."

"Everyone needs a hobby," said Addison, turning the
golden key over in his hands. "It's no concern of ours.
We're just one puzzle away from finding the treasure."

......

The team spiraled their way down the rickety steps to the
base of the tower and stood staring, flummoxed, at the
locked door.

"The good news is we found the Incan key," said Addison.
"The bad news is, it doesn't open this door."

"Well, we can't just stay locked up in here waiting for Don Miguel," said Molly.

Raj picked up a loose plank of wood that had once been a riser in the staircase. He gripped it firmly in his hands like a baseball bat. "We could bash the door down," he suggested hopefully.

"Or we could try knocking," said Eddie.

Addison figured the latter option couldn't hurt. He knocked.

A second later, a key scraped in the lock, and the door cracked open. Addison recognized the scowling face of the tall security guard with the shaved head. His hulking body filled the doorway. He looked angry and resentful, presumably from getting stuck guarding a door when he could have been downstairs enjoying a wedding.

"Well, what do you brats want?" grunted the guard.

"Only one thing," said Addison, smiling. "And you have already done it."

"What's that?" the guard asked.

"You opened the door." Addison stepped aside, revealing Raj, who took a running start and swung his plank hard into the man's stomach. It connected with a satisfying smack, like a Jell-O mold chucked from a high window and meeting the pavement.

The security guard doubled over, clutching his gut, moaning a three-part harmony of anger, pain, and disbelief.

Addison's team slipped past him. They ran, fists pumping like pistons, across the landing and down the grand staircase of the castle.

"I feel a bit bad about that," said Addison.

"I feel *great* about that," said Raj.

Addison reached the main floor and halted outside the library. "Now we just find Guadalupe and slip out of here."

"How do we find her?" Eddie asked. "She could be anywhere."

Addison never got a chance to reply. From the next room, they heard a heart-stopping scream.

Chapter Fourteen

A Wedding to Remember

ADDISON'S TEAM ROCKETED THROUGH the library and skidded to a halt at the dining room doorway. They cracked the door open a sliver and silently peeked through.

Guadalupe lay pinned to the dining room table, Zubov's hand clutching her throat. Professor Ragar, flanked by his men, smiled triumphantly. He pried a few pieces of silverware from Guadalupe's fingertips. "Where are the Cookes and their little friends?"

Addison's group pressed their eyes to the gap in the doorway.

Guadalupe squirmed under Zubov's grip and spat out a few choice Spanish words that Eddie refused to translate.

Addison noted that Zubov had already procured a new knife—a stainless-steel stiletto switchblade. Zubov brushed the hair back from Guadalupe's neck and ran the blade along the folds of her ear. "How about I pierce those pretty ears for you?"

"We should rejoin the wedding, or our host will be upset," said Professor Ragar. "Besides, we can't have any more screaming. Don Miguel is trying to unite rival gangs today—he wants no violence here."

"So how are we supposed to find those kids?" Zubov growled.

"The beauty of a castle is it has only one way in and one way out: the main gate. Wherever those kids are, they cannot escape without passing through the wedding. With any luck, they are finding the third key for us."

Ragar led his men back outside to the tented pavilion. Zubov dragged Guadalupe with her arms pinned behind her back.

Addison turned to his comrades for a strategy session.

"Let's get out of here!" suggested Eddie.

Raj and Molly bobbed their heads in wholehearted agreement.

"What about Guadalupe?" asked Addison.

"She's getting what she deserves." Eddie shrugged.

"She's always stealing. And now someone stole her," agreed Molly. "It fits."

"Let's make a run for it," said Raj.

Addison shook his head. "She helped get us this far. We can't just abandon her."

Molly, Eddie, and Raj looked at Addison with astonishment.

"She stole your wallet," said Eddie. "Twice."

"She lied about being an Amazon expert," said Raj.

"She almost got us killed," Molly added.

"She's got pluck," Addison agreed. He tried to imagine fleeing the castle and leaving Guadalupe behind, but knew he just couldn't do it. Addison drew in his breath and looked each team member in the eye. "86ers don't leave a team member behind."

"She's not an 86er," said Eddie.

"Yes, but we are," said Addison. "Look, Guadalupe doesn't have any friends or family besides us. If we don't help her, nobody will. We landed her in this, and we're going to steal her back."

"We can't trust her, Addison."

But Addison had made up his mind. He played his trump card, the one thing he knew Raj, Eddie, and Molly could not refuse.

"Code Blue."

······

Addison's team sneaked through the empty dining room and huddled by the French doors. Addison peered out at the wedding. "All right, everybody clear on the plan?"

"I'm going to sneak up to Zubov and pour a pitcher of ice water down his back," said Eddie, his voice trembling.

"Then I hit him with a catering tray," said Molly.

"I whack Ragar with a second catering tray," said Raj.

"And then?" prompted Addison.

"We grab Guadalupe and run like mad for the parking lot," said Raj.

"Good. It's not our finest effort, but we're working within time constraints."

"What are you going to do, Addison?" asked Molly.

"I," said Addison, suavely smoothing the lapels on his jacket, "will provide the diversion." And with that, he stood up and marched confidently into the wedding reception.

······

Addison decided he needed his brain juice—an ice-cold Arnold Palmer—before creating a diversion. Besides, he wanted to relax while his team maneuvered into position. Not caring who saw him, Addison casually took a seat at the bar and extended a hand to the bartender.

"Addison Cooke."

"Felix," said the bartender, giving Addison a firm handshake. "American, huh?"

"Guilty as charged."

"Me too."

"No kidding."

"Westport, Connecticut. I moved down here for the weather and never looked back. What can I getcha?"

"I wouldn't say no to an Arnold Palmer." Addison smiled.

"Coming right up," said Felix, scooping ice into a fresh glass.

Addison turned to survey the room. He noticed the seating was split down the middle; Don Héctor Guzmán's cartel sat on one side of the banquet hall, suspiciously eyeing Don Miguel's cartel on the other side.

Professor Ragar's table was located in the center. Guadalupe sat beside the Professor, clamped firmly in place by Zubov's two hands digging into her shoulders. Ragar's bodyguards roamed the room in dark suits and even darker glasses. No one had yet spotted Addison.

"Arnold Palmer," said Felix, sliding Addison the glass. "And I went easy on the ice."

"Felix, you are a rose amongst thorns." Addison took a careful sip. "Exquisite," he declared, reaching for his uncle's wallet. "Credit card is okay?"

"Open bar, Mr. Cooke. Everything's on the house."

"Then you don't mind if I try your shrimp cocktail?"

"Be my guest."

Addison plucked a fresh shrimp from the buffet and dipped it in cocktail sauce. He breathed the salty sea air, listened to the band's light cha-cha, and drank in the exotic décor of the party. "Felix, this is a lifestyle I could get used to."

"Amen, Mr. Cooke."

Addison savored the moment. His mind turned to all the history he'd learned at his uncle Nigel's knee. He remembered how Julius Caesar outfoxed the Gauls at the Allier River and conquered France. He thought of the Greeks sneaking into ancient Troy. He thought of the Americans surprising the Germans at Normandy. The trick, Addison knew, was to create a big enough diversion.

He heard a yelp from the crowd and turned to see the headwaiter pinching Eddie's ear. Eddie, caught in the act of pilfering a pitcher of ice water, turned red with embarrassment. Eddie yielded the water pitcher to the angry waiter as Ragar's men closed in on him.

Across the reception, Addison spotted Molly and Raj, clutching two filched catering trays and sprinting as a furious caterer chased them down. Raj tripped over something—possibly himself—and his tray flew from his hands to shatter a large and expensive-looking floral centerpiece. Addison's rescue attempt had officially lost the element of surprise.

Don Héctor Guzmán's thugs, easily spooked, leapt to their feet and drew guns from the cummerbunds of their tuxedos. They aimed their weapons at Don Miguel's men.

Don Miguel's men responded in kind, drawing their weapons from holsters.

Don Miguel himself flapped his hands desperately, waving the gunmen to remain calm. "Relax, there's no problem!" he exclaimed. "Try the hors d'oeuvres—they're delicious!"

Ragar's bodyguards captured Eddie, Molly, and Raj, gripping them by the backs of their necks. Addison's team's feeble rescue attempt had lasted all of twenty seconds.

From her table, Guadalupe shook her head in disbelief. She put her face in her palm, unable to watch.

Addison polished off his Arnold Palmer and set the empty glass on the felt-topped bar. He sighed. This was going to require all his powers.

······

Professor Ragar's men dragged Molly, Raj, and Eddie toward the Professor's table. Nobody noticed Addison stroll casually up to the bandstand, slip the bandleader a few pesos, and step onto the stage.

Addison gripped the microphone, feeling at home under

the lights. The mic shrieked with feedback for a second, but then Addison was off and running. *"Buenos días."* He smiled at the crowd. "How's everybody doing out there? *Muy bueno?"*

The gangsters in the audience cautiously holstered their weapons and sank back into their chairs. They clapped tentatively.

"Here's a song I'd like to dedicate to a very special professor I know who likes to kidnap orphans," said Addison. "Everyone, please put your hands together for Professor Ragar!"

A spotlight found the professor just as he was winding up to give Eddie a smack. Ragar froze, bewildered, in the spotlight.

"Let him know how much you love him," Addison told the applauding crowd. "This number is one of my favorite jazz standards, 'They Can't Take That Away From Me.'" Addison plucked the gold key from his pocket and tossed it in his hand so that it sparkled in the light. He winked at Ragar in the audience.

Addison gave the band a four count, and they came in hot. He worked the crowd, giving the old Gershwin tune all the topspin he could muster . . .

> *"The way your smile just beams*
> *The way you sing off-key . . ."*

Addison twirled the Incan key in his fingers, taunting Professor Ragar . . .

> *"The way you haunt my dreams*
> *No, no—they can't take that away from me."*

What Addison lacked in singing ability, which was a lot, he made up for in showmanship.

Professor Ragar ground his teeth and waved his men toward the bandstand. Eyes glued to the Incan key, the bodyguards released Molly, Eddie, and Raj, and zeroed in on Addison.

Only Zubov remained with Guadalupe. He pressed his stiletto to the skin of her neck so that she flinched.

Addison gave a thumbs-up to the spotlight operator and put his heart into the next verse.

> *"The way you hold your knife . . ."*

Zubov saw everyone's eyes swivel to him as the spotlight captured him in its glow. He lowered his stiletto uncertainly from Guadalupe's neck. Addison belted out his big finish.

> *"The way we danced till three*
> *The way you've changed my life!*
> *No, no—they can't take that away from me."*

Ragar's men decided enough was enough. They charged the bandstand like pillaging Vikings.

"You guys have been great," Addison told the applauding audience. "Don't forget to tip your waitstaff."

Black-suited guards hurtled onto the stage. Addison dropped his mic in a pitcher of water. The mic crackled loudly and shorted out. Somewhere, a fuse box exploded like a firecracker. The tent's generators blasted sparks from their transformers. Power cut to the tent. The band's amplifiers clicked silent. All the bright lights on the bandstand switched off.

Guards lunged for Addison. He took a running start and performed a flying leap off the stage.

••••••

Timing is everything, Addison thought as he sailed through the air and crashed directly into one of Professor Ragar's guards. They both collapsed on the ground, the man gripping Addison around the knees.

Wedding guests shouted in alarm. The furious bride used the occasion to scream at some more waiters.

Héctor Guzmán's jittery gunmen drew weapons on Don Miguel's crew. Don Miguel's nervous gang drew their weapons right back. Don Miguel stood in the middle, ordering everyone to remain calm. "This is a wedding!" he exclaimed. "Don't turn it into a funeral!"

Addison managed to roll onto his back and saw Ragar looming over him. Zubov stood beside him, glowering, Guadalupe held tightly in his grasp.

"Zubov did not think you would try to rescue this girl," said Professor Ragar. "But I knew you would take the bait."

Addison looked from Ragar to Zubov to Guadalupe. He scrambled to his feet. He considered his options and discovered he didn't have any.

"Quite," said Addison.

Don Miguel pushed his way to the front of the crowd. "Ragar, what is the meaning of this?"

"These kids crashed your daughter's wedding and attempted to rob your castle. I am getting rid of them."

"All right," whispered Don Miguel. "But make it fast or we'll spark a cartel war in here."

"I will handle it," said the professor with a slight bow. He bent close to Addison and lowered his voice. "Give me the key."

Addison clenched his teeth. "I think it's better if I hold on to it. Somehow, I don't quite trust you."

"Remember, I have your aunt and uncle. You would be wise to give me what I want."

"You can't hurt my aunt and uncle, Ragar. Not yet. You need their help if you want to have any hope of finding the treasure."

Ragar extended his open palm. "Give me the key."

"I don't think so," said Addison. "Now if you'll excuse me, Guadalupe and I are going to get out of here."

Ragar closed his palm into a fist. "Do you know how many people have died over the centuries to get that key? You cannot handle it, you little fool. The key will get you killed."

Zubov gripped his stiletto and stabbed at Addison.

Addison leapt back, but too late—the knife struck him square in the chest. He fell to the ground, stunned.

Guadalupe gasped.

"Zubov," Ragar spat, "Don Miguel wants no violence. You can't just kill a kid in the middle of his daughter's wedding."

Zubov shrugged and spoke in his harsh, grating voice. "I am just encouraging him to hand over key."

Addison coughed and slowly sat up, feeling his jacket for blood. To his confusion, there didn't seem to be any. He removed the gold key from his chest pocket, amazed. "You were wrong. The key didn't kill me—it saved my life." He looked up at Professor Ragar. "In Russia, do they call that 'irony'?"

Ragar boiled with rage. He hissed at Zubov. "Okay, you can kill him!"

But as chance would have it, Guadalupe seized that exact moment to snatch the stiletto blade from Zubov. One second the knife was in Zubov's hand; the next second it was in Guadalupe's.

Before Zubov could even blink in astonishment, Guadalupe struck him in the ear with the point of the blade. "How about I pierce those pretty ears of yours?" Guadalupe growled.

Zubov clutched his ear, howling in pain.

Guadalupe wheeled on Professor Ragar. "For the record, when you grabbed me in the dining room, I picked your wallet."

Professor Ragar instinctively checked his pockets.

Guadalupe waved his wallet before his eyes.

"There's no cash in it," Ragar said.

"General principle." Guadalupe pocketed the wallet along with Zubov's knife. Then turned and fled.

Zubov gripped his bleeding ear and screamed in rage.

Addison noticed that, at least for the moment, he was no longer the subject of attention. And for once he didn't mind. He turned and dashed after Guadalupe.

······

Addison sprinted down an aisle between tables and found his path blocked by Ragar's men. He spun in the other direction and saw Don Miguel's men. "This is a sticky wicket," Addison admitted.

He rolled underneath a table and crawled along its length, upsetting some warbling women who shrieked operatically. The general vibe of the party, Addison reflected, had certainly loosened up. Everywhere people were screaming and shouting, particularly the enraged bride.

Addison sprung up from under the table and found himself immediately cornered by one of Ragar's thugs. The man lurched toward Addison, arms outstretched. Never in his life had Addison felt so in need of a jetpack.

Out of the corner of his eye, Addison saw Molly sprinting along the dining table, sliding down its length, and landing a well-placed kick right in the guard's stomach. The shocked man stumbled backward, upset a buffet table, and hit the ground to find gravity delivering a dozen buttered lobster tails directly to his face.

"Wow," said Raj, galloping up, beaming with admiration. "Molly, you're amazing."

Molly blew the wisp of hair from her eyes. "Thanks."

Addison scrambled to his feet. "Mo, you're a pretty good soccer player. But with that kick, maybe you should consider kung fu."

Molly turned the thought over in her mind and decided she liked it.

Across the banquet, the band bravely played on. After all, they were paid by the hour. The stately waltz selected by the bandleader was the perfect counterpoint to the chaos and mayhem now consuming the party.

Furious guards chasing Guadalupe barreled over a waiter carrying an enormous platter of chowder bowls. Several dozen bowls of chowder experienced the miracle of flight. As if a thundercloud of soup had passed over her, the livid bride now discovered her hair soaked and her dress polka-dotted by several gallons of corn chowder. Hell hath no fury like a woman corned.

Eddie had problems of his own, a guard hot on his tail. He followed his natural instincts and ran straight for a buffet table. He grabbed one of his favorite kebabs and then wisely kept moving, one step ahead of the guard. After another lap Eddie circled back to the buffet table. What the kebabs really needed was some spicy sauce. He dipped them on the fly and kept on running.

Molly chased after Addison, who snatched up dishes of filet mignon and hurled them at the pursuing guards. "Addison, what do we do?"

"Everything is going according to plan!" shouted Addison optimistically. "All we need is a miracle."

"You said you don't believe in miracles!"

Raj spotted Professor Ragar and conceived a plan so utterly perfect he could not foresee any possible way in which it could fail. He grabbed a carving knife from the pig roast, clenched it in his teeth like a pirate, and shimmied up a tent pole. Reaching the top, he grabbed one of the lead tent ropes and hacked through it with his carving knife. Gripping the rope in one hand and his knife in the other, Raj leapt from the tent pole. Aiming for Ragar, he swung like Tarzan across the entire party, hollering his savage battle cry: "BHAAAAAAAAAANDARI!!!"

Raj had the very best of intentions. He could not be faulted for lack of effort. Wedding guests screamed and ducked as Raj flailed toward them. He flew past Ragar, missing him entirely. In fact, Raj's astonishing speed was broken only by the nine-foot-tall wedding cake, which met him with an explosion of whipped cream like the world's most delicious atom bomb.

"I'm okay!" Raj yelled from inside the cake.

But what Raj had failed to anticipate was that slashing the hitch knot of the lead tent rope would unravel the entire tent. As the bride screamed over the destruction of her wedding dress and her wedding cake, the rest of the party turned to watch the lead tent pole groan, teeter, and collapse. A second tent pole followed suit. Soon tent poles were dropping like dominoes. Support cables strained and snapped, plucking like broken violin strings. The massive flaps of the giant tent descended on the wedding like a collapsing soufflé.

Professor Ragar and his men found themselves trapped under the massive canvas, along with several hundred screaming guests and one rabidly enraged bride.

Addison's team ducked under the tables and scrambled on all fours. They burst free of the tent and into the bright afternoon light.

Addison turned to watch the tent sagging like an

accordion's bellows, muffling the screams from inside. Gunshots—popping like fireworks on the Fourth of July— erupted from the tent, followed by more shouting. "I love a good wedding," Addison said one more time. And he really meant it.

Molly tugged on his sleeve and together they ran.

Chapter Fifteen

Casa Azar

RAJ EXPLODED FROM THE flaps of the tent, covered head to toe in cake frosting. Every inch of him was plastered in whipped cream except for his eyes . . . He looked every bit like a vanilla-flavored ghost.

"Good work, Raj," said Addison. He moved to shake Raj's hand but thought better of it.

"What kind of cake is it?" asked Eddie, sniffing him.

"Coconut with vanilla frosting."

"Can I try some?"

Raj shrugged.

Eddie scooped a handful of frosting off Raj's neck and tasted it. He nodded his head profoundly. "It's excellent." Eddie went for a second scoop.

"We've got to keep moving," said Addison. "We can't

have our cake and eat it, too." He dashed for the parking lot, the team in tow, Raj leaving a trail of footprints with sprinkles.

Fresh gunfire crackled from the wedding. Limo drivers drew guns from their holsters, cast odd glances at Raj, and raced to duck inside the collapsed tent.

"We need wheels if we're going to make it past the bridge guards," called Addison. He sprinted among the parked cars until he saw something spectacular. He froze in his tracks. This caused Molly to smack into his back, followed by Raj, who managed to shellac Molly in cake frosting. Molly did not appreciate this.

Addison was staring at a black limousine. A very special limousine. One with bulletproof glass and armor plating. Professor Ragar's limousine, to be specific.

He checked the limousine door. It was unlocked. Addison opened it and called inside. "Aunt Delia? Uncle Nigel?"

But the limousine was empty.

"Where are they?" asked Molly.

"Elsewhere," Addison grumbled. "We have more immediate problems." He looked anxiously at the deflated tent and spotted the first of Ragar's men popping out, covered in buffet food and looking more red and steamed than the lobsters.

Addison slid into the driver's seat of the limo. "Guadalupe, can you hot-wire a car?"

"Can a fish swim?" Guadalupe poked her head inside

the car. She reached out one hand and flipped down the sun visor.

The car keys fell directly into Addison's lap. He broke out in a wide grin. "Ragar took our keys, so we're taking his." He turned the ignition, and the stretch limousine roared to life.

"Addison," asked Eddie nervously, "what exactly are you doing?"

"Slowing Ragar down."

"Really?" asked Eddie. "Because it kind of looks like you're stealing his car."

Addison chose his words carefully. "I'm not *not* stealing it."

Molly spoke Addison's language and clarified for Eddie: "He's borrowing it on a permanent basis."

Ragar's men gathered outside the collapsed tent and spotted Addison's group. With a shout, they sprinted toward Addison, reloading their guns on the run.

"Get in, chop-chop," Addison called to his team.

Molly, Raj, and Guadalupe piled into the enormous backseat of the stretch limousine.

"Eddie, hurry up!" urged Addison.

But Eddie refused to get in. "I'm not going to get into a top-tier college by becoming a car thief." He turned and trotted for the bridge.

Addison sighed and released the parking brake. He shifted into reverse, backing out of the parking spot.

Grinding the transmission, he managed to slip the car into first gear. He lowered his window, leaned an elbow out, and coasted alongside Eddie.

"How's it going, Chang?" he asked casually.

Eddie looked over his shoulder to see Ragar's men pointing at him and shouting. They sprinted down the driveway, catching up quickly.

"I've been better."

"Eddie," said Addison, "I have one more car than you do. Get in."

"You're stealing a limousine. "That's like stealing *two* cars."

"I'm not stealing, I'm borrowing. I have no intention of keeping this car, Eddie. Where would I park a limo in New York City?"

Professor Ragar's men bounded toward the moving car. They opened up deafening gunfire. Bullets whizzed past Eddie's head, their low-pressure wakes ruffling his hair.

Eddie's eyes bulged in terror. He saw no alternative. "Open the door!"

Addison sprung open his door and slid over to make room.

Eddie dove in headfirst.

●●●●●●

For a few seconds, the limousine drifted, driverless. Addison had crawled over to the passenger side. Eddie, to his immense horror, found himself behind the wheel of a moving vehicle.

"Addison, what are you doing!" screamed Eddie.

"Navigating," said Addison calmly. "You're driving."

"Me?" shouted Eddie, his pupils dilating in animal panic. He made a desperate bid to crawl into Addison's passenger seat, but Addison had already buckled himself in.

"Eddie, you have to drive. Your legs are the longest."

"But I don't even have a driver's license!"

"We're stealing a limousine in Ecuador!" said Addison, at the edge of his patience. "We don't *need* a driver's license!"

"I *knew* we were stealing!" said Eddie.

Addison found the chauffeur's hat under his seat and clapped it on Eddie's head. *"¡Vámonos!"*

Eddie slammed his door shut, clicked on his turn signal, and checked his mirrors. The rearview mirror revealed armed gang members racing up to the car.

Addison pressed the door lock just in time.

Professor Ragar's men pounded on the bulletproof windows with their fists. Two gunmen climbed on top of the moving car and opened fire, bullets slamming the reinforced windows. Cracks spiderwebbed the windshield. The gunmen kicked at the weakening glass with their boots and riddled the car with bullets.

"Anytime, Eddie!" Molly shouted from the backseat.

Eddie saw the wisdom in her words. His feet reached for the pedals. He stomped on the gas as if to stamp out a fire.

The limousine rocketed forward like it was shot from a cannon. Men flew from the roof with startled cries.

"Steer!" Addison cried, reaching across to grab the wheel.

"Oh yeah!" Eddie clutched the wheel in both hands.

The limousine careened back and forth across both lanes of the stone bridge. Molly, Guadalupe, and Raj screamed from the backseat. The crashing waves of the ocean were drawing all too near.

The gate guards at the end of the bridge waved their hands for the car to halt. Addison leaned over and blared the horn. The gate guards got the message, diving for cover. For a split second, Addison swore he could hear one of the guards shout, "Put in a good word for me with Héctor Guzmán!" The limousine flew past the gatehouse and spun onto the main road in a wild cornering skid.

Eddie gunned the accelerator so that the limousine engine sat up and barked. The massive car bolted down the highway like a racing greyhound at the starter pistol.

······

Eddie drove at breakneck speed, struggling to see over the dashboard. The limo wound its way along the cliffside highway. Only a flimsy wooden guardrail stood between the speeding car and a rather unhealthy-looking hundred-foot drop.

Molly clutched her overhead handgrip as Eddie took each curve in the road at a tire-squealing pace. "We would have been better off with Ragar's men. Eddie's going to kill us for sure!"

Addison did not disagree.

Guadalupe explored the back of the limousine. She picked the lock on the minibar and filched some candy bars, a soda, and a sterling silver bottle opener.

Raj sat in a melting puddle of his own frosting, smiling peacefully. "I've always wanted to ride in a limousine."

Addison rolled down his window and checked behind them. "Here comes Ragar!"

Six black Jeeps roared up the highway, closing fast.

"What if he shoots at us?" asked Eddie.

"Let him. We're driving *his* car."

The lead Jeep gunned its engine and rammed the back of the limousine. Molly screamed. Eddie lost control of the limo, the steering wheel spinning in his hands, the tires smoking across the highway. The limousine scraped against the cliff-side guardrails, sparks shooting off the armored body. Somehow—white-knuckling the steering wheel—Eddie managed to swerve the car back onto the road.

Without seat belts in the back of the limo, Raj slid around everywhere, getting cake frosting all over Molly and Guadalupe.

"You're lucky you're so delicious!" shouted Molly.

Underneath his white cake frosting, Raj blushed.

The lead Jeep pulled alongside the rushing limo and tactical-rammed the bumper. Once again, the limousine skidded across the highway. Eddie countersteered so hard the limo rose up on two wheels. Two hubcaps burst from the tires, spinning over the edge of the cliff. For a few breathless seconds, Addison feared the limo would follow, toppling over the guardrail and into the ocean.

"I'm too young to die!" Eddie shouted.

The heavy limousine righted itself, landing back on four wheels. Eddie's eyes bulged out of his head, his entire body wet with sweat. He weaved the car back and forth, trying to occupy both lanes.

"Honestly, Eddie. Who taught you to drive?" shouted Molly from the backseat.

"Nobody!"

"Well, it shows!"

Black Jeeps sped forward, surrounding the limousine. Gunmen peppered it with bullets. Lead struck the vehicle with deafening thuds.

"We're surrounded!" shouted Molly.

"Do something!" hollered Guadalupe.

Eddie swerved the limousine, lightly tapping one of the speeding Jeeps. The maneuver accomplished exactly nothing.

"Don't be precious with the limo, Eddie," cried Addison. "Drive it like it's stolen!"

"It *is* stolen!"

"Borrowed!"

Eddie gritted his teeth. He'd had enough of this whole business, and it was time to take charge. He ripped the wheel hard to the right, smashing a black Jeep into the guardrail. He ripped the wheel hard to the left, sideswiping the second Jeep into the third Jeep.

Molly cheered.

"Bacán," said Guadalupe, impressed.

The Jeeps were no match for the heavy stretch limo. Eddie punched the gas, and they shot forward.

Addison checked the rearview mirror. Three police cars raced up behind, joining the pursuit, their sirens blazing. "We've got more problems."

Professor Ragar's Jeeps regrouped and bore down on the limousine.

"Great!" said Eddie, his voice rising in panic. "What else can happen?"

"The highway can end!" cried Molly, pointing straight ahead.

Eddie looked up to see emergency roadblocks where a landslide blocked the highway. But it was too late.

Addison reached across to yank the steering wheel. The tires screamed, burning their rubber, as Addison willed the limousine directly for the landslide.

Eddie shut his eyes and screamed.

The limousine raced up the mound of dirt like a ramp

and went airborne. For a few seconds, Addison's heart did not beat. The limousine sailed through the air and crashed down onto the far side of the dirt embankment, its bumper shooting sparks across the asphalt. The limo continued blasting down the highway.

Eddie stared straight forward, his eyes blank with shock. *"Harika,"* he whispered.

Addison checked over his shoulder. Ragar's four-wheel-drive Jeeps slowed to maneuver around the embankment and then kept right on coming.

"Those guys are better drivers than we are," said Addison. "We'll have to lose them in town. Eddie, we're taking the next exit."

Addison yanked Eddie's steering wheel one more time. Fleeing faster than a cat flung into a dog park, the limousine roared into the zigzagging maze of downtown Casa Azar.

······

The quiet seaside village of Casa Azar had never encountered anything quite like Eddie Chang. For hundreds of years, the village had patiently endured monsoons, hurricanes, forest fires, and the occasional mudslide. But this was Casa Azar's first encounter with Eddie, and the town was wholly unprepared for the devastation that can be wrought by a panicking seventh grader at the wheel of a three-ton vehicle, on the run for his life.

Eddie's immediate strategy was to crash into everything. Terrified fruit vendors leapt out of the way, yelping as their pushcarts were punted into the air. Papaya, kiwi, melons, and passion fruit were smashed against the windshield in a delicious yet blinding smoothie.

Addison flicked on the windshield wipers. He rolled down his window and scraped gobs of fruit away with his hands.

A street vendor hollered in Spanish as they passed. "¿Qué estás haciendo? Where did you learn how to drive?"

"We're from New York," shouted Eddie in Spanish. "This *is* how we drive!"

Eddie slung the giant limousine through increasingly narrow alleyways, constantly fearing the car would get stuck. He struck a cart full of squawking chickens, freeing them from their cages. He obliterated a coconut stand, sending an avalanche of coconuts rolling into the street. But through it all, Ragar's Jeeps maintained their close pursuit, followed by the wailing sirens of the Ecuadorian *policía*.

Eddie sped through an alley so narrow it clipped off both side-view mirrors.

"It's okay, Eddie," said Addison, "you weren't using those anyway."

Eddie jerked the wheel and gunned the limo down an

even narrower alley. The brick walls shredded the paint from both sides of the vehicle. Sparks flew from the metal doors. The limo burst out of the alley and into a public square. Ragar's Jeeps formed a line to the right. The *policía* barricaded the left.

"Find a shortcut!" cried Addison.

"I'm on it." Eddie promptly plowed directly through a supermarket.

The limousine smashed through the front windows and into the cereal aisle. It crashed through frozen foods and baked goods before blasting out the rear wall of the store, onto a new street.

"Eddie, that was a grocery store!" called Molly from the backseat.

"So?"

"So, the only type of building you're supposed to drive through is a car wash!"

Eddie kept his foot glued to the gas. His wipers scraped broken eggs and banana peels from the windshield.

He emerged at a large intersection and steered the limo onto a roundabout. Professor Ragar's Jeeps chased him around, followed by the *policía*. Round and round they went. Soon Eddie caught up with the last police car. They formed a sort of merry-go-round around the roundabout. It was no longer clear who was chasing whom.

Molly fought her dizziness in the backseat. "I think I'm going to hurl."

"Save that for later," suggested Addison. "We have more important things right now."

Eddie finally pulled off the roundabout, smashing postal boxes and public telephones as he struggled to steer the limousine.

A dozen more police cars joined the chase.

"Wow," said Guadalupe, "I can't believe I went a whole day without being chased by the police."

Eddie sped into the town square before realizing it was a trap. *Policía* barricaded all the streets ahead.

"Where do I go?" Eddie hollered.

"Right!" called Addison.

"Left!" yelled Guadalupe.

"Faster!" shouted Raj.

"Stop!" Molly screamed.

Eddie tried to do all four things at once. The limousine spun out of control and crashed spectacularly into the town fountain. Their enormous splash sent a flock of terrified pigeons fleeing for the suburbs.

The limousine was suspended half in the fountain and half out. It teetered as if bobbing for apples, the rear wheels spinning uselessly in the air.

"Benedict Arnold!" said Molly.

"Guy Fawkes!" cried Addison.

"The police!" yelled Eddie.

Sure enough, the *policía* skidded to a halt, leapt out of their cars, and surrounded the limousine at gunpoint.

......

Hands over their heads, Addison's team sloshed through the fountain to stand dripping in the cobblestone square. The *jefe de policía*, or chief of police, folded his arms and glared at them angrily. Except for his oversize mustache, the *jefe* did not look like a man with a sense of humor. He ordered the group to get down on their knees and place their hands behind their heads.

Guadalupe sized up the situation and decided she wanted no truck with it. She took off running. Before the *policía* could give chase, she was across the square, a blur of arms and legs. She scaled a drainpipe the way a monkey climbs a banana tree. She dashed across a rooftop and disappeared.

Addison stared after her, his mouth open in shock.

"Traitor!" shouted Molly, though Guadalupe was too far away to hear.

"Addison, I told you we couldn't trust her, but you just had to go and call a Code Blue," said Eddie, bitterly.

The words rang in Addison's head, but he was too upset to speak. He turned his full attention to Professor Ragar, who parted the gaping crowd. On his right was

Don Miguel and on his left was Zubov. They approached the *jefe de policía*. The *jefe* saw Don Miguel and bowed low in greeting.

"They ruined my daughter's wedding!" Don Miguel snarled through clenched teeth. He was so angry he had the complexion of a man being strangled.

"They cut my ear," barked Zubov, still clutching a hand to the wound. "And they keep taking all my knives," he muttered under his breath.

"They stole something precious that belongs to me," hissed Ragar.

The *jefe de policía* bowed low, again. His voice trembled, just a little. "They will be locked up at once, Don Miguel."

"Good," said Professor Ragar, leaning close to the *jefe* and paralyzing him with his cobra stare. Ragar pressed a wad of pesos into the *jefe*'s palm with one hand, and gestured to Zubov with the other. "My associate will come to your prison tonight to visit them. Let him into their cell and look the other way."

The *jefe* looked to Don Miguel, who signaled his assent with a stiff jerk of his chin. The *jefe* smiled desperately at Ragar and nodded his head. The wings of his mustache flapped like a heavy bird struggling to take flight. "At midnight. While my men are switching shifts."

Professor Ragar smiled. He bent down to where Addison

was kneeling. His thin, gloved hand reached inside Addison's blazer and removed the golden key.

"Where are my aunt and uncle?" Addison asked through gritted teeth.

"They are still with me. You stole the wrong car." Ragar gestured to a black sedan with tinted windows. "But don't worry, you won't be alone for long. Zubov will see you soon."

Zubov smiled at Addison, his thin lips curling around the points of his teeth.

Professor Ragar admired the golden key in his hand. He leaned close to Addison so the *policía* could not hear.

"When I open the treasure vault," his whispered, his breath in Addison's face, "I will finish your aunt and uncle."

"Why do this? Just take the treasure and leave us alone."

"You mean your aunt and uncle never told you?"

"Told me what?"

"Oh, my young Cooke," purred the professor, patting Addison on the cheek with one velvet-gloved hand. "This isn't just about treasure. I cannot leave you and your darling sister alive. You see . . ." Ragar leaned very close to breathe into Addison's ear. ". . . there is a prophecy."

Professor Ragar turned to the *jefe*. "Lock them up." Ragar turned on his heel and strutted back to his motorcade. He and his men climbed into their black Jeeps.

The *jefe de policía* sized up Addison's team. He swelled up his chest to look official and smoothed the upturned corners of his mustache. "License and registration?"

"It's in my other car," said Addison.

"Identification?"

Addison reached for his back pocket and stopped short. He sighed.

"What now?" asked Molly.

Addison turned sheepishly to his friends.

"Guadalupe stole my wallet again."

Chapter Sixteen

The Stickiest Wicket

ADDISON AND HIS TEAM, exhausted and filthy, sat huddled in a dark Ecuadorian jail cell. The stone floor was damp with mildew. Spiders crawled along the moss-covered walls. Molly clutched the aching burn on her leg from her jungle tangle with the anaconda. Eddie gripped his stomach in hunger. Raj shook cake frosting from his hair.

"It could be worse," said Addison.

"How?" asked Eddie.

"Today's Monday. We could be in school."

"Oh God." Eddie buried his face in his hands. "And I already missed a piano lesson this weekend. When I don't come home from school today, my parents will definitely know I'm not sleeping over at your house—they're going to kill me!"

"Not if Zubov kills you first," Molly said helpfully.

"We still have a chance," said Raj. "Before the guards frisked us, I managed to hide something inside my sock."

"What is it?" asked Molly.

"Something awesome." Raj dropped to one knee, rolled up his pants leg, and produced a tiny kit from his sock. "My lock-picking set!"

Raj sprang to his feet, raced to the dungeon door, and discovered it was solid iron. No bars, no visible keyhole. Raj slowly stuffed the lock-picking set back in his sock. He slumped to the ground, defeated.

"I guess we'll just make ourselves comfortable," said Addison. He sensed the team was scared. "The thing is to focus on the positive."

The group stared at Addison morosely.

"We're on the final puzzle," Addison said, mustering his optimism. "The last key said the treasure is on *'top of the world, above a sacred valley in a palace in the sky.'*" Addison riffled through his backpack and tossed Molly his copy of *Fiddleton's Atlas.* "Mo, see if you can find us anything about a sacred valley."

Molly glumly flipped through the index. She had little interest in *Fiddleton's Atlas,* but seeing as she was stuck in prison, she figured she had plenty of time to catch up on her reading.

Addison pursed his lips in concentration and began pacing. "'On top of the world, in a palace in the sky.' Where is the top of the world?"

"The Incas might have thought the mountains were the top of the world," Raj offered.

"Yes!" Addison exclaimed. "The peaks of the Andes are among the highest on the planet."

"Guys, there *is* a sacred valley. There's a whole chapter on it." Molly read aloud from *Fiddleton's Atlas*. "'The Sacred Valley is the Incan name for the Urubamba Valley near Cusco.'"

Addison looked over Molly's shoulder. "So what's so special about this Sacred Valley that it deserves a whole chapter?"

"It says you need to walk through the Sacred Valley to get to Machu Picchu."

"Machu what-u?" asked Eddie.

"Machu Picchu is only the most famous Incan archaeological site in the world. It's an abandoned palace on top of a mountain." Addison resumed pacing the small floor of the dungeon. "It all fits. The first clue was about the underworld, the second clue was about the end of the world, and the third clue is about the top of the world. It's a sort of progression. You see—we're almost there!"

"Addison," said Eddie, "I don't know if you've noticed, but we're locked in an Ecuadorian prison."

244

"I'm not a details guy. I think big picture."

Molly decided she'd had it. "Addison, you are the world champion at pretending nothing's wrong."

"If we get upset, we don't think clearly," Addison replied. "It's like Raj says, 'The first rule of survival is not to panic.'"

"Zubov is coming to kill us at midnight! And once Ragar finds the treasure vault, he's going to kill Aunt Delia and Uncle Nigel!"

"Maybe he was making an empty threat," Addison offered. "You know, a lot can happen between now and midnight."

"We ruined a gangster's wedding," Eddie declared. "So even if Ragar doesn't come for us, Don Miguel will."

"Plus we destroyed the entire town," added Raj. "So even if Don Miguel doesn't come for us, we'll be in jail for years!"

Molly summed things up. "We're either going to spend the rest of our lives in prison, or we're going to spend the rest of our lives dead."

Addison could feel the fabric of his team slowly tearing. "Guys, let's just take a deep breath here."

"No, no more smooth talk," said Eddie. "I'm mad and I'm hungry and I have a right to be mad. And hungry. Mostly hungry. But also mad. Really mad."

"Why are you mad at me, Eddie? How is this my fault?"

"This isn't what we signed up for! If I die in prison and my parents find out, I'll be in *real* trouble."

"We'll figure this out—we always do," said Addison.

But Eddie was in no mood to have his mood improved. "You pressured me into lying to my parents, flying to South America, and stealing a car. Now armed gunmen want to kill me! If I'm dead, it severely hurts my chances of getting into a good college!"

"Is that all you care about?" shouted Addison. His uncle Jasper had taught him there was never a reason to raise one's voice outside of the horse track, but Addison was beginning to suspect there were exceptions to this rule. "Getting into trouble with your parents? You care more about your own stupid problems than saving the Incan treasure."

"I *do* care about the stupid treasure," said Eddie, "but not if it means dying in a stupid prison."

"I *don't* care about the stupid treasure," said Raj. "I came along because Addison said it'd be our last adventure together."

"There was only one reason to come on this stupid journey. To help our stupid family. But all I ever hear Addison talk about is finding the stupid treasure." Molly turned to Addison. "So what is more important to you, Addison? The stupid treasure, or your stupid family?"

Addison knew everyone was upset with him. This was

a time to choose his words carefully. "Both? Treasure *and* family?"

"Typical," said Molly.

Everyone retreated to their own corner of the cell.

Addison wanted to say something uplifting but found he was too exhausted. He sunk down to the stone floor and leaned his head against the rock wall. He wondered if Zubov would come to finish them. He wondered if they could survive the night.

......

No moonlight pierced the windowless cell, but everyone sensed it was late. Despite their tiredness, no one could sleep. They were all waiting for Zubov.

Addison broke the silence. "Eddie, what time is it?"

Eddie checked his watch for the hundredth time. "Eleven thirty-five p.m. Or twenty-five minutes to Zubov."

"He's probably on his way," said Molly.

"Maybe if we all attack him at once, we have a chance," said Addison. "We did it before."

"He's expecting that now," said Eddie. "He'll be pre-pared this time."

"I can't take this anymore!" said Raj, springing to his feet. Finding footholds in the mortared rock, he snaked his way up the wall, searching for an escape. He climbed until he reached a utility box near the ceiling. Bracing himself, he found a safe perch on a stone outcropping. It supported his weight. He set to work on the utility box with his lock-picking set. "Somebody count to ten!"

Eddie began counting but lost interest after he passed two hundred.

The group waited in resigned silence for midnight. Eddie called out the passage of time . . . 11:55 p.m. 11:56 p.m. 11:57 p.m. . . .

Finally, after twenty-two minutes of fiddling, Raj yelped in triumph, "I got it!" The lock popped like a cork, and the utility hatch swung open.

"What do you see?" asked Addison.

"Utility pipes. Some sort of water main."

"Does it lead anywhere?"

Raj gripped the largest pipe with both hands. It jiggled when he shook it. He shook it some more; it was definitely loose. Maybe, Raj reasoned, if he shook the pipe hard enough he could crack the masonry of the outer wall. "Hey, guys, I think I've got something!"

Raj yanked hard on the rusted pipe, and it snapped. A geyser of freezing water blasted into his face. He yelped, sliding back down the wall to land in a wet heap on the ground. On the plus side, the cake frosting was now washed clean from his hair.

The team hollered as icy cold water sprayed everywhere.

"I lost my lock-picking set!" Raj groped around the floor in the gurgling torrent.

Frigid water filled the sealed dungeon at alarming speed. A second pipe burst, and then a third. Water now blasted from several holes in the rock wall. It gushed past everyone's knees and kept on climbing.

"Raj, you have not improved our situation!" shouted Addison.

"Eleven fifty-eight," cried Eddie.

"We're going to drown in here," called Molly. The water already lapped around her waist.

"I was just trying to help," said Raj.

"Everybody shout and maybe someone will hear us," Addison said.

As one, the team hollered at the top of their lungs. But they were locked deep in the basement of the old police station and there was no one to hear their cries.

As the water surged past his chest, Addison began to wrap his mind around the very real possibility that he might drown.

"I don't want to die," said Eddie. "I've never been to a Yankees game."

"I've never even been to the Empire State Building," said Raj.

"I've never been to New Jersey," said Molly.

"You're not missing much," said Addison.

The water bubbled higher, lifting their feet off the ground. Molly treaded water furiously, struggling to keep her head aloft. Soon their heads reached the ceiling. They were running out of air in the sealed cell.

"I'm sorry for drowning us!" shouted Raj. "I didn't mean to!"

"I'm sorry for crashing the limo into the fountain and getting us thrown in prison!" cried Eddie over the rushing torrent.

"No, I'm sorry!" Addison's breath came in fast and thick. He knew he didn't have much time to say what he needed to say, but he knew it needed to be said. "I'm sorry for getting you into this whole mess. I pressured you to come with me—I called the Code Blue. I got swept up in the treasure hunt because I was obsessed with beating Ragar. But Molly was right all along. I forgot what's really important. It's not about treasure, it's about—"

"You're not going to say something sappy, are you?" Eddie interrupted. "I mean, because that would be awful. If we all died here just while you were making some cheesy speech."

"Eddie, I was trying to apologize. I mean, we're 86ers. And if this is the end, I'm glad I got to spend it with—"

"All right, we get it," said Eddie. "If you're going to get all sentimental, I'd rather just die already!"

The water surged past their necks.

"Just let me say this," said Addison. "I'm sorry I trusted Guadalupe! We risked our lives saving her from Zubov, and she completely ditched us."

"Fine," said Eddie. "Apology accepted."

The team had an inch left of air. They pressed their noses against the ceiling.

"Addison, are we going to die?" asked Molly.

"You ask a lot of questions, Mo."

"We could use a miracle."

Addison treaded water with the last of his strength. He took one last gulp of air. "I don't believe in miracles."

$$\cdots\cdots$$

The next thing Addison felt was a massive explosion that rattled his bones. What little wind was left in his lungs was knocked out of them. He watched the earth execute a few somersaults. The tumbling world performed a double backflip into a flawless half gainer.

Addison opened his eyes, coughing and sputtering. He assessed his situation. The wet object he was lying on was definitely the ground. The dark glittery thing above him was almost certainly the night sky. The stuff filling his lungs was fresh air. Very little of this made any sense to him.

Molly, Eddie, and Raj lay flopped on the ground, gasping for breath. They were surrounded by chunks of broken rock and cement in an alleyway. Addison's brain wheezed and turned over, struggling to find first gear.

Addison sat up to see Guadalupe sitting in the cab of an idling tow truck. Slowly, his mind began to catch up with the tide of events. The big truck's steel tow cables were clamped to exposed chunks of rebar covered in cement. Guadalupe had ripped out the entire dungeon wall.

"Guadalupe, what are you doing here?" Addison asked in amazement.

"You guys helped me, so I'm helping you."

"Where did you get a tow truck?"

"Five-finger discount," Guadalupe winked. She gunned the engine.

"But how did you know to come at the last possible moment?"

"What last possible moment?" asked Guadalupe. "It took me six hours to find and steal this beautiful truck."

Stunned *policía* emerged from the headquarters, pointing and shouting. In the middle of the group was a tall man in a black leather jacket: Zubov.

"Addison," said Molly. "This was a miracle."

"You're welcome," said Guadalupe. "Time to go!"

Addison's team picked themselves up off the ground, amazed to be alive, and piled into the crew cab of Guadalupe's tow truck. Addison rode shotgun. Molly sat next to him, mashed up against the gearbox. Raj and Eddie crammed into the back with the tools.

Guadalupe handed Addison his wallet back with a wink. She spun the steering wheel and floored the gas. The truck leapt forward, sending the *policía* scattering. She snapped the wheel 180 degrees and squeezed the truck down a side street.

"*Bacán*," said Addison, impressed. He watched the *policía* receding in the rearview mirror. "We should have let you drive the limo."

A few resilient police cars gave chase, sirens flashing. Guadalupe checked her mirrors, grinned, and gunned the engine. She led them on a harrowing flight through the tiny alleyways of Casa Azar.

"Have you ever seen a 'spinning duck'?" Guadalupe shouted over the roar of the engine.

"What's a 'spinning duck'?"

"Hold on tight!"

Guadalupe whipped the truck around a corner and spun the wheel, skidding the truck smartly into a parallel parking spot. It fit like a hand in a glove. She killed the lights and engine. "That was the spin—now everybody duck!"

Addison's team hunched down as the string of police cars rounded the corner, gumballs flashing. The *policía* rocketed past the parked truck, blazing north through the empty town.

Guadalupe waited a few heartbeats before restarting the engine. She pulled out onto the highway heading south.

"Well," said Addison, "I don't think they will welcome us back in Casa Azar."

"First New York, then Olvidados, and now Casa Azar," said Molly. "We're running out of cities we're allowed to be in."

"There are plenty more cities for us to be kicked out of, Mo," said Addison reassuringly.

Guadalupe realized with a touch of pride that it had taken her less than twenty-four hours to become wanted by the Ecuadorian police. She was eager to put the country behind her. The team took the winding seaside road south toward Peru.

Nobody noticed a distant car in the rearview mirror, driven by a man in a dark leather jacket.

III

THE
INCAN
TREASURE

Chapter Seventeen

The Cliffs of the Andes

THE SACRED VALLEY LAY nestled in a saddle of the Andes, the longest mountain range in the world. Already the afternoon sun cast the long shadows of the peaks across the grassland below. Guadalupe pulled the tow truck over to the shoulder of an abandoned dirt road.

The team climbed down from the truck cab, stretching their aching limbs. They had traveled straight through the night, sleeping and driving in shifts. Everyone except Eddie was allowed a turn at the wheel. Now they turned and gazed up at the mountain, Addison double-checking his compass and atlas.

"It's still a healthy climb."

"Let's just hope we're there before Ragar," said Molly.

"Well, let's get moving."

"Not me, *amigos*," said Guadalupe. "This is where I say good-bye."

"What about the treasure?" asked Raj. "Aren't you curious?"

"We're so close," said Addison. "And we can use your help."

Guadalupe shook her head. She turned to face Addison. "I haven't been completely straight with you."

Addison braced himself. He was getting used to this from Guadalupe.

"I'm not an orphan," she said simply.

Addison shook his head. "I don't follow."

"Most of what I told you is true. The part about my mother remarrying. And how I don't like my stepfather. But they didn't die in any car accident. I just ran away."

Addison and the others listened quietly.

"I left my mother and brothers back in Bogotá," Guadalupe continued. She took a deep breath. Honesty seemed exhausting for her. "You guys took a risk saving me at the castle, even after everything I did to you. You didn't abandon me." She forged ahead. "The more I think about it, the more I realize I abandoned my family. And I should go back."

Addison nodded his head. "I have to admit, I always

assumed you were in this for the gold. I mean, escorting us across the Amazon when you weren't a guide. Following us all the way to Ecuador . . ."

"You were right." Guadalupe lifted one shoulder and dropped it.

"What changed?"

Guadalupe sighed and shook her head. "Some people you just don't rob." She turned to walk back to her truck but Molly stopped her and hugged her. Eddie and Raj patted her on the shoulder as well. Guadalupe gave Addison a hug and turned to climb back in her truck.

"Will you write to me?" asked Addison.

"Sure. I've got your address."

"Great," said Addison. "Wait, how do you know my address?"

Guadalupe pulled his uncle's wallet from her pocket and tossed it to him.

Addison caught it one-handed. "You picked my pocket when you hugged me just now, didn't you?"

"Sorry." Guadalupe smiled. "Old habit."

"Here." Addison reached into his jacket pocket and held out his hand. "It's the wallet you stole from Professor Ragar." He shrugged. "I thought it might have useful information."

Guadalupe took the wallet from Addison, turning it over in her hands. "But when did you . . ."

"When I was sitting next to you in the tow truck last

night. You were speeding away from the police. I figured your attention was diverted."

Guadalupe looked at Addison as if seeing him for the first time, her eyes filled with newfound respect. *"Bacán,"* she said at last. "You're all right."

She swept her long black hair from her face and over one shoulder, her bracelets tinkling. "Keep in touch, Addison." She hugged him one last time.

Addison's voice faltered. His cheeks felt flushed. "Okay," he said simply.

Guadalupe climbed into the cab of the truck and started the chuckling diesel engine. She waved through the open window, set the truck in gear, and rumbled down the country road. Addison watched the truck grow smaller until it finally turned a bend and disappeared.

••••••

Addison led the group across the Sacred Valley. At first, he couldn't see what was so sacred about it, there being so many thorns and pricker bushes. But eventually, the low regions gave way to pristine forests of alder and coral trees that blanketed the gorges and ravines in richly scented air. Climbing higher, the evergreens opened to reveal meadows of orchids, maize, yucca, and sweet potato. Great clouds of mist turned the tops of the conifers into vague brushstrokes, and by the time the group ascended to the base of the cliffs, Addison felt he had crossed into a fairy-tale landscape.

"There it is," he said at last, pointing to a few tiny specks far up on the peak. "Machu Picchu is at the summit of that ridge, on top of the mountain."

"Well, where do we go?" asked Molly, staring up the cliff. "Is the treasure vault in Machu Picchu or just somewhere nearby?"

"I don't know," said Addison. "I don't know how to narrow it down. Ragar has the key. And I didn't have time to make a copy of the clue." He sat down on a rock and shook his head.

"Well, I did," said Molly. "In the tower's eyrie, before we brought it down the ladder." From her pocket, she produced a scrap of paper with a pencil tracing of the key.

Addison leapt to his feet, beaming with pleasure. "Molly, you are my second-favorite Cooke."

Eddie uncrumpled the paper and translated the clue.

"The top of the world holds the treasure of the Incas.
Above the sacred valley in a palace in the sky,
Supay's mouth is open wide to swallow up the brave.
Beware the curse of Atahualpa or you will surely die."

"The Incans weren't interested in making this easy for us," said Addison.

"I guess we just look for Supay's mouth," Eddie shrugged.

"Where's that?" asked Molly.

"Probably on Supay's face."

"It's at the top of the world," said Addison. "That's all the clue tells us. Now, c'mon, let's hurry. We have to assume Ragar is two steps ahead of us—he has the same clue we do, plus a head start."

The team began hiking up the steep winding path along the bitter edge of the cliff face. They climbed ever higher into the rising mist. At the tree line far below, a dark figure flitted silently through the grove, catching up.

......

The cliff path grew more narrow and treacherous the higher Addison climbed. Soon fog hid the valley below and obscured the path ahead. Addison felt like they were hiking through clouds.

Addison ran the fingers of his left hand along the cliff face. To his right was a thousand-foot drop. He placed each step directly in front of the other to keep inching forward along the ledge. A stiff wind buffeted the group, stinging their squinting eyes. They clung to the rock for fear of being swept away. Addison's pulse beat double time and then switched to a jazzy triple-time swing. Peering over the ledge, the world plummeted away into fog. It was impossible to know how far one would fall before hitting the earth.

Growing light-headed, Addison stumbled. His shoe sent rocks cascading over the precipice.

"Careful," said Raj, tightening his bandana. "A hundred and forty-seven hikers die every year in rockslides. One false step, and you'll be wrapped in the dark cloak of eternity."

"Thank you, Raj." Addison did not find Raj's information helpful at all. He gulped for air, made it a few more steps, and stumbled again. This time Raj grabbed him by the sleeve.

"Addison, if you slip, you'll die. And you won't like that."

Addison pressed himself to the cliff face, gripping vines for support. In his mind, he heard thunder and lightning crashing all around him. He stopped and sat down, hugging his knees. He shut his eyes. "I can't do it," he said at last.

"What's the matter with him?" asked Eddie.

"It's his fear of heights," said Raj.

Molly sat down next to Addison, who buried his face in his knees. "C'mon, you can do this."

"I can't."

"Addison, talk to me," Molly whispered.

Addison swallowed hard. Finally, he answered. "It's Mom. It makes me think of Mom."

Molly looked up at the sheer cliff walls and down at the thousand-foot drop. Understanding dawned in her eyes. "You saw what happened to Mom that night?"

Addison nodded. "There was nothing I could do. Nothing except watch."

Molly nodded.

"I wish I could go back there and do something."

"It wasn't your fault." Molly shook her head. "You were just a kid."

"I miss her."

"Me too." Molly looked at him. Then she gazed out at the remote landscape, veiled in fog. She took a deep breath and let it go.

"If they were here, they'd know what to do."

"I'm here," said Molly, "and I won't let you fall." She helped him to his feet.

Addison rose unsteadily. Raj put a hand on his shoulder. Eddie, too. They took one step. And then another. Addison willed his eyes open. He forced himself to look at the steep cliffs, the clinging vines, the open air falling away beneath them. He focused his eyes on the path ahead.

Molly, Eddie, and Raj didn't say anything. They just held on to Addison, his arms, his shoulders. And together, very slowly, they climbed the cliff path, Addison's footing growing surer with every step.

······

The steep path narrowed to a sliver of rock that spanned the length of the open cliff face. Addison's team side-stepped along the granite, their bellies pressed to the cold stone. Wind shrieked in their ears, and their shoes scraped pebbles from the path, sending tiny rocks skittering a thousand feet over the precipice.

Raj, leading the way, paused at a dangerous curve in the rock. A deep furrow, tall and wide as a redwood tree, was carved into the cliff. "What do you guys make of this?"

The group peered upward at the strange rock formation, but wisps of fog, high above, obscured the top of the stone chute.

"Maybe it's from water erosion," Eddie suggested.

"If it's not Supay's mouth, then we have to keep moving." Addison's fingers were growing cold from gripping handholds in the granite.

The team sashayed along the cliff face, buffeted by blustering gales that drew tears from their eyes. Their legs began to shake from exhaustion.

A few minutes later, Raj came upon another, identical furrow worn into the cliff. "Déjà vu."

"I don't see any way we could have gone in a circle,"

Addison mused. "I mean, we're going in a straight line."

"Two identical columns carved in the rock." Eddie shivered against the pummeling blasts of frigid air. "It can't be a coincidence."

"Well, if it's not a coincidence, what is it?" Molly asked.

Addison stared up at the carved hollow groove, snaking its way up the cliff. Circling gusts briefly parted the fog above. He saw the twisted furrow narrow to a point, a hundred feet above. Addison squinted his eyes in concentration. And suddenly, his brain did a backflip. "I get it."

"Get what?" Eddie asked, shouting above the howling wind. "Tell me before I freeze to death!"

"The Incas carved a sign into this rock. But they carved it so large we missed it entirely."

"Okay." Molly shivered. "So what's the sign?"

"Remember the shield carved in the stone wall in the basement of the Cathedral of Lost Souls?" Addison called over the wind.

"The one that opened to the secret door."

"The very same," said Addison. "And remember the shield El Mozo carried in his portrait at the castle?"

"Sure."

"Now imagine this entire cliff face is the surface of an enormous gray shield. What symbol would be in the middle of El Mozo's shield?"

Molly grasped it at once. "Supay's skull!"

Addison nodded excitedly. "Those twin hundred-foot columns carved into the rock—those are ram's horns—"

Molly picked up Addison's thread. "So Supay's skull is carved into the cliff somewhere right below us."

Addison nodded. "We couldn't see the carvings on our climb up because of the fog . . . plus five hundred years of vegetation."

"It's just a theory," said Eddie, staring doubtfully at the treacherous wall of granite.

"There's only one way to test it," said Addison. "And if it's right, we'll find Supay's mouth carved into the rock."

"Supay's mouth is open wide to swallow up the brave," Eddie recited.

The team groped their way diagonally downward, from toehold to toehold, working their way toward the center of the cliff face. Their hair blew in their faces, their clothes flapped and fluttered like a ship's sails in a squall.

"My hands are icicles," said Eddie. "I can't hold on much longer."

"Keep going," said Addison. "We'll make it."

"My toes are so frozen they could shatter!"

"You should have worn cleats," said Molly through chattering teeth.

At last, Raj spotted a ledge bulging from the sheer cliff wall below. "Wish me luck," he said, and let go of the rock.

"Raj, wait!" shouted Molly. But Raj was well on his way. He slid twenty feet down the slick granite to land in a crouch on a stone outcropping.

"It's okay!" he yelled.

The rest of the team followed suit, hollering as they slid down the chute. They collapsed on the rocky outcropping, exhausted.

For a few minutes, they did nothing but catch their breath. Every step was exhausting in the high elevation.

Raj stood up and peered at the overhanging spar of the cliff, filled with tangles of vines. "The good news is, we're alive. The bad news is, I don't see anything that looks like Supay's mouth."

Addison swatted away a few vines. "This is a thorny problem," he agreed, pulling some prickers from his palm. "I wish I had my brain juice." Addison folded his arms and paced, deep in thought.

"A samurai makes every decision in the space of seven breaths," Raj put in helpfully.

"That's sound advice. My uncle Nigel has his own three-step process for solving problems. He sits down, thinks really hard about it, and if he still can't solve it, he takes a nap."

"I don't know if we have time for that," said Molly.

Addison decided a rest wouldn't hurt. He found the patch of rock face most well padded with vines. He sat down, leaned his back against the vines, and was quite surprised when he fell inside the mountain.

······

Addison landed on his back inside a dark cave. He yelped, parted the vines, and scrambled back outside onto the cliff ledge. The Cooke brain was never as razor sharp as in moments of adversity. Addison quickly surmised that the hanging vines hid a cave opening hollowed into the cliff wall.

"Well, that happened," said Addison, summing things up. He brushed himself off and got to his feet.

"I guess your uncle's method works," said Raj, peering through the tangled mass of vines into the cave opening.

Molly began scraping away the old and rotted vegetation, clearing them away from the rock. Eddie, Raj, and Addison pitched in. The vines fell away to reveal a shocking sight.

The massive open jaws of a skull were carved into the stone. Carved, gnarled teeth sprouted from the floor and ceiling. Addison spotted two demonic eyes carved into the cliff wall high above, flanked by the towering, twisting ram's horns. The gaping, screaming jaws formed an open cave leading deep inside the mountain.

"Supay's mouth," Molly whispered in awe.

"Not more skulls!" Eddie exclaimed. "What is with El

Mozo and skeletons? Didn't he have any other hobbies or interests?"

"It is creepy up here," Raj agreed. "All day, I've felt like someone is watching us."

"El Mozo's behind all of this," Molly declared, gesturing at the cave. "If he was working with the Incas and had all that gold, he could afford to build the Cathedral of Lost Souls and the Castle on the Edge of Forever. He could afford to build this hidden mountain cave and help the Incas hide their treasure."

"Look over here," said Raj. "Footprints. Lots of them."

Addison edged closer to Raj and examined a cluster of sandy footprints at the cave's entrance. He spotted an odd circular mark, the size of a quarter, pressed into the dust. The track appeared every few feet beside a large set of boot prints. Addison pointed. "Do you know what this circular mark is?"

Raj squatted down and studied the print. He slowly nodded his head. "A walking stick."

Addison turned to his team and lowered his voice to a whisper. "Professor Ragar is already here, somewhere inside this mountain."

"His group could have climbed up this morning, or even last night," suggested Raj. "That's why we never spotted them."

"And they placed the vines back over the cave entrance

when they entered," concluded Addison. He yanked down a few long vines, coiled them, and looped them over his shoulder. "Mountaineering rope," he explained.

Raj nodded his approval. He searched the underbrush and armed himself with a heavy stick.

Eddie stared into the impenetrable darkness of the cave. His voice caught in his throat. "We're really going to do this?"

Raj quoted the final clue, " *'Supay's mouth is open wide to swallow up the brave.'* "

Addison took a breath and summoned his courage. "I guess we're the brave." And with that, he stepped into the darkness.

Chapter Eighteen

The Hidden Cave

ADDISON'S FLASHLIGHT PIERCED THE gloom. A low stone ceiling arched overhead. He crept stealthily down the corridor. Each footstep scuffing the stone floor echoed loudly in the silent cavern.

Carved stone skulls adorned the walls, painted red and black with ochre and pitch. Addison's flickering flashlight cast macabre shadows that capered and leered. In the play of the light, the skulls appeared to howl, laugh, or scream.

The path wound deeper into the mountain, dank and musty with the centuries. The team climbed higher, feeling the elevation in the thinning air. The cave walls were painted with scenes of horrific Incan massacres. The Spanish conquest was recorded in gruesome detail; native people impaled on spears and stabbed with pikes.

At last, they reached a stone crypt carved into the wall of the cave.

"Whose grave is this?" whispered Molly.

Eddie blew away a few centuries of dust and read the inscription on the tomb. He gasped. "El Mozo."

Addison removed his cap and the group stood for a moment in respectful silence.

"How did he die?" asked Molly.

"Pizarro's men caught up with him in a town called Cusco, not far from here," said Addison. "They defeated his army and executed El Mozo in the city square, along with two hundred of his followers."

"The Incas must have buried him here to guard the tunnel," said Eddie, his eyes wide in the darkness.

Raj scanned the dusty footprints on the cavern floor. "Ragar's men passed this way. They're ahead of us, somewhere up this path."

"I don't think El Mozo would want the professor's men taking the treasure," said Molly.

"I don't want the professor's men taking the treasure, either," Addison said. "Let's keep moving."

The path wound past the time-gnarled bones of what looked to be a deer, perhaps dragged into the cave by a cougar many years past. Addison's flashlight batteries decided to call it a day. The light faded to yellow, then orange, and then finally went kaput. The group was plunged into total darkness.

"Now what?" said Molly.

"Well, this—" began Addison.

"Addison!" Molly interrupted. "If you say 'this is a sticky wicket' one more time, I swear—"

"Okay, fine," said Addison. "This is a tricky pickle."

Molly sighed. "Not much better."

"Don't worry, guys, I've got this." Raj used his Swiss Army knife to saw off one of his pant legs. This he tied around his stick, forming a torch. He attempted to light the pant leg with a match, but it didn't catch. Instead, it was Raj's stick that burst into flames, shot sparks, emitted a horrible stench, and promptly flamed out.

"Hm," said Raj.

"It was a good thought, but your stick was too flammable." Addison groped in the dark and grasped the leg bone of the dearly departed deer. "Let's have another pant leg."

Raj sawed off his other trouser leg and Addison tied it around the femur. This Addison rubbed in the pitch of one of the stone skulls. He handed it to Raj. "Light her up."

Raj set match to torch, and the pitch burned as steadily as a living room lamp.

"Onward and upward," said Addison.

The team continued deeper into the darkness, the cave walls seeming to press in on them. At one point, Addison thought he heard distant footsteps following far behind, but when he stopped to listen, the sound vanished. He decided it was the echo of the rocky tunnel.

Eventually, the path narrowed so severely they were forced to walk single file. Addison stopped and beckoned for light. Raj held the torch high so its light reflected off the mica in the walls.

Just ahead, a wooden bridge arched across a deep crevice in the rock. The chasm was dark and bottomless. The ancient timbers of the rickety bridge were splintered and rotten.

"Do we trust it?" asked Eddie.

"Ragar did," said Raj.

Addison considered the obstacle. "The Spanish knights would have weighed a lot in their armor. The Incans probably used this to their advantage." He shifted the coil of vines from his right shoulder to his left and turned to the group. "We cross the bridge one at a time. That way there's not too much weight on it all at once."

One by one, each stepped gingerly across, hardly daring to breathe. The wood planks creaked and groaned their complaint. At last the team was safely on the other side.

"If Ragar gets the gold, how is he going to get it across this bridge?" asked Eddie.

Addison took another look at the chasm below. "Very carefully."

The team continued, winding their way up the narrow tunnel. The granite walls were slippery and glistening with humidity. Before long, the chute widened into a large cavern.

Raj froze, pointing to a vast mosaic of painted tiles carved into the stone floor. He raised his flickering torch to reveal the pattern. "A dragon!"

"Pachamama, the mother of the world," said Addison. "She's an Incan goddess who takes the form of a dragon." He admired the jagged teeth and the green, yellow, and purple scales of the wings. It was too dark for him to make a sketch. "Pachamama has a special power, but I can't remember what it is."

"Can she breathe fire?" asked Raj. "Or make lightning?"

"Invisibility?" asked Eddie.

"I can't remember." Addison scratched his chin in thought. "I just remember it was dangerous."

Eddie took a step forward.

Addison snapped his fingers together. "Wait—Eddie, don't step on the mosaic!"

"Why not?" Eddie asked, stepping onto the mosaic. His weight was already planted firmly on a stone tile when it sunk an inch into the ground. His heart sunk with it. He froze, realizing he had just triggered another booby trap.

A deep rumbling from the cave walls shook the cavern. Eddie didn't know what was coming, but he was fairly certain he wasn't going to enjoy it.

"I just remembered Pachamama's power," called Addison. "She causes earthquakes!"

Eddie didn't need time to mull things over. He turned and bolted.

A massive boulder plummeted from the ceiling and crushed the tile where Eddie had been standing.

Eddie sprung from tile to tile, bouncing like an Irish step-dancer. Wherever he leapt, boulders followed, raining from the ceiling.

"Eddie, stop stepping on those tiles!" Addison yelled.

Deadly boulders crashing around him, Eddie hopped in frantic circles like a frog in a frying pan. "Where do I step?" Eddie flapped his arms, as if willing himself to remain airborne.

Addison threw down his bundle of climbing vines and sprinted for Eddie, grabbing him by the collar. Fists pumping and feet flying, he half led and half dragged Eddie across the cavern and dove into the opposite tunnel. The sound of crashing boulders ceased. For a minute, Addison and Eddie lay on the ground gasping for breath.

"The Incas didn't want conquistadors stealing the gold, so they built that rickety bridge," said Addison, climbing to his feet and dusting off his jacket. "They wanted only devout Incans to find the treasure, so they built a trap for anyone who doesn't know about Pachamama."

"I stepped on Pachamama and disrespected their god," said Eddie. "Sorry I nearly got you killed."

"I should have spotted it sooner," said Addison. "My aunt and uncle must have led Ragar's men around the edge of the wall to avoid the trap. We'll have to be more alert now."

Molly and Raj carefully inched their way around the perimeter of the mosaic and safely joined Addison and Eddie in the low tunnel.

"I wonder what trap is coming next?" Raj said a little too eagerly.

"I'm dying to find out," Eddie said sarcastically.

"Poor choice of words," said Molly.

Raj stepped to the front of the group. "I'll take point position."

"Okay, everyone follow Raj like a line of ducklings," Addison instructed the others. "And nobody touch anything!"

Peering into the gloom with his torch, Raj carefully probed and tapped the surrounding rocks with his stick. Step by step, he carefully led the group along the passageway. At last, the narrow path opened up into a high-ceilinged chamber.

A great chasm spread wide before them. The sheer drop descended into the darkness, its depth impossible to fathom.

"It must go all the way to the heart of the mountain," said Eddie in an awed whisper.

"I have very little interest in finding out," said Addison. He examined the path ahead and grimaced. The only way to cross the chasm was by hopping across scattered stalagmites that grew up like stepping-stones. The stone spikes were so massive, a person could balance on them if they were careful and not overly concerned with personal safety.

"What are the Incas testing for here?" asked Molly. "Balance?"

"Bravery," said Raj. "Supay's mouth opens wide to swallow up the brave."

"I'll bet he swallows cowards, too," said Molly.

"Great," said Eddie, staring into the bottomless chasm and shivering.

Raj tossed a pebble into the crevasse. Everyone listened. If the pebble ever landed, nobody heard it.

"Addison, are you going to be okay with this?" asked Molly.

"Well, I can't really see how high up we are in the darkness. So that helps."

Raj took the lead, followed by Molly, followed by Addison. Eddie brought up the rear.

Addison hopped to the first stalagmite, and then the second. On the third, he almost lost his balance, overshooting his mark in the dim light of Raj's torch. His feet scrambled for purchase, but he held on. He made it to the next stone spike, and then the next.

It was on the sixth stalagmite that things went horribly awry.

Addison took a powerful leap and stuck the landing, even in his slippery dress shoes. But the stone decided, after millions of years of just staying put, that it was time for a change. The ancient rock cracked and tipped forward like a falling tree. Addison felt his world plummeting.

Addison's rock smashed, domino-style, into Molly's, which crumbled and crashed into Raj's. For a few heart-rending seconds, all three clung to their stalagmites, suspended in space, their feet dangling over the void.

Somehow, Raj still clung to his torch. He wrapped his legs around the enormous stone spike and squeezed tight.

Addison waited for his rock to collapse, sending him careening into the darkness. But for the time being, the great stone held. He dug his fingers into the crumbling rock and gripped it with all his strength. "Eddie, do something!"

Eddie stood on his stepping-stone and gaped. Alone, his was the only rock that held strong. He watched his friends clinging for dear life. "Like what?"

"My ropes!" cried Addison. "They're still in the earthquake room!"

"I can't go back there! I'll die!" yelled Eddie.

"We're dying right now!" Molly shouted.

"She's right," gasped Addison, gulping down his fear. Already his hands were growing sweaty and his grip was loosening on the rock. "You've got to go, Eddie!"

Eddie swallowed hard. "All right. But there better be a ton of gold in that treasure vault."

"There will be seven hundred and fifty tons! Just hurry!"

Eddie turned and retraced his steps across the jagged stones. He sprinted back down the dark tunnel and reached the destruction of Pachamama's chamber. Broken rocks lay scattered across the mosaic.

Eddie tiptoed around the perimeter of the room, his back hugging the wall. In the dark, he tripped over a stone that clattered onto the booby-trapped tiles of the mosaic. Eddie held his breath, but the stone was not heavy enough to trigger the avalanche. He wiped sweat from his forehead and kept moving.

At last, Eddie inched to the far end of the chamber and yanked Addison's vines from under a fallen boulder. "Okay," Eddie whispered to himself, staring back across the mosaic. "Now I just have to do this all over again."

......

Addison clung to his fragile stone with the last of his strength. "How are you doing, Molly?"

"My arms are cramping."

Addison felt his own grip weakening. "Raj, how about you? Can you hold on a little longer?"

"This is fantastic." Raj smiled, hugging his rock like a koala bear hugs a tree. "I never did anything like this in Manhattan."

Addison heard Eddie's shoes skittering along the far chamber. "Eddie, hurry!" he shouted, his tired fingers trembling. "Molly can't hold on any longer!"

Eddie's face appeared over the lip of the giant rock.

"What took you so long?" Addison gasped.

"I'm happy to see you, too." Eddie anchored his vine rope around the stalagmite and tossed Addison the free end. "And for your information, I was very, very busy trying to not die."

Addison reached into the void and grabbed the vine rope.

"Can you make it, Addison?" Molly called.

"I think I can." For a terrifying moment, he let go of his stone, the vine taking all his weight as he dangled in space. Somehow, the fear of heights no longer seemed to control him. He climbed his way on top of his rock, panting with the effort.

"Faster, please," said Molly.

Eddie wrapped a length of vine around his waist. He belly-crawled along Addison's stepping-stone. Together, they wriggled onto Molly's boulder and dropped her a vine.

"It's about time," she gasped, grabbing the rope.

"You're welcome," said Eddie, quoting Guadalupe. He hauled Molly up. Eddie was still ghostly white, but he was no longer trembling.

When they all reached Raj, he handed up his torch.

"Wait," Raj said, staring into the inky void below him, "I just want to enjoy this a moment longer."

"C'mon, we're on a tight schedule." Addison dropped Raj a vine.

Together, they crossed the last stepping-stone and reached the far side of the chasm. Eddie bent double and took deep gasps of air.

"Were you scared?" asked Molly.

"Nope," said Eddie. "I was terrified."

"Well," Addison said, clapping Eddie on the shoulder, "you saved our lives."

Eddie straightened his back and stood a little bit taller. *"Harika,"* he said. And he meant it.

The team ducked into the next tunnel and followed its snaking twists and turns deeper into the mountain. In the darkness, Addison lost all sense of time. Maybe a half hour passed, maybe an hour. There was nothing for it but to keep walking.

"I hear voices," said Molly at last, halting in her tracks.

Addison listened and heard them, too.

Raj doused the torch. The team crept forward through the darkness, shrouded in the gloom. Flickering lights loomed up ahead.

The group carefully peered around a bend in the path. Before them, the tunnel opened into an enormous cavern. And there below, in the main chamber, stood Professor Ragar.

••••••

Addison and his team crawled to a safe vantage point, a ledge overlooking the sprawling chamber carved into the rock. The massive cavern was supported by pillars etched with hieroglyphics. Flaming torches lined the walls. The entire structure spanned a chasm where a river ran directly through the mountain, bubbling and gurgling in the darkness hundreds of feet below.

Professor Ragar, miraculously clean and resplendent in his white suit, gazed down the long stone corridor that led to the treasure vault. He was flanked by his men, who carried mining helmets and climbing gear. At their feet, bound in ropes, sat Aunt Delia and Uncle Nigel.

When Molly spotted them, she nearly called their names out loud, but Addison silenced her with a finger pressed to his lips. Together, the team wriggled closer on their bellies to spy on Ragar.

"Next," Professor Ragar barked to his men.

A short, pudgy bodyguard stepped up to Ragar nervously. The professor held out the three Incan keys: one of stone, one of silver, and one of solid gold. The man hesitated before finally choosing the stone key.

"Good luck," said Ragar.

The guard nodded. He unbuttoned his suit jacket and inched timidly toward the treasure vault. He ducked through the gaping jaws of a massive stone skull, stepping carefully over its stone teeth. He crept down the limestone hallway, his furtive eyes darting left and right like a high-stakes gambler who's just placed an astronomical bet at a Ping-Pong match.

A stone step sunk beneath the man's foot, triggering a booby trap. Iron spikes jutted from the wall. The fleet-footed bodyguard leapt and managed to dodge them. He was apparently faster than Ragar's last bodyguard, who still hung impaled on the spikes like a shish kabob. The iron points retreated into the wall, dragging the corpse back into the shadows.

Panting with adrenaline, the trembling bodyguard reached the end of the hallway and stared at the locked door of the enormous treasure vault. The great door was heavy limestone, two stories high, and covered with ropes of gnarled vines crosshatched with a fretwork of cobwebs.

There was a single keyhole in the door. The man shut his eyes and muttered a fervent prayer under his breath. Finally, his hand shaking, the man inserted the stone key. It fit. He cautiously turned the key until he heard the tumblers click. The man grinned, and for a brief moment, he was truly hopeful.

Then a trapdoor snapped open beneath him, and he plummeted into the river a hundred feet below with a terrific splash. The water churned as caimans rolled and twisted and snapped their jaws. The man's screams echoed until the trapdoor slid shut.

From their hiding place, Molly recoiled in horror. "Were those crocodiles?" she whispered.

"Caimans," Raj corrected.

"I can't believe he's using his men like guinea pigs," Eddie exclaimed.

"You mean *cuy*," Raj corrected again.

"How do caimans even live down there?" Molly asked.

"The river must run right through the mountain. You see, caimans eat a variety of fish, including perch, piranha, and paiche, all of which—"

"Shhh," said Addison. "Here comes the next contestant."

A tall, gangly bodyguard now stood before the treasure vault door. Soaked in sweat, he gingerly removed the stone key from the keyhole. He paused; so far, so good. The bodyguard rested the stone key on a convenient ledge. He now inserted the silver key.

It fit, clicking neatly into place. Taking a deep breath, the guard turned the key in its lock. "I think I got it!"

"Very good," said Professor Ragar. "Is the door opening?"

"I think so!"

The bodyguard was technically right. A door was opening, just not the door he would have preferred. The trapdoor once again sprung open, swallowing the man. He plummeted a hundred feet to begin a new chapter in his life as alligator food. Thankfully, a rather short chapter.

From their hiding spot, Molly cringed again. "Did they

really need alligators down there? Wouldn't it have been enough just to fall a hundred feet?"

"You try having your land stolen by the Spanish," said Addison. "See how friendly it makes you."

"Also," said Raj, "caiman."

"Got it."

Addison corralled the team into a whisper conference. "We need a plan. I'll be the diversion."

"What do we do?" asked Raj.

"First, you guys hide. Then I'll run in and grab their attention. Ragar's men will chase me back down this hallway. When the coast is clear, you guys rush in and open the treasure vault."

"And also rescue Aunt Delia and Uncle Nigel," said Molly.

"Naturally."

"Why do you always get to be the diversion?" asked Raj.

"Yeah!" said Eddie. "I don't want to be the one to open the treasure vault. Everyone who tries to open it ends up in a caiman pit. I've made myself very clear on my preference for not being eaten by caimans."

"Eddie," said Addison, "I live my life by only one rule: don't end up in a caiman pit. And I wouldn't wish a caiman pit on anyone. But we have to get rid of Ragar's men if we want any chance of rescuing Aunt D and Uncle N."

"I don't vote for any plan that ends with me being eaten."

"You guys are being too loud," whispered Molly.

"Molly, this is important," said Addison. "We need to figure this out."

"What's important is that we not get caught."

"Here's an idea, Mo. We put *you* in the caiman pit to satisfy their hunger. Then the rest of us are safe."

"Here's an idea," said Molly. "Shut your trap!"

And it would have been sound advice. For at that moment, Zubov stepped up behind them, drawing a brand-new knife. He grinned, showing his sharpened teeth. His blade flashed in the torchlight. "Hello, kids."

Raj yelped in surprise.

Eddie looked for an escape route.

Molly wasted no time. She wound up and kicked Zubov hard in the shins. A jolt of pain shot up her leg. Molly howled in surprise and toppled over, clutching her foot.

Zubov smiled at Molly. He slowly lifted his pant leg, revealing burnished leather Stetsons, tough as aged cedar wood. "New boots."

He whistled loudly, signaling Ragar's men down in the cavern below. Zubov closed in on Addison's team, tossing his bowie knife from his left hand to his right. "New knife."

"How long have you been following us?" asked Addison, playing for time.

"All night," said Zubov. He grinned and tapped his pointed teeth together, making a hideous clicking sound.

"I would have killed you sooner, but I needed you to lead me back to the professor."

"Yes, about this whole killing business," Addison began. But he didn't have time to finish his thought.

Zubov drew back his arm and hurled his knife at Molly. She dove to the ground, scraping her shins on the rock. The knife flipped through the air, clattered over the precipice, and tumbled into the ravine. "Ha!" Molly shouted triumphantly.

Zubov only smiled and clicked his teeth again. He spread open his leather jacket, revealing a knife belt taped around his chest. Two dozen fresh blades gleamed in the flickering firelight. He drew two knives, spun them in his hands, and tapped them together like drum sticks. "I've got all day."

Molly swallowed hard. "Why don't you put those knives down and fight us fair?"

Zubov shook his head. Ragar's men climbed the ledge and emerged behind him. They outnumbered Addison's group. Zubov smiled. "I don't fight fair. That's why I win."

Addison's team shrank backward. There was no escape.

Zubov lunged for Molly, grabbing her by the arm. She twisted and squirmed, but Zubov was clamped to her like a conjoined twin. He bent forward to bite her, his sharpened teeth snapping the air an inch from her ear.

Molly discovered that she hated to lose. She wound up and kicked Zubov as hard as she could. This time, she aimed a few feet higher than his shin.

She caught him completely by surprise.

Zubov turned purple and crumpled to his knees, wincing.

"I don't fight fair, either," Molly said.

Professor Ragar's crew swarmed in and tackled Addison's team. They struggled, but were no match for the grown men. Addison felt himself thrown to the ground. A boot slammed down, pressing his face into the cold rock.

Chapter Nineteen

The Treasure Chamber

ZUBOV AND HIS MEN herded Addison's team into the main chamber. The high-arched ceiling gave the cavern the feeling of a cathedral. The marbling of the ancient rock, millions of years old, created dazzling patterns that reflected in the torchlight.

Aunt Delia and Uncle Nigel looked up at Addison's group in amazement.

"Addison Herbert Cooke," Aunt Delia exclaimed, "what are you doing here!?"

"*Herbert?*" said Eddie, stifling a laugh.

Zubov gripped Addison by the scruff of his neck.

"It's okay, Aunt Delia," said Addison. "We've come to rescue you!"

Zubov hurled Addison to the rocky floor. He landed next to Aunt Delia and Uncle Nigel. Zubov's men tossed Molly, Eddie, and Raj on the ground beside them.

"Guy Fawkes!" said Molly angrily.

"Language, Molly!" said Aunt Delia.

"But Addison says it!"

"Raj and Eddie," Aunt Delia continued, shaking her head in bewilderment, "do your parents realize you're here?"

"Kind of," said Eddie. "We left a note."

"Yes, Mrs. Cooke." Raj nodded his head emphatically. "We told them we're with you."

"You're all supposed to be in school right now," Aunt Delia said. "It's a Tuesday!"

"This is a dangerous situation," Uncle Nigel put in. "How did you even get here?"

"Yes, about all that . . . " Addison began. "If we ever get home, you may want to call your credit card company."

Professor Ragar interrupted the family reunion, clapping his gloved hands together for attention. "Wonderful! All the Cookes in one place." He ran a gloved finger over his thin mustache, an idea solidifying behind his icy eyes. "Dr. Cooke!"

Mr. and Mrs. Cooke both answered, "Yes?"

"I am running low on volunteers." Ragar gestured toward the treasure vault. "Perhaps the Cooke family can be of assistance?"

"Jump in a lake and eat *cuy*," said Molly flatly.

Professor Ragar snapped his fingers. His men hauled all the New Yorkers to their feet and shoved everyone toward the treasure vault door.

"Open the vault," said the professor, handing Uncle Nigel the gold key, "or I feed you to the crocodiles."

Raj was about to correct Professor Ragar about the caimans, but a quick glance at Ragar's scowling face made him think better of it.

......

The Cooke family, plus Raj and Eddie, ducked through the open jaws of the stone skull.

"I swear," said Eddie, "if I have to walk through one more skull on this trip . . ."

"Relax," said Molly. "It's probably your last."

That clammed Eddie up.

Together, the group crept down the long narrow hallway.

"I should be the one to open the vault," said Aunt Delia. "I wrote my graduate thesis on Incan technology."

"Forget it, Delia," said Uncle Nigel. "It's far too dangerous. Let me."

"What about us? We came all this way. If we're going to die, I should at least get to see some gold first," said Eddie.

"I can help open the door," said Raj. "I used to own a lock-picking set."

Addison spoke up. "Maybe it's not the gold key, you guys. I mean, it seems too easy, doesn't it? If this is the final door to the treasure, it must contain the hardest puzzle of all."

"Well, if it's not the gold key, what other key could it be?" asked Molly.

"I have no idea. But the solution to the puzzle might be in one of the Incan books I read."

"Books are your answer for everything," cried Molly.

"Books *are* the answer to everything."

"Who told you that?"

"I read it. *In a book.*"

By the time they reached the treasure vault door, everyone was arguing.

Aunt Delia held the gold key aloft in her hand. "It must be this one—gold represents treasure."

"No, Addison's right—gold is too obvious." Uncle Nigel took the stone key from the ledge and shook it at her. "The stone key makes the most sense. Whoever opens the vault should not be seeking silver or gold, they should seek only illumination."

"Who opens a treasure vault to seek illumination?"

"We do!" snapped Uncle Nigel in his crisp British accent. "We're not fortune hunters; we're archaeologists!"

"But Ragar's men already tried the stone key!"

"Are you positive?"

"Yes! You don't have your glasses on, and I do."

"Well, maybe he turned it the wrong direction. Let's see if the key fits." Uncle Nigel tried to fit his stone key into the door while Aunt Delia tugged at his arm.

Molly and Raj wrestled over the silver key. Eddie clung to the wall, convinced the caiman pit would swing open at any moment.

Addison concentrated on the puzzle, trying to block out the sound of everyone arguing. He remembered that a samurai makes every decision in the space of seven breaths. He realized he didn't have that much time. Three breaths, at best. He closed his eyes, tuned out the shouting voices, and was pleased to find a solution in only two. "I've got it."

But nobody heard him.

Just as Uncle Nigel managed to get his stone key into the keyhole, Addison raised his voice and shouted, "I've got it! Everybody *listen!*"

Everyone paused their fighting to look at Addison.

"The Incans believed the treasure vault would only open for someone who learned from King Atahualpa's mistakes," said Addison quietly.

"Sure," said Uncle Nigel, not at all sure where Addison was going with this.

"So what was Atahualpa's mistake?"

"Instead of fighting the Conquistadors he fought his own family," said Molly.

"That's right," said Addison. "Atahualpa fought his brothers. And he fought his parents. So his family's armies abandoned him. By himself, Atahualpa was easily beaten. That was Atahualpa's curse."

Aunt Delia and Uncle Nigel looked at Addison, brows furrowed.

"Don't you see?" asked Addison. "Ragar can never open the treasure vault because it won't open for just one person. It will only open for a family."

Addison walked to the vault door and wiped away centuries of dirt, cobwebs, and vines. And to everyone's amazement, there was not just one keyhole in the door, there were three.

Addison took the three keys in his hands and stretched his arms wide. But the keyholes were spaced far apart so no one person could turn them all at once. Addison turned to his family. "I can't do it alone."

He handed the stone key to Raj and Eddie, the silver key to Aunt Delia and Uncle Nigel, and the gold key he shared with Molly. Together, they all inserted their keys into the locks. "Now," he said. They turned their keys in unison.

And for the first time in five hundred years, the treasure vault opened.

••••••

The immense stone door swung inward, revealing a sprawling chamber as large as a gymnasium. Uncle Nigel took a torch from the wall and stepped inside. Addison's team followed.

Before them lay treasure beyond their wildest reckoning. Gold vases filled to the brim with sparkling emeralds. Bright silver statuettes of birds and flowers inlaid with blue sapphires and crimson rubies. Crowns and tiaras studded with topaz, crystals, pearls, and diamonds. And everywhere, mountains upon mountains of glittering gold and silver coins.

Molly took off running, sliding belly-first down hills of gold. Raj tossed priceless gemstones over his head like confetti. Eddie whooped for joy, diving headfirst into a heap of gold coins.

It hurt more than he was expecting.

Addison stood with his uncle, marveling at the sight. "The legend was true," Uncle Nigel said, shaking his head in wonder. He put an arm around Addison. "How did you solve the clues? I didn't even know you spoke Spanish."

"I had help. A lot of help."

Aunt Delia picked up one artifact after another,

stunned by the craftsmanship. "Most of these are pre-Columbian, I'm sure of it," she said breathlessly. "Look at this bounty. It will take years to classify."

Uncle Nigel lifted his voice to Molly, Raj, and Eddie, who were having a snowball fight with gold doubloons. "Remember, don't remove any treasure from the vault. This belongs to Atahualpa and his people."

"Not anymore," said Ragar, stepping into the vault, followed by his men. "It's mine now." His bodyguards wheeled wooden carts into the treasure vault and began shoveling them full of gold coins.

Uncle Nigel pointed at the stone pillars by the door. "If you knew anything about Incan hieroglyphs, Vladimir, you would be able to read that warning."

"Oh really, what does it say?"

"This treasure belongs to the Incas. It does not leave."

Professor Ragar sighed. "It belonged to them five hundred years ago. It's mine now. And unfortunately, Dr. Cooke, I no longer have need of your expertise." He stooped to pick up a handful of priceless coins and let them cascade through his fingers. "I knew the Cooke family would serve a valuable purpose. But now that I have the treasure . . . you're cooked."

The professor gestured to Zubov, who stepped forward with a long coil of rope. "Zubov has been looking forward to this part even more than the treasure."

••••••

Addison and his team were hauled back into the main chamber. Ragar's men tied them all to stakes. Addison's hands were jerked behind his back and bound with rope, his spine pressed against the wood.

Zubov yanked Molly's ropes extra tight. "Nice knowing you."

"Wish I could say the same," said Molly.

Zubov looked at her evenly and nodded. "You've got heart."

The bodyguards collected ancient timbers from the walkways and heaped them at the Cooke family's feet. Zubov split kindling with his new blades, spreading the shavings across the timbers.

"Why kill us this way?" asked Eddie.

"Ragar wants to burn us alive, just like Atahualpa," said Addison grimly.

"At least it's not the caimans," said Molly.

Eddie nodded. "Still, this is not how I would prefer to go. Don't we at least get a final meal?" He watched the kindling piling up at his feet and then anxiously eyed the burning torches of the gallery. The walls were lined with stone-carved skulls, their jaws yawning open in silent screams.

"Addison," Molly said quietly.

"Yes, Mo?"

"This is a sticky wicket."

Addison nodded his agreement.

Professor Ragar stepped forward, a burning torch in his gloved hand. He leaned close to Addison and Molly, flames dancing in his eyes. "Ah yes, the final two."

"The final two what?" Addison struggled against his bonds, but this only made the knots grow tighter.

"Cookes," breathed Professor Ragar.

"Vladimir, leave them out of this!" snapped Uncle Nigel. "They're just kids. Do what you want with Delia and me, but let the kids go."

Ragar leaned close to Molly, his vampire skin smelling of musty attics and sour wine. "So many Cookes . . ." He patted her cheek and she flinched. "All must be killed, to fulfill the prophecy."

"You don't really believe in that nonsense, Ragar," said Uncle Nigel.

"Of course not." The torch hissed and spat in the professor's hand. "But Malazar believes it."

Molly swiveled to look at Addison. She mouthed the words, *Who is Malazar?*

Addison did his best to shrug—no easy feat when tied to a stake.

"Why be loyal to him?" asked Uncle Nigel. "He's a murderer."

"Ten years I rotted in that prison. Malazar saved me from the gates of hell." Ragar pressed his angry, mottled burn scars close to Uncle Nigel's face. "This is—how do you say?—the least I can do."

Ragar set his torch to the kindling. The timbers smoked, sparked, and ignited.

He stood back to admire the growing flames. "Now," Professor Ragar said, turning to smile at Addison, "you will die like your parents."

••••••

Ragar turned on his heel. His men followed him out of the chamber and into the treasure vault.

Addison wriggled to face his uncle. "What is this prophecy? And who is Malazar?"

"And what does Ragar know about our parents?" asked Molly.

"Our family has many secrets," Aunt Delia said sadly. "There is a lot we haven't told you yet."

Addison watched the forked tongues of flames licking higher. "Now might be a good time!"

"It doesn't matter now." Aunt Delia closed her eyes. "You were too young, and you're still too young."

The flames snapped and jumped, devouring the kindling. Addison felt the growing heat inching closer to his toes. He decided this was it. He took a deep breath.

"Molly, Eddie, Raj, I'm sorry I got you into this. Aunt D and Uncle N, I'm sorry I couldn't save you."

Eddie perked up his ears. "Addison, are you getting all sentimental again?"

Addison's eyes watered from the rising smoke.

"We're the ones who are sorry," said Aunt Delia. "We never wanted any of this for you."

"I'm sorry I didn't spend more time with you guys when I had the chance," said Uncle Nigel.

"I'm sorry everyone's so sorry," said Molly.

"I'm sorry I have to listen to this," said Eddie.

"I'm not sorry about anything!" said Raj.

The crackling flames grew louder. Addison coughed from the smoke. He tried to ignore the heat growing by his feet.

"Well, I'm sorry we're all going to die," said Addison.

The flames rose ever higher. There was no way of slowing the spreading fire. Raj, Eddie, and the Cooke family were going to be burned alive.

Chapter Twenty

Atahualpa's Curse

ADDISON SHUT HIS EYES, clenched his teeth, and waited for the pain to come. He thought about the ancient samurai and realized he didn't want to die afraid. He forced himself to open his eyes.

He watched Ragar's men struggle to push a cartload of gold out of the treasure vault, ignoring Uncle Nigel's warning. The cart must have weighed half a ton and was tricky to maneuver through the doorway. The men rolled the gold along the corridor toward the open jaws of the stone skull.

Addison looked down at his feet to see smoke rising from his dress shoes. The flames crept dangerously close to his pants. He looked over at Raj, whose pants were sawed away at the legs. Raj was gritting his teeth.

"Hang on, Raj!" he shouted.

"Hang on for what?" asked Raj.

"Atahualpa's curse!"

Ragar's men pushed their gold cart out of the mouth of the giant skull and felt a stone slab shift. The men froze in their spot, worried they had sprung some sort of booby trap, and probably not a good one. They listened for a few seconds in anxious silence, but no trap revealed itself.

The men sighed in relief.

Addison watched the rising flames dart higher around the cuffs of his pants.

"Wait, did you hear that?" asked Molly.

Addison listened intently and became aware of a distant rumbling deep within the mountain. A growing thunder of ancient gears grinding and churning, building to a roar that shook the rock walls of the cavern.

Ragar's guards set down their heavy gold cart and wondered, for the first time, if perhaps they should have heeded Dr. Cooke's warnings.

Hindsight is always 20/20.

The massive stone jaws of the skull slammed shut, trapping the bodyguards inside the corridor. The treasure vault door also crashed shut, sealing Ragar, Zubov, and their men inside. The main entrance to the chamber boomed shut as well, sealing in Addison's team.

The ceiling was lined with hundreds of stone-carved

skulls. Their jaws opened wide and blasted sand into the chamber. The sand jetted into the cavern from all sides, forming massive torrents that quickly spread across the floor.

Addison heard Professor Ragar, Zubov, and their bodyguards pounding against the door of the treasure vault, screaming as they were slowly buried alive. In Addison's own chamber, the sand continued to rocket from the carved skulls. It covered the floor one inch deep . . . two inches deep . . . three . . .

The raging flames touched Addison. The cuffs of his pants ignited, the blaze racing up his legs. Just when he could no longer stand the heat, the sand reached him. It enveloped his feet and ankles, gradually extinguishing the flames. Soon, the sands squelched the fire entirely. Addison's team cheered in relief. But the sands only rose faster, filling the chamber . . .

"Not to be picky," said Eddie, "but this *also* isn't how I would prefer to die."

"Well, what do we do about it?" cried Aunt Delia.

Addison looked to Uncle Nigel and remembered his advice. "Always use your environment," he said confidently. Addison realized, however, that at the present moment he was tied and bound to a stake. So he wasn't entirely sure if this advice was applicable. It's all well and good to go around saying things like "Use your environment," but Addison's useful environment was currently restricted to the few square inches he could actually reach with his tied hands. Yet as the sand quickly pooled around his knees, thighs, and waist, Addison realized he had options. His bound hands could, in fact, reach into his own back pocket. And there he discovered something significant. Something truly useful. Something undeniably helpful when one is tied up in rope . . .

Zubov's butterfly knife.

Addison managed to frantically saw through his ropes by the time the sand reached his stomach. He quickly reached Raj and cut him free before the sand reached Raj's shoulders. Together they reached Eddie, Aunt Delia, and Uncle Nigel.

Molly screamed for help. "Addison," she called before her mouth disappeared under the rising sands, "I'm the shortest!"

Addison looked over in time to see Molly disappear beneath the sands.

......

Addison fought desperately to reach Molly, but found himself mired in the sand. "Help! Molly's trapped down there!"

Raj did not believe in destiny. But he occasionally suspected that he must have a purpose in life, that all the survival books he devoured in the library would someday, somehow, amount to something.

He realized this was his moment. "I know what to

do," Raj said, amazed. "This is like quicksand, and the way to survive quicksand is to lie flat—it evenly distributes your body weight." He grabbed Addison's butterfly knife and wriggled across the sand on his belly. He was able to cross the rising dunes without sinking. "Hang on, Molly!" Raj reached the spot where Molly had disappeared. "BHAAAAAAAANDARI!!!" he shouted with all his might. He plunged his head into the sand.

Raj burrowed down until only his bare ankles stuck out of the dune. Addison marine-crawled across the sand as he saw Raj do. He drew closer and pulled on Raj's ankles. Uncle Nigel yanked on Addison's ankles.

Inch by inch, Raj emerged from the sands, followed by Molly. She coughed and sputtered, but she was alive.

Addison was stunned. "Raj, one of your survival skills *actually worked!*"

Molly smiled up at Raj and gasped, "Thank you, Raj!"

Raj brushed sand from his hair and smiled shyly.

Still the sands rose. It shot from the mouths of the stone skulls in gushing torrents. The mounting pressure blasted several skulls clear off the walls, so the sand poured into the room even faster. It pounded Addison's head with crushing weight. His team coughed and gagged from the billowing dust, swirling clouds of dirt clogging their eyes, ears, noses, and mouths. They choked and struggled for breath.

"What do we do?" Eddie shouted.

"Stick together," called Addison.

Following Raj's lead, Uncle Nigel belly-crawled his way to a stone pillar. He clung to it like the mast of a sinking ship. The group managed to drag one another, hand over hand, toward the pillar. But fresh sand piled on their shoulders and backs, freezing their movement.

The blasting sand, in stinging jets, rose high enough to extinguish the wall torches. The chamber gradually plunged into darkness. The mountain creaked and groaned, giant cracks fissuring the rock.

"Either we suffocate in here, or the ceiling collapses on us!" shouted Uncle Nigel.

Addison didn't favor either of those two options.

Cracks splintered the cavern ceiling, raining debris in a deadly cascade. The overhead crevice widened as the ancient rock crumbled. High above, a shaft of light pierced the gloom, illuminating the growing cleft.

"There!" Addison cried. He eyed the thickly knotted stone vines carved around the pillars. The image of his mother clinging for her life on the battlement flashed across his mind, but he swallowed it down. "We climb."

Addison's team gripped the stone vines encircling the giant pillars. It took all their strength to hoist their bodies free of the mounting sand. The pillars held strong, and Addison's group pulled themselves higher, grappling their way up the rock.

"Up there!" called Raj. A sliver of sunbeam glimmered

from the crag in the cave wall. Working together, they clambered toward the light.

"Take my hand," said Molly.

"Thanks," said Addison. And she helped him up.

Hands gripping stone, they reached the crevice where the sunlight broke through.

······

The group crawled out onto the summit of the mountain, pulling themselves up with the last of their strength. They coughed and sputtered, blinking sand from their eyes and patting it from their hair. They inhaled the fresh air in deep gulps like floundering fish.

The Cooke family, plus Eddie and Raj, struggled to their feet and took their bearings. They were standing in Machu Picchu, the Lost City of the Incas. The white stone palaces of the ancient city, terraced into the mountain, glowed in the auburn rays of afternoon light. The team, dirty as chimney sweeps, shook dust from their clothes and admired the view from the top of the world.

Addison was the last to rise to his feet, his fire-scorched dress shoes clattering on the rock. He set his hands on his waist, watching the dust still rising from the crag in the mountain. "All that treasure lost," he said wistfully.

"You guys are the real treasure," said Aunt Delia, squeezing Addison's and Molly's shoulders.

"Oh please," groaned Molly, "Don't ruin this moment."

The team watched the setting sun inch toward the Pacific, its last rays bathing the Incan palaces in gold.

"Atahualpa's treasure will remain where it belongs," said Uncle Nigel. "With the people who built this temple."

"Amen to that," said Eddie. He turned to walk away, looking for a pathway down. A single gold coin clattered from Eddie's pants. Another coin dropped from his sleeve. And then a torrent of treasure spilled from where it was stuffed into his shirt and pants. Spanish doubloons, Portugese cruzados, and Incan ingots of solid gold. Coins poured out of Eddie like a Vegas slot machine. It took a full minute for the last coin to clang to the ground and rattle to a stop. Eddie offered a guilty smile.

"We're archaeologists, not treasure hunters like Professor Ragar," said Uncle Nigel. "We have to return it, Eddie. The treasure belongs here, in Peru."

Eddie sighed, but Addison stepped in. "Wait a second, Uncle N. Wouldn't it help archaeology if we showed this treasure in a museum? Get more kids interested in history? Spread the story of Atahualpa? Five-hundred-year-old Incan treasure—it could be that big exhibit you're looking for."

Uncle Nigel frowned, but Aunt Delia spoke up. "It would help the museum, Nigel," she said thoughtfully. "And it could save our jobs."

"It'd be a great exhibit," put in Molly.

"And, of course," Addison added, "we'll return the gold to Peru as soon as the exhibit is over."

Uncle Nigel scratched his chin, weighing it in his mind . . .

Chapter Twenty-One

——————•——————

Home Again

HUNDREDS OF STUDENTS FILED into the packed exhibit at the New York Museum of Archaeology. A large replica of the Incan treasure room dominated the main foyer. Students climbed over the teeth of the massive stone skull, crept past replicas of iron-spiked booby traps, and glimpsed actual pieces of the Incan gold inside the treasure vault.

Addison, Molly, Eddie, Raj, and Uncle Nigel stood by the information booth and stared at the mob of museum visitors that looped all the way down the front steps and around the block. Raj waved across the atrium at his three sisters. They smiled and snapped photos.

"We're a hit," said Addison.

Uncle Nigel beamed. It was only a month since their return from Peru, yet it felt much longer. There was so much preparation required to mount the new exhibit.

A voice rang out from the crowd.

"Dr. Cooke! Dr. Cooke!" The museum director, a rotund and fussy Swede named Helmut Ingleborg, squeezed his way through the wall of people. Helmut was perpetually out of breath and red-cheeked with excitement. "What a stupendous success, no?" he cried, clutching Uncle Nigel's hand and shaking it until Uncle Nigel's glasses slipped down his nose.

"Thank you, Helmut," said Dr. Nigel, embarrassed by the attention.

"This exhibit has rave reviews, isn't it?" Helmut laughed, his eyes twinkling. His command of English was questionable at best, but he made up for it with enthusiasm. Helmut turned to Addison's team. "The fact that tiny adults helped discover this treasure is a big news story." He waved his arms at the immense crowd of schoolkids. "Just look at all the tiny adults coming to the museum now!"

Helmut took Addison's hand and pumped it like he was starting a lawnmower. He pinched Molly on the cheek, which she tolerated with heroic self-control. "We'll see you at the opening gala tonight!" chortled Helmut. And he disappeared into the throng of visitors.

Uncle Nigel turned to Addison's team. The noisy crowd pressed in from all sides. "You guys want to get out of here?"

Addison's team nodded as one.

"C'mon," said Uncle Nigel, "I've got a surprise for you."

......

Uncle Nigel led the group onto the museum's rooftop garden. It was a secret place few people knew, offering a dazzling panorama of New York City. The garden contained dozens of private hammocks, hillocks, and hideaways that Addison felt were perfectly designed for reading a book.

"Why did you take us up here?" asked Molly. "What's the surprise?"

"Well, I remember sending you and Addison to get dinner from the vending machine when I was too busy with work . . ."

"And we never ended up getting anything," said Molly. "On account of being hunted by convicts."

"The upshot is, I still owe you a proper dinner," said Uncle Nigel.

Molly nodded her head emphatically.

Uncle Nigel led them to a Japanese pagoda by the meditation pool. And there sat Aunt Delia with plates, napkins, and several steaming boxes of Frank's Pizza.

Molly was so overwhelmed she nearly fainted.

Addison supported her with one arm. "Deep breaths, Mo."

The team shared stories over dinner. Peru felt so long ago, they now found they could laugh about most of it. Raj reenacted Eddie's wrestling match with a skeleton under the Cathedral of Lost Souls. Eddie pantomimed Raj's brazen vine swing across the chasm in the Amazon. Twilight fell over the city, and the stars glowed in the sky.

"I'm glad we got some family time before the gala," said Aunt Delia, finishing the last slice of pepperoni.

"Do we have to dress up tonight?" asked Molly, who would rather put on a straitjacket than be forced to wear a dress.

"A lot of important donors will be there," said Uncle Nigel. "And they'll want to meet the people who uncovered the Incan vault. Tonight, if all goes well, we can save the museum."

······

Addison dearly loved a black-tie gala. He knew how to match his tie knot to the width of his shirt collar. He knew how to match the width of his tie to the width of his lapels. He knew three different ways to fold and fluff a pocket square. And he now wore a tie bar like the one he'd admired on Professor Ragar. Addison was a person completely at home in a suit.

The gala filled the museum's atrium. A string quartet played Bach next to the Aztec temple. Guests in tuxedoes sipped cocktails by the reflecting pool that once held a half-dozen electrocuted bodyguards.

Addison and his team spent hours smiling and greeting donors. Addison enjoyed telling stories about Peru. He met a few city councilmembers and even the mayor. After a few hours, however, he grew tired and restless. Talking about adventures was not the same as living them.

He polished off his second Arnold Palmer and made his way to the bar. He handed his empty glass to the bartender. "Another AP, please, Trisha."

"Are you sure you don't want to slow down, Addison?" Trisha asked.

"Make it strong and keep 'em coming. I've been shaking hands and getting my cheek pinched for three hours and there's no end in sight."

"Coming right up, Addison." Trisha grinned, scooping ice into a glass.

Addison rested an elbow against the bar and turned to survey the room. He spotted Eddie gorging himself on chicken kebabs at a buffet table. He then noticed Raj, sweating with concentration, trying to bring his hand as close as possible to the open flame of a buffet heater. Addison thought ahead to eighth grade and wondered what the future held. They wouldn't stay young forever. People grow, people change, people move away. Addison decided that no matter what, he needed to make this upcoming summer vacation count.

Trisha the bartender slid over a fresh Arnold Palmer. Addison took a long pull.

Molly joined him at his side. "What is that, your second Arnold Palmer?"

"Third," Addison admitted.

"Pace yourself."

"It's my one indulgence." He shrugged.

Eddie and Raj approached.

"Have you tried this chicken satay? It's just like Turkish kebabs, except from Asia!" Eddie polished off a skewer and had six more ready on deck.

Uncle Nigel joined the group. "Enjoying yourselves?"

Eddie's mouth was too full to answer, but he nodded vigorously.

Helmut Ingleborg parted the crowd, red-faced with excitement. "Dr. Cooke!"

"What is it, Helmut?"

Helmut was too riled up to breathe. "Donations are pouring in. The museum had a good year tonight."

"Well, that's good news."

"That's not what I came to tell you! I just got off the phone with our sister museum in Hong Kong. You must return to fieldwork at once! They've unearthed a hidden Song dynasty fortress in the Gobi Desert!"

"Incredible," said Uncle Nigel, his eyes lighting up. "How fast can I get there?"

"The museum is already chartering a plane, no?"

"Excellent. I keep a bag packed in my office. I can order provisions and hire a crew once I arrive in China . . ." But as soon as the words left his mouth, Uncle Nigel thought better of it. He looked at Addison, Molly, Eddie, and Raj.

"On second thought," he said to Helmut, "you'll have to find someone else. I've traveled too much lately. I need to spend more time with my family."

"But this is impossible, no?" Helmut's hands flew up over his head. "You are the most qualified to lead this expedition, isn't it!"

"I'm sorry, Helmut, I just can't."

"Take us with you," suggested Molly.

"Yeah," said Eddie. "It's almost summer vacation. We won't miss any school."

"And we were helpful on the last trip," said Raj.

Uncle Nigel shook his head. "Raj, aren't you and Eddie still grounded for flying to South America without permission?"

"Only for two more weeks," said Raj eagerly.

Addison saw his window of opportunity. This would require all his powers of persuasion. He stepped forward. "Uncle Nigel, I racked up a lot of transportation charges on your credit card. If you make us your research assistants for the summer, we can work off the debt."

Uncle Nigel's eyebrows shot up. He was impressed. "Wow, Addison, that's actually pretty responsible of you. But still, I can't just jet you off to China."

"Why not? The trip is an opportunity for us to spend time together," said Addison.

Uncle Nigel mulled this over.

"And if the museum is already chartering a flight," Addison pressed his point, "it makes dollars *and* sense."

Aunt Delia emerged from the crowd. "Do you have room on that flight for one more? I'm the number two Song dynasty expert at the museum."

"Who's the number one expert?" Molly asked.

All eyes turned to Uncle Nigel. "All right, everyone. Clear your summer schedules, get your travel visas, and start learning Mandarin." Uncle Nigel smiled. "We're going to China."

THE END

Watch for more adventures of

COMING SOON!

Author's Note

......

The history of the Incan treasure is stranger than fiction.

The story begins when Francisco Pizarro conquered Peru in 1532. Pizarro lured Atahualpa to the main plaza in Cajamarca, Peru, by promising a safe parley. When Atahualpa arrived, Pizarro simply ambushed him. Atahualpa's Incan guards were terrified by the sight of Spanish horses and sound of Spanish guns. The Incan guards fled, and Atahualpa was easily captured.

The Spaniards locked Atahualpa in the "Ransom Room" that still stands in Cajamarca. Atahualpa offered to fill the room once over with gold and twice over with silver, in exchange for his release. By the dimensions of the room, this amounted to 3,366 cubic feet of gold and 6,732 cubic feet of silver.

King Atahualpa's general, Rumiñahui ("Stone Face"), was given two months to gather and deliver the treasure to the Spaniards. When Pizarro executed Atahualpa before the due date, Rumiñahui never delivered. Though he was eventually captured and tortured to death by the Spanish, Rumiñahui never revealed the location of the Incan treasure.

Pizarro squabbled over lands with his fellow conquistador, Diego de Almagro, and eventually ordered him decapitated at the prison in Cusco. Diego de Almagro's son, nicknamed "El Mozo," was half Native American. Vowing to avenge his father, El Mozo raised an army of supporters and attacked Pizarro's palace at Lima, Peru, on June 26, 1541.

Pizarro was somewhere between sixty-two and seventy years old at the time of this surprise attack. While trying to buckle on his armor, Pizarro managed to kill two of the attackers with his sword. While his sword was trapped in a third man, the attackers slit Pizarro's throat. He fell to the ground and was stabbed repeatedly. Pizarro drew a cross on the floor in his own blood and called out to Jesus Christ before dying. In 1977, Pizarro's decapitated head was discovered in a lead box, hidden in a secret basement niche in the cathedral at Lima, Peru.

After assassinating Pizarro, El Mozo briefly became governor of Peru. But El Mozo was soon captured by the Spanish at the Battle of Chupas on September 16, 1542. He was executed in the city square at Cuzco.

After five hundred years, it is difficult to know the fates of Pizarro's Famous Thirteen knights. Pedro de Candia was a firearms expert who was killed by El Mozo at the Battle of Chupas. Domingo de Soraluce eventually became the ruler of Panama and attempted to sail home to Spain with a fortune in gold. He died at sea, and his ship was robbed before it reached port.

Over the centuries, many treasure hunters have met their death pursuing the Incan gold. A Franciscan monk named Father Longo, an Ecuadorian miner named Don Atanasio Guzmán, a British sea captain named Barth Blake, a Scottish treasure hunter named Erskine Loch, an American geologist named Bob Holt—these are just a few of the adventurers who met violent or mysterious deaths while seeking the Incan treasure.

Whether or not the treasure is cursed is a matter of speculation. Whether it is hidden in Ecuador or Peru is also a matter for debate. If the towns of Olvidados and Casa Azar exist, they are too small to be found on any map. As of the publication of this book, the location of the Incan treasure remains a mystery.

Acknowledgments

Thank you to my family and friends, without whom I would be far too well adjusted to consider a career in writing. Special thanks to Brianne Johnson, Dana Borowitz, and Beau Flynn, for their help and encouragement. Many thanks to my brilliant editor, Michael Green, and to my younger editors, Christopher Adler, Evan Parter, Leila Pagel, and Harper Oreck. Lastly, thank you to Scott Carr, for inviting me to the party.